Reject Squad

GUIDE ME HARDER

JAYCE CARTER

ENTWINED PUBLISHING

Guide Me Harder
ISBN # 978-1-80250-621-1
©Copyright Jayce Carter 2025
Cover Art by Kelly Martin ©Copyright December 2025
Interior text design by Entwined Publishing
Published by Expanse, an Entwined Publishing imprint

Published in 2025 by Entwined Publishing, United Kingdom.

Entwined Publishing is a division of Totally Entwined Group Limited.

Entwined Publishing books by Jayce Carter

The Omega's Alphas
Owned by the Alphas
Shared by the Alphas
Saved by the Alphas
Protected by Her Alphas
Caught by Her Alphas
Tamed by the Alphas
Claimed by the Alphas
Exposed by Her Alphas
Trained by the Alphas
Reclaimed by Her Alphas

Ready or Not
Fake It 'til You Make It
Opposites Attract
Third Time Lucky
Enemies Closer

Grave Concerns
Grave Robbing and Other Hobbies
Hell Raising and Other Pastimes
Saving the World and Other Bad Ideas

Dark Sanctuary
Bound by Fear
Trapped by Doubt
Buried by Despair

Nemesis
The Corpse Princess
The Resurrected Queen

Larkwood Academy
Silenced
Whispers
Screaming

The Devil's Luck
A Devil of a Time
Devil May Care
Run Like the Devil
The Devil's Due

Black Heart Auctions
Selling Innocence
Buying Time
Taking Chances

Flocking It Up
Flock This
Out of my Flocking Mind
Flock Around and Find Out

Reject Squad
Guide Me Harder

Collections
Sun, Sea and Sinful Delights
Secret Santa: To Catch a Fox
Cupid's Academy: Stolen
Hot Bite: Summer Trips and Other Reasons to Get Naked

GUIDE ME HARDER

Dedication

To all the girls who are disappointed in real men — enjoy some fictional ones!

Chapter One

Yun

This is my last chance.

The warning rang in my head on repeat, over and over again, reminding me that I couldn't fuck this up. No matter how often I'd screwed it up in the past—and I had, plenty of times—I couldn't let that happen *now*.

I'd worn a fitted suit, something the Guild had gotten me. Normally, the expensive fabrics and marvelous craftsmanship would have landed far outside my price range, but the Guild offered some perks to members. They helped out with work expenses, and since I'd never used those services, they'd approved the new outfit with ease.

The woman who worked at the upscale clothing store had sworn up and down that I looked wonderful, and, to be honest, I'd hardly recognized the girl I'd seen in those large mirrors in the changing room. She'd appeared put together, as though she had everything sorted out in her life.

Well, minus the bags under her eyes, the ones that came from chronic, crippling insomnia.

Still, whether I looked the part didn't change how I felt—entirely unprepared. I doubted anything short of a complete rewrite of my entire life would change that.

Someone walked by on the street, peering toward me with an untrusting side-eye.

So, maybe standing in front of an office building for what had to have been ten minutes was suspicious. I could almost picture the Guild giving me an earful should I get the cops called on me for loitering.

Just go for it.

My knuckles ached from the hard, dark wood of the door after I knocked. The nameplate hanging at eye level read *"Reject Squad."*

The name had me nearly shaking my head. That wasn't their actual name, of course. Officially, on all the documents, I'd been paired with Squad S412. Reject Squad was what others called them in jest, while people sneered and spread whatever rumors were going around at the time.

Just how many of those rumors were true?

It was impossible to tell because they never addressed any of them. Instead, they reveled in the lies, in the rumors, in the way people talked shit about them.

And I'm supposed to join this clusterfuck?

Yeah, I was, because this was it for me.

The door opened and a man with long, dirty-blond hair looked out, so tall that he at first looked not at me but over my head and past me. He lowered his gaze to mine.

Would he yell at me?

Espers weren't known for having great temperaments.

Or perhaps he'd order me in, tell me to start guiding right this moment.

My stomach rolled at that thought, at the fear that swarmed through me like a million crawling bugs.

"Where are the cookies?"

His words caught me so off guard that my brain struggled to come up with anything in response.

He turned his head slightly and called past him, into the darkness of the building which I couldn't see into, "I don't see any cookies." He faced me again, his brows furrowed as though this cookie debacle were the great, lingering question of our generation. "Did you hide them or something? Did you forget them? One time I got sent to the store for mac and cheese and I ended up spending all the money Carter gave me at this taco truck outside, so I came back without anything. It's fine, here." He reached into his jeans pocket, then shoved a fistful of money at my chest until I took it more from surprise than anything else. "That's enough. No tacos this time, though." He closed the door in my face.

Which left me standing there with what — when I looked down — turned out to be at least eight hundred dollars in fifties and twenties and no idea what the fuck had just happened.

Part of me wondered if I should just leave. Was any job worth this? These guys were insane, right? That was the only explanation.

Except, the words of the Guild president again whispered through my mind.

My last chance.

If I failed here, if I didn't make this work, I had no idea where I'd land.

I just knew it wouldn't be good.

Which meant no matter how crazy this seemed, I needed to make it work.

Should I go get cookies? Maybe this was a test, like they wanted to ensure I had what it took to work with them?

I felt like walking in blind to an exam that I hadn't known about or taught.

Just as I accepted the idea that I'd need to turn around and go to the store, the door opened again.

I expected that strange man to return, asking about baked goods, which was why it surprised me to find someone else there. He had dark hair, a bit messy and long enough to fall to his cheekbones, with waves through it, though I wondered if they'd stay if he brushed it properly. He wore a button-up shirt, light blue, and had the sleeves rolled up and over his forearms.

"This isn't the cookie girl," he shouted into the building, again making me wonder if they'd all lost their minds. Perhaps they'd gone too long without a guide and were well and truly corrupt—just in a far less murdery way than most of them went. When he turned back toward me, he had an almost charming smile painted across his lips, though something about it screamed in my head not to trust it—or him. "Sorry, come in. My name is Carter."

I followed him, still clutching the cash against my chest, and got my first look at the interior.

The outside had been rather nondescript, just another small business or office building, surrounded by similar doors that housed lawyers and real estate agents and new-age doctors who claimed to cure rich people with crystals but usually only cured them of their money.

No one would have expected to find this just past one of those doors.

The space was large, with stairs near one side that wound up to a second floor. This ground floor was open, though, with a kitchenette on one side and a large couch facing a huge flat screen mounted on the wall across from it. A few desks sat in the space, awkwardly placed as though they weren't sure what to do with the room.

Some of the desks had papers on them, purposeful stacks, as though the owner worked through them at their own pace, while others appeared to never have been touched at all.

And the thing that would have completely thrown any person? A full wall with a glass front and weapons locked inside. Guns, knives, something that I felt pretty sure was a missile launcher. While the rest of the space was an absolute mess, that area remained perfectly organized, along with a desk just before it that had a load of paperwork across it.

Yeah, this was *not* the office of a civilian.

"If she isn't here with cookies, who is she?" the man who had answered the door asked from his spot on the couch, his arm thrown over the back as he watched me.

"This is the guide that the Guild sent."

Another head popped up from the couch as though summoned by that. "Guide?" This man looked nothing like the other two, with short hair gelled back like some old-timey gangster and tattoos that painted him like a new generation gangster. He had a neck tattoo of bird wings wrapped around his throat and an eye at the center. He wore a black shirt with a V-neck and long sleeves, meaning I couldn't see any more of him, but I had a feeling that his tattoos went a *lot* further than that.

He stared at me before flashing a smile so lewd I nearly blushed. I didn't need to read thoughts to have a pretty good idea of what exactly was on his mind.

"Don't get excited," Carter warned as he took a seat at the desk with the weapons behind it. "You know the Guild wouldn't just send us any old guide."

"What's wrong with her, then?" the tattooed man asked as though I weren't there.

"She doesn't bring cookies, that's what's wrong," the long-haired man answered, his voice sullen. Was he actually *pouting* over such a thing?

"If you would shut up, I might be able to figure it out." Carter shook his head, then gestured at the seat across the desk from him. "Ignore them — they're like children. They think any attention is good attention. The one who answered the door is Kenyon, and the delinquent-looking asshole beside him is Ingram."

I swallowed hard, the names making this all feel more real as I took the seat he'd offered and tucked the money into my pocket, unsure what else to do with it.

We sat in silence for a long moment, awkwardness creeping in.

"That means you're supposed to say your name," Kenyon whispered from the couch, loud enough that everyone could hear it, as though I hadn't worked out basic social norms.

I fought back the desire to remind him that I did just fine, that it was they who had caused this weirdness. Who could keep their wits about them when surrounded by lunatic espers?

"My name is Yun Moore," I offered, keeping my hands in my lap.

It was a trick I'd learned years before, to never put my hand out for a handshake. Other guides might be fine with casual touching, but I sure as fuck wasn't. "The Guild sent me here."

Carter waved that off, as though unimportant. "Yeah, yeah, the Guilds like to talk and work things out, our opinions be damned. Still, this isn't a squad people are usually champing at the bit to join up with. Ingram might have the tact of a seven-year-old, but he isn't wrong. Why'd you pull the short straw?"

His words lashed out, the sting not dulled despite the way he said them—lighthearted, as though we were having any casual discussion.

I pulled my shoulders back, refusing to be looked down on. "That isn't any of your business. You need a guide, and the Guild thought I would be compatible. I can assure you I'm capable of it."

"What rank are you?"

"S."

He didn't seem impressed, though why would he? My understanding was that this squad had all Rank-S espers—the highest rank there was—so they would expect a comparable rank when it came to a guide. If guides and espers had differing levels, they didn't work as effectively together. He made a soft sound, then moved on. "So, you're willing to be our guide?"

Willing felt like far too accepting a word. Forced to? Had no choice? Sure, those were accurate, but willing?

Technically, maybe.

"Yes," I said instead of voicing the rest of it. "But I have some requirements. I don't do any physical guiding."

Ingram choked from the couch, as though something had lodged in his throat, then started to cough. When he finally caught his breath, I could have sworn I heard "Fucking pity" quietly from him.

"That means you'll need to guide far more often, and you'll get run down quicker. That seems like an absolutely terrible idea."

I closed my hands into fists to keep my expression stoic. It wasn't an unusual response to a rather unusual boundary.

Sure, some guides put limitations on the type of guiding they did—especially at first. They might say they wouldn't kiss, wouldn't engage in sexual acts, but few completely refused physical contact at all. The natural draw between espers and guides meant even those rules, when made, rarely lasted long.

The process of guiding was made easier by physical contact, more so when fluids were involved. Removing the corruption—twisted energy that accumulated inside an esper as they used their powers—had to happen. Without that, the corruption would eventually overwhelm them and drive them mad, turning them into little more than crazed monsters themselves. It meant espers *needed* guides to keep them sane.

"Those are my limits," I repeated, my voice firm, unwilling to even suggest a softening.

Kenyon hadn't spoken again, watching us, his gaze moving back and forth like a kid watching his parents fight. Ingram had lain back down, his interest waning at the realization that he wouldn't be fucking me.

Fine by me.

The less interest any of them had in me, the better.

"That seems like a losing proposition for us. We get saddled with a guide who can only do a portion of the job?" Carter leaned back in his chair, his gaze hard even if his voice still sounded friendly and casual. "I mean, I get why *you're* here. You're out of options, aren't you?"

I sat up straighter at that. Sure, I had a reputation, but I'd hoped it hadn't gotten this far. This squad never attended meetings or functions, so how the hell would they know anything?

"You got kicked out of your last six squad assignments. In fact, I think the last one, you put an esper in the hospital for a week."

I flinched as I recalled that day. The way his body had struck the ground, the heavy thud, the stares of others as they tried to work out what had just happened.

Me, a guide, had just put a Rank-S esper on his ass, flat out on the concrete floor.

It wasn't something people saw, and sure enough, by the end of that day, I'd gotten a call from the Guild telling me my assignment had been pulled.

They'd been nice about it, of course. All 'it just wasn't a good fit,' as though we were boyfriend and girlfriend getting let down easy.

I knew the truth, though.

They were afraid of me. It wasn't the first time, but it had to be the last. If I screwed up again, if I found myself on the outs with another squad—well, I had nowhere else to go.

"That was confidential," I muttered softly. I couldn't exactly deny it, but they shouldn't have known about it.

"Nothing in this world is confidential," Carter pressed. "And that isn't the first time you've done that. Seems the normal guide defense system is a bit supercharged for you. Let me guess—the president told you this is your last stop, right? This is it for you. If you can't make it work here, they're going to cut you loose."

"They can't afford to lose guides," I argued.

"Useful ones, sure, but you're defective. You do more harm than good to the squads you're assigned to. And that's over the fact you can't even do basic physical guiding, right? So what exactly is it you think you're going to do for us?"

I closed my eyes for a moment. I didn't want to show weakness, but better this, better to collect myself and start again than say something I couldn't take back.

I've been through worse than this. Some shitty, low-grade squad isn't going to make me feel inferior.

After my pep-talk, I met his gaze again. "You need a guide, and I'm here. Is there really anything else to talk about?"

"Sure there is. This, sweetheart, is called leverage. You need us, so don't pretend like you're holding all the cards."

Just like that, all that control I'd told myself to exercise snapped. Maybe it was his smirk, or the disinterest from Ingram, or the way Kenyon still watched us silently, or, fuck, maybe it was the stack of money tucked into my pocket, but I rose and slammed my palms against the desk. "You want to talk about leverage? You might have looked into me, but don't think you're the only one who knows things. You're my last chance — you're right. But I'm your last chance, too. You've been fucking around for years, doing the bare minimum to keep your registration status. You've probably run off every guide who steps foot in this place — and who can blame them? Who would want to work with a bunch of fuckups? My bet is that they assigned us together because we're *both* on our last shot here. So don't you even try to talk about leverage or look down on me. You need me just as much as I need you." As my tirade wound down, as my words slowed and I realized just what the fuck I was saying, some of that bravado drifted away.

What if I pushed too hard? What if he kicked me out?

Espers were known for being proud — after all, they got their ego stroked from the moment they appeared, always told what good heroes they were, always coddled.

In my experience, they didn't tolerate it well when people poked that belief.

A rough laugh left Carter, quiet at first, then growing as it went on. He wiped a finger beneath his eye, then leveled an amused smirk at me. "Well, well, well, who knew that the Blizzard had such a temper?"

His use of my not-at-all-fond nickname told me that, despite him acting like he knew nothing, he actually knew a hell of a lot.

"Enough games," I snapped. "Do we have an understanding?"

He set his elbows on the desk and leaned forward, something in his expression warning me not to trust him. He might smile, he might laugh, he might act like my friend, but he sure as fuck wasn't. "Sure, Blizzard. Welcome to the Reject Squad."

Chapter Two

Carter

"When will she get here?" Kenyon popped something into his mouth—no doubt a sugary treat. Despite his age, he still ate like a child.

It was a good thing the Guild paid us well because if they didn't, Kenyon's food delivery budget alone would put us under.

"She's supposed to get here at nine," I told him for the fifth time in the last hour. I doubted he'd really forgotten, but rather that the ADHD disaster couldn't wait for more than a few minutes before his patience ran out and he had to check in again. "Why don't you go check to make sure her room is ready?"

He huffed before trudging away.

Not that I could blame him.

As I worked on a stack of papers on the desk, sorting through the jobs that had come in to decide which we'd take on, my mind kept going back to *her*.

Yun Moore. Twenty-six years old. Rank-S guide. The few details in her file told me so little it was almost laughable. I didn't care about what was in the file—that was only the Guild's opinion of her.

It never told the true story.

That story sat in the shadows of her eyes, in the way she'd held herself back, in the truth that she'd never dare reveal willingly.

I blew out a breath and reminded myself I didn't care.

Or, it was better to say I only cared as much as I had to in order to keep our squad registered and running. Anything else?

Not my circus. Not my fucking monkeys.

A crash from upstairs followed by a shouted "I'm fine" from Kenyon reminded me that I had my own monkeys and they were a fucking mess already. No reason to go looking for more problems.

Still, the fire in her eyes when she'd lectured me…

I'd gotten myself off twice last night to the memory. What the fuck was wrong with me? Why the hell was I into some little spitfire guide who refused to even hold hands during guiding? That was so not my type, and a mess not even worth getting close to.

Especially considering what she'd done to espers in the past.

That had me sitting back in my chair, letting it lean in a way I would suggest no civilian do. It balanced on two legs, and the slight adjustments that allowed it to remain perched that way eased my mind as I thought.

Guides had a slight defense, an ability to repel an esper with a short burst of energy, but it was intended as a way to shock an esper back into their right mind should they lose control. I'd never before heard of one that could actually *harm* an esper. It seemed impossible, and if it hadn't been so well documented throughout her lifetime, I wouldn't have believed it at all. I'd have chalked it up to an old wives' tale, to something meant to scare espers into behaving and keeping our grubby little hands to ourselves.

But too many instances of it existed for me not to believe.

Which meant I needed to ensure we watched ourselves around our little guide — it seemed she bit.

"You know, you're not very observant for an esper."

I frowned at the voice that seemed too real. My mind was pretty fucking amazing, wasn't it?

Then, the very face of the woman I'd assumed I'd conjured up appeared above me, causing me to lose that precarious balance and topple to the floor. My head hit the hardwood, making me wish I'd gone with Kenyon's idea for carpet.

She didn't move — not to help me or apologize. Instead, she crossed her arms and stared down at me.

At least it gave me a nice look at her from an altogether new angle.

And she *was* rather pretty. She had pale skin and eyes so dark it was hard to tell iris from pupil. Her hair was black and fell to her shoulders, the strands with a slight wave in them. She was thin, her frame small, and fuck did she have contempt written all over her features.

Who knew that was my type?

"You're early," I said.

She turned her wrist, the screen of a smartwatch flashing to life. "No, I'm right on time. What sort of esper doesn't notice someone walking into their office?"

I rolled over and got to my feet with the same slow lumbering I tended to use. No reason to show how quick or agile I was—I preferred being underestimated. It was the same reason why I spoke like a fool, so others let their guard down around me. "Espers feel a draw to guides, but we also don't view them as threats, which means our senses don't always notice them." I lifted my eyebrow at the bag of groceries slung over her shoulder. "Did some shopping?"

She reached in and pulled out a package of...

Cookies.

The sight nearly had me laughing again. Leave it to this girl to entertain me, to show me amusement I hadn't expected at all.

Her cheeks tinged pink. "Well, he did give me money for them."

"He gave you a few hundred. That's about ten dollars' worth."

She shrugged and tossed the cookies on the kitchen counter. "Consider the rest a delivery fee and tip."

Which told me she could probably use the money.

Guides were taken care of—very well, for those who made their espers happy—but that didn't mean they had it easy. Plus, given her responses before, I had to assume she wasn't one of those babied ones who got gifts all the time.

"You travel light, don't you?"

She frowned, no comprehension on her pretty face.

"You didn't bring things to stay here. No clothing, no personal items. Girls need things like that." I waved my hand to encompass the multitude of things that women seemed to have to have. We'd had a few female guides come, and they always showed up with ten bags—usually expecting us to carry them all.

She turned and hiked a finger over her shoulder, pointing at a backpack slung there.

A backpack that couldn't have held more than a couple outfits — maybe.

"So is the rest of it in a car? Do we need to go get it?" Even as I asked, I ensured my voice sounded just as annoyed as I felt about the prospect of doing just that.

"This is it."

Another thought hit me, even less pleasant. "Did you keep your Guild apartment because you don't think this'll last?"

Maybe the girl just didn't want to move all her items for an arrangement she figured would fall apart quickly, anyway. I didn't blame her for it, but it still bothered me. It was as though she'd written us off before we even got to try.

Sure, it was going to fail, that was obvious to anyone, but she didn't have to act as though she knew it.

"This is everything I have," she pressed, her brows inching toward each other as though she didn't like the conversation. "I don't have much."

"Why not?"

"Why have more than I need?"

I frowned as I took in the one bag, which couldn't possibly have enough clothes or goods for a person, right? It was good that we didn't live in the cold, because a proper jacket sure as fuck wouldn't fit in there.

Well, we got paid more than enough to get her anything she was missing. She'd have to accompany us on missions, after all, which meant if we got called away to Alaska or where-ever-the-fuck the Guild sent us, she'd need proper goods.

"I'm surprised you didn't complain about staying here," I pointed out instead of harping on her belongings — or lack thereof — anymore. "I figured you'd start talking about boundaries or something like that."

"Believe it or not, I'm actually a competent guide. I know that staying close means I can offer better guiding, and not having to go far afterward is better for me."

Because you're going to be exhausted. That was the part she didn't mention, but she didn't have to. The reality was that if she refused any sort of physical guiding, then taking care of our squad was going to push her to her breaking point.

The reason for staying close often was that as guides and espers got more intimate, the odds that they'd end up having sex were almost hundred percent sort of thing. Living together made that all easier.

In her case, it was because she planned to run herself into the ground and didn't want to drag her ass far to sleep when finished.

Which didn't sit real well with me.

It was part of the whole esper thing, part of knowing that my life and sanity depended on guides, that I didn't like to see one hurting.

Not my problem.

"Well, let me show you your room and do proper introductions." I pushed away the thoughts, the questions, the unease. She just needed to do her job, and nothing else mattered.

The Guild would get off our asses and we could go back to our quiet little lives so long as this worked out. If we all knew where the others were coming from, if we accepted that this was strictly business, all the better for everyone.

I headed up the stairs, the soft strike of her sneakers against the steps telling me she followed.

I pointed at each door as we passed. "This is the bathroom, but each room has its own, too. This is Ingram's room, here is Kenyon's, mine, Shear's, and yours is here."

"Shear?"

"Right. He wasn't there yesterday. Look, you'll meet him at lunch today." I figured that was the most that anyone needed to know at the moment. It was best not to push things too much by making her think about that nut job.

Instead, I went to open the door to her room, only to have it pulled out before I could get there. On the inside stood Kenyon, a huge, goofy grin on his face.

I was about to ask what he'd done — that smile said it was probably something that was going to annoy me — when I spotted a wad of towels on her bed.

What the fuck?

"It's a swan," Kenyon explained, gesturing with both his hands like he was some woman on a game show, his expression full of unearned pride.

And again, I was reminded that I was surrounded by idiots, even though by this point I should have grown used to it.

"It looks like a very sad blobfish," Yun said before I could come up with anything.

Kenyon frowned, looking back at the atrocity. "Look, this is the body, this is the neck." He set his hands on his hips, shoulders drooping. "It's harder than the video made it seem."

"Why would you even do this?" I asked.

"You said to get her room ready. I thought it would be welcoming, like at a hotel."

"Is there candy on the pillow?" I rubbed my eyes as though that would take away the headache.

"It's a chocolate." He smiled like the dumbest six-year-old showing a horrible stick figure drawing to his mother. I'd met Kenyon's mother — I knew damn well that she spoiled him, always had.

Even now, with him being a powerful esper who fought monsters for a living, his mother came over once a week to wash his socks.

It was her fault he was this stupid.

"Thank you," Yun said, her tone implying she wasn't sure what else to say, the inflection rising at the end as though it were a question.

Which was a pretty fair reaction to most of Kenyon's antics.

"Go on," I ordered with a finger toward the stairs. "Let her get settled in. We're going to have lunch at noon, and we can get to know each other better then."

Kenyon nodded, his jovial attitude undimmed by my direction. Ignorance really was bliss, which explained why his stupid ass was perpetually happy.

Once he left, Yun slid past me and into the room. I leaned my shoulder against the doorframe, giving her space. "This room is yours. None of us will enter it without your permission. If you need something, let me know and we'll get it."

She didn't thank me, but I understood that. The fact was that we didn't do this out of the goodness of our hearts. We weren't offering her shelter and protection and whatever she needed because we were just that nice. She was paying for it with her body, by guiding us, and I had no doubts that anything we spent or gave was a paltry repayment in return.

"You've got a few hours, so get settled in. Noon. Lunch."

She nodded but said nothing else, so I shut the door behind me and let her be.

She was a necessary evil, a part of life for espers whether we liked it or not. In the end, after our little talk, I'd come to one conclusion for sure.

We were using each other, and in my experience, that made for the most dangerous and often best partnerships of all.

Chapter Three

Yun

Putting my items away always felt wrong. It was like cutting a round pie into square pieces — it just made my bones itch.

Maybe it came from the fact that each time I did it — when I folded my socks and underwear, placing them in drawers, and hung my meager outfits — it was never long before I had to repack them.

Setting down roots had never worked for me, and each time I had to unpack, it reminded me of it. It hurt worse, having to repack it all, like tearing those roots from the soil.

Which meant that at the last two places I'd gone to, I'd failed to unpack at all. I'd seen no reason to.

Living out of a backpack was fine with me. I had a few outfits, my bag organized, clothing the type that didn't wrinkle. It meant I didn't need any time to get 'settled in' as Carter had put it. Instead, I'd used the time to explore the room.

It was nice. Not as nice as a few others I'd been in, of course. The output of a squad determined its financial compensation. Since this squad barely kept their registration active, it meant they didn't make what the other, more famous ones did.

Of course, I didn't mind that. I'd lived with little, needed even less, so this was more than adequate. A bed, a desk, a bathroom with a tub deep enough to have my knees and tits below the water at the same time. This was everything I needed and then some.

I checked the space for any signs of cameras, then added my one change that I always made — a new door handle with a lock only I had the key for. I'd learned this little trick after my second squad, who'd kept sneaking into my room after missions to steal my panties.

Sure, an esper could break the door down if they wanted, but this at least made me feel as though I had some control.

Carter might have told me it was my space, but I knew better than to believe any esper.

No one showed up as I made the change, the small screwdriver I kept in my bag making quick work of the job. Within two minutes, I had the old handle off and the new one on. A check that the key worked, and I shut the door again, satisfied with a job well done.

I found nothing questionable. The men were weird, sure, but they hadn't struck me as dangerous.

Well, no more than any esper.

I went to the bedside table, my sleeping pills in hand. I didn't appreciate questions, so I preferred to hide them.

When I pulled open the drawer, however, I slammed it shut immediately, as though that would stop my brain from processing what I saw.

I paused, letting my mind reset. Maybe when I opened it again, I'd be wrong.

I'd be *happy* to be wrong.

Except when I slid the drawer open a second time, gripping the small black pull — yep, still there.

Spread out like some pervert's buffet were more sex toys and associated items than most adult stores kept on hand.

They weren't tossed in all willy-nilly, either. Nope. Someone had carefully placed these. I could almost imagine them testing the layout.

Should the dildo go to the left of the nipple clamps? No, no, the right is better.

There were condoms, lube, vibrators of all shapes, sizes and type, dildos, clamps, wipes. I pulled open the cabinet below the drawer, unable to process it all, only to find that space also sullied with more of this shit.

Floggers were hanging, and more clamps — these on chains — along with masks, gags, blindfolds.

What the hell was wrong with these men?

I shut both the cabinet and drawer far more carefully this time, then shook my head and tucked my pills back into my bag. No way would I put my precious, innocent sleeping pills into that depraved den.

I'd made myself clear, hadn't I? Just what the fuck were these men expecting?

Maybe they were left over from the last guide?

I shuddered as I pictured any guide stupid enough to let espers use things like that on them. Sure, I'd heard stories, heard guides talk about the 'perks' of a session, but I'd never once understood that drive.

Guiding was a part of life, a hated task that I had to complete. It wasn't pleasant, and it sure as fuck wasn't sexy.

Other guides might get wet from a session, but I was broken, snapped too early and unable to heal back into the normal form.

So if they thought this was what they were getting?

They were in for a fucking surprise.

A few hours later, the steps of the stairs didn't so much as creak beneath my feet. I'd heard that when espers moved into a place, they overhauled everything. The structure usually needed to be reinforced to withstand the general life of an esper.

This meant that the construction was always top-notch.

Despite the fact that Reject Squad was fairly well mocked, it seemed they were no exception to that rule. When I reached the bottom of the staircase, I found the table already full.

The three I'd already met—along with one new face—sat along the two sides of the rectangular table, with an empty plate at the head, clearly meant for me.

Yeah, this looked exactly like an interrogation.

Not that it shocked me. Some squads were so happy to have a guide that they didn't give a damn about details. Any guide willing to take on a squad like this deserved a bit of questioning, however.

Not to mention that there had to be a certain level of trust between espers and guides. They had to interact so much, had to put faith in one another. I didn't much want to answer questions—nor ask them—but that didn't mean I couldn't understand the desire.

I headed over, ignoring the way they all stared at me, and took the spot obviously meant for me. When I sat, I peered at the food there—a sandwich and fries. Neither appear overly culinary but edible enough.

"The information they sent us said you didn't have dietary restrictions," Carter said. "Is there anything you don't like? Anything we should get or avoid?"

I knew it really didn't matter, but something about that felt like giving away trade secrets, like telling them things they didn't need to know.

Sure, them finding out I hated carrots but loved apples probably wouldn't hurt me, but I still had found that telling espers anything never worked out in my favor.

"Nothing. It's all fine by me."

Carter said nothing, but a glance in his direction said he didn't believe me. Still, he shrugged, the same disinterest he often had. "You've met Kenyon and Ingram already." He gestured at each man.

Ingram hardly looked up from his plate, but Kenyon offered an excited wave that didn't all at fit the way he looked.

"This is Shear."

And *that one* caught my full attention. The last member of the squad, the one I hadn't met yet. I understood why, and for a moment, wondered if they'd hidden him on purpose to keep me from running out the moment I'd laid eyes on him.

He had eyes so bright blue that they could pass for neon. He had dark, curly hair piled on top of his head in a messy bun, the sides of his head shaved, and stark angles on his face that would have been fantastic on the cover of a magazine but seemed like way too much in real life. He was startling in his appearance, but even more so in the intensity of his gaze. He didn't say hi to me, didn't seem to acknowledge me—just stared.

"She's lying," he said softly, his voice distant.

"About what?" Carter asked.

"Everything." Shear blinked quickly, as though waking up, then peered down at his plate and picked at the items there.

"Stay out of my head," I snapped when his words made sense. He must have been a mentalist, one of the rare espers capable of telepathy, of mind reading, of any number of scary-as-shit skills. I turned my gaze on Carter, anger thrumming through my blood. "You never said you had a mentalist here."

"I figured you'd know who we had, and I didn't think it would matter."

I pressed my lips together, hating the way I felt violated by just that tiny bit of interaction. Mentalists were the *worst*. I'd only dealt with one, and after that?

I'd refused to take jobs that forced me to interact with them. If I'd known…

Then I'd have done nothing, since this was my only option. It was easy to be up in arms when a person had choices, but I sure as fuck didn't.

So instead, I just cast another glare in Shear's direction. "Don't get into my thoughts."

"They're messy," Shear said, his gaze down. "I don't want to be in there."

Yeah, well, neither do I.

At least we could agree on that.

"So, let me give you the rundown," Carter said. "Kenyon is a healer, and Ingram over there is a stealth specialist."

I nodded, though I had to admit it surprised me a bit. Kenyon was so boisterous, large and rather dumb, I'd assumed he was combat. Ingram, with his flashy tattoos, hadn't struck me as stealth based at all. In fact, I couldn't imagine that man blending in *anywhere*.

"Aren't you going to ask me what I am?" Carter asked, a hint of false hurt in his voice.

"Why would I?"

"Curiosity?"

I made a point of rolling my eyes in as least a respectful way as possible. "It's obvious. You have to be combat specialized. It's the only thing missing to be a functional squad. Plus, given all the weapons were right behind your desk, it makes sense that you'd be the one using them."

Carter grinned widely, and it seemed an honest smile for once. "Well, good to know we haven't been saddled with an idiot."

"If it was an idiot I could fuck, I'd prefer it," Ingram added on.

Carter offered him an exasperated look, then returned his gaze to me. "On that subject, you're sure about the whole no-touching thing? I mean, that's a pretty hard line there. I've never seen a guide able to hold on to something like that."

I shook my head in a quick jerk that caused my hair to spill forward from behind my ear. "Absolutely not. No touching at all."

"What if you change your mind during?" Kenyon asked. "I mean, guides do that, right? They think they want one thing, then get into the mood halfway through." The way he said it implied he'd experienced that before.

And he wasn't wrong.

At least not about normal guides.

I just wasn't normal.

"I won't change my mind. I've been a guide with the Guild for almost ten years, and I've never once changed my mind. I wouldn't get my hopes up if I were you, thinking you were different or something. You're not."

Ingram snorted. "You say that now. Give it a few weeks and we'll see what tune you're playing. Don't worry, little snowflake, when you change your mind, I'll be more than willing to fuck you." He drew his lips into a lopsided smile. "Until then, feel free to use the goodies I left you."

I should have figured it had been Ingram, given the little interaction we'd had so far. It seemed like something he'd do.

"Goodies?" Kenyon asked. "Did you leave some for me, too?"

Ingram snickered. "I don't mind sharing."

Kenyon peered at me, his smile wide and stupid and hopeful.

"Trust me, you don't want any." Even as I said that, I thought about how hilarious it would have been to show Kenyon what Ingram had stored there. Of course, dumb or not, Kenyon *was* an esper, and given what he'd said earlier, he wasn't as innocent as he might have seemed.

Kenyon pouted but went back to his food, seeming easy to distract, which worked perfectly for me.

"How do you keep in touch about missions?" I asked. "I have to make sure I prepare if we'll be traveling or anything."

Kenyon tilted his head like a confused pup while Ingram snickered. Shear didn't even acknowledge my question, but Carter pointed toward the fridge. "There's a whiteboard."

I frowned as I looked in the direction he'd gestured to find a small whiteboard attached to the front of the fridge door. The sight was so absurd that I couldn't help it before I got up from the table and went over to the fridge.

If I tilted my head, sure, those could almost appear to be words written on it? Maybe it said Tuesday, January 64th?

"*This* is your method for keeping track of jobs?"

Carter sounded almost hurt when he responded. "Hey, that's kept us on track for years!"

"We have a board?" Kenyon asked as he scratched his head.

"I thought it was a grocery list," Ingram said.

"That explains why Carter never buys the yogurt I keep adding to the list," Shear said.

"Yogurt? I thought that said yoga. I wondered why I kept going to that damn yoga class every week by myself," Carter huffed.

I couldn't even bring myself to respond as I stared at these four men, wondering if stupidity was contagious. These were espers, right? I wanted to yank all four of them down to the Guild and get them retested right now, because at the moment, I found it hard to believe such a thing. They seemed far too chaotic and dumb for me to even consider how they'd enter dungeons and fight monsters.

They were idiots.

I rubbed my hands over my face. "We need to have a way to schedule and communicate," I explained, wondering how I became the esper whisperer all of a sudden. Normally, the squads I'd worked with all ran smoothly. They had someone in charge and they all fell into line.

Sure, they were people, which meant they made mistakes, they let loose, but they took their jobs seriously.

These men seemed to take *nothing* seriously.

"We have a group text," Kenyon said, turning his phone around to show me.

And just like that, I wished we had eye bleach. The thread appeared to be nothing but gifs—ones of cats from Kenyon and mostly porn from Ingram.

This was how they got anything done?

That explained why they got *nothing* done. How could anyone complete anything in this mess? The only thing in order that I'd spotted so far was the weaponry cabinet.

Then again, I guess having guns lying around was probably a pretty bad idea and a step too far for these fools.

Carter handed me something, and it took a moment to realize it was a cell phone. "You're in the group text already. Don't worry."

I stared down at the phone, the thing nicer than anything I'd had in…well, perhaps forever. I tried to hand it back. "I don't need this."

He folded his hands behind him, a sure sign he didn't plan to take it back. "Sorry, those are the rules. You're in this squad, we need to communicate with you. Think of it as a perk."

I sighed, hating the feeling of owing anyone anything. Worse, something about the surprisingly large and light phone felt like a collar, like a tether holding me to them. Still, they weren't wrong. Wasn't I the one complaining about how we needed to be able to plan, to know our schedules? How was that going to happen without a phone?

And I certainly wasn't in a position to get one myself. Being a guide had its advantages, but some of the downsides were that we didn't really have credit scores or documentation to sign contracts on our own.

So I set it on the table and took my seat again, a quiet awkwardness in my chest that I couldn't shake. I muttered out a sullen 'thanks' before focusing again on my food.

"We'll work on a schedule," Carter offered, tone soft as though trying to appease me. "But we don't do a whole lot to worry about."

"How many jobs do you take on a month?"

"Four, maybe? Usually local stuff. We get called in if a dungeon opens close by, but only in emergencies. Otherwise, they leave us alone for the most part."

I shuddered at the mere mention of a dungeon. It was difficult to hide that reaction, even after all these years.

Funny, given that was what everyone talked about around me. What else did espers have to say? Still, it never failed to conjure up horrors I'd rather not ever think about again.

I pushed it aside, relegating those feelings to the darkness reserved for my past. "You're all S-Rank. Why aren't you called into more dungeons?"

Carter lifted one of his dark eyebrows. "You really don't know much about us, do you?" He let out a dark chuckle. "We're S-Rank, sure, but we aren't the *good* ones, you know, the ones they put on television that play up for the cameras real well. Plus, we aren't huge fans of doing dangerous work, so we usually hang back. If it's bad enough, they'll call us in to help mop up around the entrance, but that's it. So don't expect a ton of travel."

And, boy, didn't that make my day…

I'd managed to avoid most dangerous work as a guide. Some guides, the flashy ones, they got stuck right outside a dungeon, helping the espers who needed guiding during large-scale operations. I'd never been one of them, so I'd gotten to stay back to help after my squad arrived back to their place.

It served me just fine. I saw no reason to put myself into danger any more than I had to.

Still, it made me glance around the table at the four men here.

No, not men, but espers.

I'd dealt with lots of them over the years, all different types, different ranks, different ages, but they were similar in their need for approval, in their desire to prove themselves. Sure, they had pressure on them. I wouldn't pretend like they had it that easy or anything—I wasn't that short-sighted—but they'd always struck me as show offs.

Espers and squads tended to battle for top rankings, wanting to see themselves on the news, wanting to prove themselves. In fact, it was so bad near the top that people threw each under the bus just to get ahead.

Which was why I had no idea how to take these four who didn't give a fuck about those sorts of things. It went to explain why they had such a bad reputation, didn't it? They really didn't care about doing anything, so maybe they deserved all that hate and ridicule, after all.

At least, that was how they seemed.

I ate slowly, unsure how to put that together, how to understand or interact with these men. Normally, I knew what espers wanted, could tolerate them, could control them just by understanding them. I never enjoyed it, but it at least felt safer because I understood it.

These four, though, they didn't follow any of the rules I was accustomed to. It made me uneasy, had me watching them with a new wariness. Espers were dangerous, sure, but they'd been easy to predict before. If these four didn't do as I expected, if they didn't follow the trends I knew of, how was I supposed to deal with them? How was I supposed to stay a step ahead?

The answer escaped me, so I focused instead on my food. I'd need to pay attention, to learn the new rules, because I knew better than most that my survival could depend on it.

Chapter Four

Ingram

The beast moved before me, a lumbering, mindless, rage-filled monster. It had slipped through a small portal, escaped a dungeon, as a few of them did now and again. Most dungeons opened fully, allowing espers to go inside, trapping civilians inside at the same time. Those were the best-known type, the ones that made the news. Occasionally, though, smaller portals would open for short periods of time, like tears in the fabric of our world, with monsters escaping through them before they closed and disappeared again. These portals could be open for only a matter of a few minutes, gone before anyone knew about them. They were rarely ranked or remembered.

Shear was sensitive enough to notice them, however, as was I. We felt the disturbance, even the slight one caused by unstable portals. Only a fool would enter them, but we didn't mind picking off the beasties that got through. It was hardly a workout for Rank-S espers like us, but given the tension in the house, I appreciated the chance to get out.

The Guild wouldn't even bother to send anyone, given it was a low level. They'd view it as too insignificant to waste time on. It meant they wouldn't order espers there, but we did as we fucking wished.

Shear had confused the monster that had gotten free, forced it to move away from the community of homes and toward an open park which, given the late hour, was entirely empty.

Better this way. I preferred avoiding the risk of collateral damage. Our jobs were hard enough as it was without needing to deal with civilians. Some screamed, attracting the attention of the monsters, and others — the worst kind — actively tried to help, which just made things harder.

If they got themselves offed, that wasn't my problem. I didn't plan to lose any sleep over an idiot putting themselves in danger. The problem was that when the news got wind of it — or, god forbid, a video — the Guild liked to point fingers and blame us, and Carter ended up angry over it all.

I didn't need to have him bitching at us over anything else — it happened enough already.

I moved through the shadows, in the space between this world and the dungeons, not quite here but not elsewhere, either. It hid me from everything, turned me into a mirage, allowed me to move fast, unseen, until I arrived just behind the beast.

It was twisted, just as they all were, as though some strange intelligence that had seen animals and nightmares had mixed them until it spat this vile creature out. This thing ran on four legs, its chest wider than its hips, its feet tipped with claws, the face more like that of a horse with fangs.

I could still recall the first time I'd seen a beast like this, when I'd come face to face with one before I'd turned into an esper. Back then I'd been little, just a kid, all skinny and attitude in that gangly stage before I actually put on muscle. I hadn't known back then that I'd be one of the few who would change, who'd turn into an esper. There weren't any tests, nothing to figure it out, not until it happened sometime in the teenaged years.

The monster had charged out of the forest line back in Oregon, bigger than anything I'd seen before, roaring so loudly the ground shook beneath my feet. It had startled me so much that I hadn't been able to even move, to jump out of the way.

And I'd done nothing.

I'd just stood there watching as that thing bounded right at me.

The moment it had towered over me, close enough that the rotten scent of its breath hit me, when I realized that I was looking straight at my death, something had gotten between us.

An esper.

My first time meeting one, in fact. It wasn't like they usually hung out in poor-ass little towns, not unless they had good reason, and that reason was a portal that had opened a few miles away.

My mom had told me to stay inside, and I'd ignored her, like kids do, wanting to get a glimpse of the portal.

It wasn't on TV, it was in my own fucking town, and I just knew the other kids would be talking about it come Monday.

It was funny to think that I was that esper asshole now. I'd thought he was some hero back then, amazed that he'd jumped between that beast and me. He was bigger than life, willing to face off against a monster like that.

And now I stalked something far more dangerous without breaking a sweat.

What I hadn't known back then was that the esper had been a B-Rank, which was the reason he was out that far, mopping up strays who'd gotten past the line.

On the other hand, here I was with an A-Rank beast that would have wiped the floor with that esper asshole, assuming he was still alive.

It wasn't like espers usually lived long or happy lives.

"Finish it." Shear's voice in my head grated on my nerves as it always did. I'd gotten used to it, as used to that bullshit as anyone could ever get, but that didn't mean I liked it.

Still, telling him to knock it off didn't matter. He never fucking listened, assuming he even understood anything.

At least Kenyon was an honest-to-fuck idiot. It was hard to blame him for much when he couldn't help it.

Shear was smart—too smart. He just didn't understand what being a human meant. Maybe that came from spending so much time looking into people's brains. Anyone would go fucking insane from that.

Still, he wasn't wrong. I slipped in close to the beast, watching as it shook its head back and forth in confusion. No doubt Shear had fucked their brains up so much they had no idea which way was forward. I had no idea what nightmares he'd planted there, how he'd warped the world around it.

I'd experienced it a time or two when my mental shield had failed, when I'd gotten caught up in a wide-cast illusion, and it wasn't anything I wanted to feel again.

I slid out of that shadowy realm just beside the hulking monster and closed my hand around its throat. A quick jerk caused a sickening crack of bone, and the body fell into a useless, still heap in the dirt.

Shear came up beside me. "It's farther away from the portal than they usually roam."

I turned my gaze toward the portal that had opened but not remained open. "Sometimes they're more stupid than usual."

Shear pressed his lips together, those weird fucking eyes of his glowing even in the dark. "It's different. The way they move, the way they travel. It's with purpose."

"You're just being paranoid. What are you, six, believing in ghost stories? You need me to check for monsters under your bed, tonight?" I didn't hide my mocking tone in the least. Let him hear it—he deserved it.

"No. I can check it myself." He shook his head, as though he'd worked through options, then tossed them aside. "Something is different. Something is coming."

"That's cryptic as fuck and more than a little annoying. Either say something useful or don't, but don't pull that bullshit."

Shear inched his eyebrows toward each other and shook his head again. It reminded me that as difficult as he was, as annoying as his words were, I should just have been fucking thankful that I didn't live inside that fucked-up skull of his.

I had no idea what nightmares swam around in there, but if the things he cast into other people's heads were any indication, it wasn't a great area.

I lifted my arm to look at my watch, then hit the button for a cleanup crew. It pinned the location, and a moment later, a response told me they'd gotten the request and were sending people out.

No reason to wait around for it. At this point in the night, no one would come wandering this way, and even if they did? A dead monster was a hell of a lot less traumatizing than a live one.

Shear and I headed back to the office, and I remembered why I preferred working with him compared to anyone else. Shear remained silent most of the time. Sure, he could read my thoughts if he wanted — and sometimes even if he didn't want to — but he didn't fill the space with pointless talking.

And if I wanted to, he let me.

Kenyon never shut up, and Carter always felt the need to bitch at me over something I wasn't doing right. They were both always on my ass, but at least Shear knew how to shut the fuck up for a while.

I drove — Shear tended to get distracted, and I didn't need to get anything broken in a wreck — and in another twenty minutes, I pulled the SUV into the underground garage space, accessible from the front of the building. A two-car garage was almost unheard of right off the beach, so finding it had been worth every pretty penny we'd spent on the beachfront property.

Shear said nothing as he left the car and headed inside, going up to his room in a way that would have been rude from anyone else. We made exceptions for him, though, and honestly?

Sometimes I preferred him to leave so I didn't have to deal with his weird-ass personality.

I frowned as I stepped inside, the feeling strange. It didn't take long for me to identify the source.

Guiding.

Not direct guiding. That was stronger. It was the difference between a slice of apple pie and just picking up a slight whiff of it. With Yun in the house, a subtle guiding effect took over, something that would ease espers in that space. It wasn't enough to save one, of course, not enough to really stop corruption, but it reminded me why S-Rank guides were so fucking prioritized.

This could make the difference for some, this slight feeling of peace. Sure, a part of me fucking hated the idea of anyone affecting me that way, even in the positive, because I wanted to do shit on my own.

The other part of me, however, felt the gentle stroking of that power and wondered what she'd feel like if I slid into her. I wanted to watch her squirm beneath me, her fingers digging into my arms, her hips rolling. I wanted to taste the sweat that beaded up on her chest, to take her as she took the corruption from me.

I shook my head to dislodge the fantasy.

Was I a pervert? Yeah, I sure fucking was. I didn't mind testing boundaries, but I drew my own line at whipping my dick out where it wasn't wanted — and so far, that guide had made it clear she didn't want it.

I didn't think that would last, of course.

I headed up the stairs, taking them two at a time. We'd driven for a total of forty minutes for what was a thirty-second fight — if I even wanted to call it a fight. It hadn't taken much out of me, other than winding me up and making me crave more.

That's how it always was, though.

I wanted *more*. More of what, I had no fucking idea. Just more. More fight, more purpose, more reason, more guiding.

It all wrapped around me as I showered until I felt as though I couldn't breathe.

This feeling inside me hadn't gone away, not for a fucking minute, though it lessened when I did one specific thing.

I grabbed my phone, water droplets still running down my bare skin, over the intricate lines of the tattoos that covered me, and sent a message.

It didn't take much, just a few words. I didn't even bother to pay attention to who I sent it to — anyone with a star by their name in my contacts would do.

The response was fast. An immediate yes and an address.

This clawing need for more, this hunger that never found satiation, it only quieted when I lost myself in the body of someone else.

Sure, I was a pervert and a man whore and a fucking bastard, but it was the only damned time I found even a moment of solace.

Chapter Five

Yun

Yep, everyone is looking at us...

I much preferred flying under the radar. Being an S-Rank guide meant people knew about me, of course, but I never enjoyed basking in that sunlight like others.

Like Mercy, over there.

Mercy wasn't her *real name*, of course. Or, at least, that was what I assumed. She was the Guild's perfect little guide, so they'd probably renamed her just to make her look better.

Who could resist the blonde guide named Mercy who looked as though she could walk any runway?

She smiled brightly as she greeted people, sweet but not too sweet, nice but not too nice. She gave off, 'you could fuck me if you play your cards right' in just the right amount to make simps of everyone who came in contact with her.

"You know her?" Carter asked from beside me.

"We've met," I hedged, a discomfort settling deep in my stomach. "Have you met her?"

"By which you mean, has she guided me?"

I blew out a breath and turned my gaze from her, unwilling to answer Carter. The answer was yes, that I absolutely wanted to know about that, but I sure as fuck wasn't about to *say* that. It made me sound like some scorned girlfriend.

Carter snickered softly. "Yes, she's guided me before."

"I didn't ask."

"But you were curious."

"You sure think you mean more to me than you do."

"You're not even a *little* curious?"

Yes. "Nope."

"Yun?"

I managed to hold in a groan before looking up and finding the very guide discussed standing just before me.

And as much as I hated it, she looked even more perfect up close. Usually, from this distance, people could spot the problems. The blemishes, the way one boob was larger than the other, *something*. It was like when high-def TV became a thing and newscasters stopped looking so good.

Leave it to Mercy to still look fucking perfect.

"Hey," I said with an awkward wave, smiling as though I hadn't just been dreading this very interaction.

She hugged me in the same overly friendly way she reacted to me every time we met. It always made me uncomfortable, of course, but it was hard to get too mad at her. She was like an excited puppy—she meant nothing by her actions, and it was my hang-up, not hers. When she moved away, she offered me a bright smile, as though we were best friends. "I didn't think you'd be coming today."

"Yeah, me either."

Truth be told, I'd *tried* to get out of it. I hated coming to Guild meetings like this, but Carter had insisted. It seemed even Reject Squad had to show up from time to time, whether they wanted to or not. This was one such meeting, where the higher-ups had demanded both their presence and mine.

I'd rarely gone to these before. Even when part of a squad, they'd always let me off the hook and allowed me to stay back.

Guides weren't always required, after all. The information presented in these had more to do with upcoming dungeons, with staffing issues, with territory line changes. Those were the jurisdiction of espers, not guides.

However, Carter had absolutely refused to hear any of my excuses when I'd tried to stay back. Instead, he'd just assured me that there would be good food.

As though *that* made it better.

So here I was, dressed in simple black slacks and a long-sleeved, white, button-up shirt. It was nothing compared to a few of the other guides around.

Mercy wore a white dress like some angel, and she had an honest-to-god *ribbon* hanging down from her hair. What the fuck? Was she trying to play the part of an eight-year-old?

The guides tended to be easier to spot than the espers, since they stuck out. They wore colors, somehow seemed softer, and often had on far more expensive clothes, a stark contrast from the all black of the espers.

They stood as the showpiece that the squad wanted to display as a symbol of wealth.

I glanced down at my clothing, suddenly uneasy. I hadn't dressed up, and Carter hadn't asked me to.

Was it because we all already knew I was defective? Because we all knew the old saying of putting lipstick on a pig?

The weight in my head, the discomfort lessened all at once. It was almost enough for me to ignore how it had happened — *almost*.

I twisted, my gaze finding Shear across the room, those eerie blue eyes locked on me.

"Stop it."

He huffed a soft breath and turned away, as though he'd let me have my little tantrum.

"So how are you liking your new…assignment?" Mercy stumbled on that last word, as though unsure how to phrase it. It felt like when a person gets divorced and moves into a tiny apartment. People want to be nice and ask about it, but they also know it's a huge downgrade, so wonder if they should mention it or not.

"It's fine," I said, words tight. No reason to say anything more, and 'it's fine' was as honest as I could get. "It's only been a couple of days."

A couple of entirely uneventful days. I had dinner with them most evenings, and one or two of them disappeared at any one time. I had no idea what they were doing, but so far, they hadn't asked for any guiding.

It meant that it had been pretty boring. A lot of playing on the laptop they'd supplied, and a lot of reading.

Though I knew my time off would end soon. No esper could go forever without guiding, after all, which meant I'd have to earn my keep sooner rather than later.

A little fact I tried hard to ignore.

"What about you?" I asked to take the focus off me.

"Oh, same for me."

"Not going to settle down?"

"I'm not the type to get tied down. I prefer working freelance." Which meant she often handled the espers at the portals, taking care of the high-risk issues, filling in when squad guides got overwhelmed. It also put her out in front of all the cameras, a place she excelled.

Her gaze moved off me, to Carter, and boy did her expression change. It amazed me, really, as I wasn't sure I'd *ever* seen that smile of hers fade. "Carter," she said, voice tense.

If he noticed the reaction—and I'd bet he did—he didn't let on. Instead, he smiled as though they were best of friends. "Hey, Mercy. Lovely dress."

She glanced down as if she'd forgotten what she had on. She patted the white fabric, her words short. "Thank you. I should get going." Her gaze returned to me, and was that…pity? "Call me anytime, Yun."

Her words felt like a lifesaver she'd thrown out to me.

But why?

I held back my questions. That wasn't the reaction of a guide who simply felt bad about who I'd gotten saddled with. Instead, it was personal, had only started when she'd gotten a look at Carter, like there was some history I didn't want to know but perhaps needed to know.

I turned to ask when a voice broke out through the large, open room. "We are going to get started, so please find a seat."

That silenced the questions, pushed them aside for later, as Carter held his hand out to gesture me forward, to lead me to a table near the back without touching me.

Just what did Mercy know that I didn't?

And did it even matter?

Chapter Six

Shear

I focused my attention toward the stage and not on the rest of the turbulent room, not on the espers that surrounded me, the guides dotted about, and certainly *not* on the woman who sat beside me.

In fact, I tried to make that space a void where nothing could get in or out. I pretended it didn't exist, limiting my skills so *she* couldn't distract me.

Yet distract me she did.

Something about her forced my darker instincts to rise, as though she called to the corruption that swarmed inside me.

Why?

What made her different? Special?

In my experience, everyone was special, which meant no one really was. We were all just bad copies of one another, all mimicking the behavior of others to get accepted into whatever little tribe we found ourselves near. Instinct compelled people, even espers, to form groups, to use social structures for our survival, and it meant that people ended up much the same at the end of the day.

So why couldn't I write Yun off as I did others? Why did she interest me in a way no one else had? It wasn't a great feeling, not entirely, but rather like those intrusive thoughts that told people to throw themselves off tall cliffs.

The reasons behind it hardly mattered. Instead, I needed to focus on how to react.

Why something was the way it was didn't change the course of action to take, after all.

"We are three months out from the next stable dungeon appearance." The speaker was Jin Foley, a debuff esper, S-Rank, who ran most of the planning for Guild-wide offensives. He was young, at only twenty-two, but even I had to admit to feeling impressed when I had seen him move through a battlefield just two years ago.

The Guild president sat off to the side of the stage, appearing much older than he had just a few years ago, as though time had suddenly moved faster. He rarely spoke much at such meetings anymore, leaving the running of the Guild to the younger crowd. Instead, he'd morphed from a powerful esper capable of great things to a figurehead.

"After the stable dungeon, The Edge, appeared six months ago, it came to our attention that the casualty numbers were far higher than they should have been. The reality is that we can't expect squads who never work together to show up for a large-scale offensive and collaborate perfectly on the spot. We do not want a repeat of that fiasco, so we will be hosting joint missions for the next three months in preparation. These missions will put those of you with cooperative powers together, to help you work through difficulties, prior to the dungeon opening."

"So we know where the dungeon will open?" someone called from one of the front tables.

Jin shook his head. "We know it will be in the southwest of the United States, but nothing more than that. That's why, in the days before, we want all squads prepared at the Guild staging center in Tucson, ready to move out. From there, we can be at any potential location in a few hours."

My lip lifted on its own, though I agreed with the reasoning. I had gotten used to working with my squad, had gained a certain level of comfort with them. The last thing I wanted was to end up stuck with a bunch of strangers, to have to exist in close quarters.

Learning to close out people was a difficult skill, and the more trust I had with a person, the more time I spent around them, the easier the task was for me. Having to spend time in close proximity to others was bound to strain me.

And, as much as I would love to think we wouldn't be expected to participate—as we often weren't—we wouldn't have gotten called here if they didn't intend us to play some part.

"Is everyone here going?" some idiot called out.

Some idiot meaning Kenyon, sitting at the end of our table.

Jin looked back, squinting as though our seat rested so far toward the back of the room that he could hardly see us. "Yes. Every squad called in here will be part of the local groups. We will also call in other squads from farther away, but they will come near the end for backup. We want to keep this to the Western Section for the main work."

I rolled my eyes at that, at the games these fools played. They cared about territories, about how their group looked compared to another. We were all part of the North American Guild, but loyalty rested with the individual sections within NAG—and their acronym was fitting. At the end of the day, the *Guild* was what controlled everything about our lives, and they didn't mind fucking us over for their own benefit.

They wanted to prove that *we'd* taken care of this ourselves. They wanted to pat themselves on their backs and talk about how great they were, how they'd handled the dungeon all on their own.

It reminded me of how every esper in the Guild acted as well, all scrambling over the corpses of those who came before to try to reach some top spot, as though that would justify our tenuous position in the world.

"You're seriously going to let Reject Squad in?" a voice asked from the crowd.

"Didn't we learn our lesson before?" another chimed in.

"Things are bad enough as it is—why make it worse by letting them come?"

Person after person spoke up until a low murmur rushed through the space. I could pick up each one if I wanted—even if I didn't—but I tried to ignore it.

None of the insults were new or all that inventive. No one had thought about it too deeply nor spent the energy to at least come up with something creative.

It meant that no matter what they volleyed, nothing landed.

I'd rather not be there either.

I'd seen what doing the so-called right thing got a person, and I wanted nothing to do with that. I preferred not to make the same mistake more than once.

Carter rose, and for a moment, the room quieted. Was he about to say something profound? Something that would reassure them all that we were meant to be there? To remind them that despite all appearances, we were still S-Rank espers who were more than capable?

"I know you're all concerned, and trust me, I understand." *A good start.* "I want to assure you that I don't want to be there anymore than you want me there. To make up for it, I'll bring brownies."

Wonderful.

I sighed at the sudden silence that engulfed the room, as not a single person in there knew how to react to such absurdity.

Then again, that was Carter's move. He knew exactly how to throw people off their game, how to toy with them, how to play the part of an idiot so he could get them to follow his lead.

This was no different. Beneath that amused smirk, I sensed the things he kept hidden.

The fear. The anger. The pain.

Something stabbed back through that line, like a needle slipping into the center of my brain, and if I didn't recognize it at his warning to stop poking around in his mind, I might have believed he had nothing to do with it—given his completely unchanged expression.

He sat back down, the scratching of his chair against the tile floor loud.

After another awkward heartbeat, Jin spoke up as though the exchange hadn't happened. "Every squad here has been chosen because we think you'll bring something important to this offensive. I will send all the relevant information along with the upcoming schedule of training to your squads. I have complete confidence that we will be able to face this danger as we have others, that we will overcome as we always have. This will be the third time some of you have faced this dungeon. Many of us have lost good people to it. However, we will absolutely not allow The Pitt to win."

The Pitt.

The name sent a general unease through the entire room. Sure, anyone with a calendar knew it was coming, that the appearance of the stable dungeon was going to happen soon, but hearing the name never failed to put any esper who had faced it before on edge.

That wasn't what caught my attention, though.

Instead, it was a sudden blast from my side, from the little guide perched there between us. Her expression didn't change, her body language didn't change, but her mind? All the little synapsis inside that secretive, illusive little brain of hers lit up like a fucking Christmas parade.

Well, it seems someone has a history...

Chapter Seven

Yun

The Pitt.

No matter how many times I tried to purge that place from my memories, the very name conjured it all right back up like a shitty magic trick. I stood in the bathroom, splashing water on my face to try to clear away the energy coursing inside me.

The water remained freezing cold no matter how long I'd left it on warm, but maybe that was better. The slight shock to my system helped clear my mind.

Shear had stared at me as the meeting had closed, suggesting he'd caught wind of something. I suspected that despite his presence in this squad, he was far too good an esper not to feel something. I could school my features, I could keep myself from reacting outright, but even I couldn't control my feelings.

I'd excused myself with a weak reasoning of needing a bathroom break. Most men knew better than to ask questions when a woman said that, so they'd let me go without interrogation or complaint.

It gave me a moment to try to gather myself.

I'd known it was coming, of course. The Pitt opened every ten years like a fucking alarm clock put on snooze, showing back up just to fuck everyone over again. I'd just ignored it, hoped that it would never be *my* problem again.

Who would have thought that the fuckups of the NAG would get put on the front lines? That *I'd* end up right back there?

I leaned forward, gripping the sides of the sink, desperate for something to help me gather my wits and shove the feelings that seemed far too large back inside my shattered psyche.

"Well, if it isn't the Blizzard."

The hated name echoed off the bright, tiled walls in the restroom, giving me what I needed to stand straight and turn around.

There stood a woman who appeared vaguely familiar. I couldn't place her, but suspected I'd interacted with her at some point. Then again, espers sometimes ran together after a while.

"You actually show up here?" she asked, her toned arms crossed. "You've got more balls than I figured."

I nearly asked her who she was when it hit me.

Rosalind. The last time I'd seen her, her face had looked different—but horror will do that to a person. No wonder I didn't recognize her, what with the sneer of disgust on her features.

It also explained *why* she had that look.

Anyone who saw a guide put down a member of their squad would probably not be too thrilled with them

"I was here with—"

"With Reject Squad. Yeah, I know—I saw. At first, I was pissed you would show your face here after everything you've done, but you know what? It makes sense that you're with *them*."

The words chafed, but I refused to let her see she'd gotten beneath my skin.

Besides, she wasn't *entirely* wrong, not after what had happened.

"I'll be going." No reason to fight with her over any of this. She had reason to feel the way she did, and to be honest, I didn't want to be here any more than she wanted me here.

Plus, with the information discussed in the meeting, I wasn't anywhere in my right mind. Even if I could have handled this sort of exchange normally, I sure wasn't up to it right now.

I went to pass her, angling my body so I didn't brush against her, when a strong current gripped me and shoved me back. My heels skidded against the tile floor, my cheeks so warm I worried they might have burned from the blast of hot air.

My back struck the hard tile, knocking the air from my lungs.

I blinked quickly, tears rushing from my eyes—not because I cried, but because of the searing air. When I could clear my vision enough to see, I spotted Rosalind before me, her lip curled up on one side.

Right, she could control weather—specifically wind and heat. It was easy to forget—or ignore—the specific abilities of espers. Guides could do a single thing, but espers had a nearly unlimited well of powers to pull from, and keeping it straight had always seemed like far too much work.

This reminded me of Rosalind, however, of what she wielded. She was only an A-Rank, of course, but an A-Rank could kill me just like an S.

"You think I'd let you just walk out of here? You get to walk away and pretend like you didn't do a damn thing? What, just because you're a guide?" Spittle hit my face as she spoke, a testament to her anger — as though my being trapped against a wall didn't make the point just fine?

"I'm a guide," I said, my voice cracking from the hot air that surrounded me. "Do you really think hurting me here is going to go well for you?"

"You think being a guide is a shield for you? You're defective, nothing but a useless guide who hurts those you're supposed to help. We'd be better off without having a time bomb like you around."

She isn't wrong.

The feeling of her powers restraining me scratched at my already wounded psyche. It was the worst time for this, but she was lucky she hadn't physically touched me. I doubted I could handle that, even if I agreed with her.

If someone ended things, wouldn't everyone be better off?

If I wasn't around anymore, I couldn't hurt others, wouldn't experience pain myself. The temptation to just give in hit me — probably because I hadn't defended myself on purpose so far. It had simply been that innate instinct for survival that had protected me before.

Just as I gave in, however, as I accepted this as the logical end to my life, the heat disappeared.

I collapsed forward, my knees striking the tile so hard my teeth snapped together. I braced my weight on my hands, breathing in greedy lungfuls of air, realizing just how little oxygen had been around me.

When I lifted my gaze to see why she'd decided not to kill me, I found a sight I sure hadn't expected.

Carter stood there, Rosalind dangling by the throat in his grasp, gripping his wrist as she kicked her legs. His eyes shone bright purple, casting a glow over Rosalind's face, and he appeared every bit the monster espers could be.

The most terrifying thing, though? The one that really set me off?

The way he kept smiling. He didn't glare, didn't sneer. Instead, he still had an entirely unhinged smile on his face, as though he had no connection to rational thought anymore.

The sight, along with news of The Pitt and Rosalind's attack, proved too much for my mind. After the lack of sleep, the lack of so many things, I found myself swallowed up by the blackness.

I had no idea how long I remained unconscious. I didn't dream, didn't fight against the wonderful void of nothing that occurred when under. Instead, I let myself rest in it, unbothered by anything.

The world came back slowly, hazy, a moment of bliss before reality struck again—as it always did. I found myself on a comfortable bed, a familiar one, instead of the tile I vaguely recalled smacking my face against as I'd passed out.

I opened my eyes, blinking away the remnants of sleep. It wasn't good sleep, not the type where you woke refreshed, where you stretched your arms and inhaled deep breaths to energize.

Nope, this was the sort that happened when you fall back asleep, but not for long enough. It was like waking up after an impromptu, accidental nap, when drool coats your cheek and your mouth feels full of grit.

I expected to find myself alone, but instead, a broad back met me.

I gulped hard, but at least they sat on the side of the bed, faced mostly away, without any contact at all.

Carter.

I recalled how he'd looked in that bathroom, holding an A-Rank like she were nothing more than a pile of yarn and with about that much fight to her. Sure, he was a higher rank, but that didn't explain how he could do that so easily.

And his eyes...

I jerked backward at the memory, having seen similar eyes in the past. My back struck the headboard as I tried to get distance between us, everything inside me screaming to get away, to do whatever it took to escape.

He turned, and I expected to see purple, to see that vicious shade of violet that haunted me.

Except...he looked normal.

His smile had the softened edges again, none of the signs of corruption that I'd seen in the bathroom.

Had I imagined those? Were they just sparks of my brain where the past mingled with the present, where my trauma forced me to relive things that I'd rather have forgotten all about?

"You with us again?"

"What—" My voice cut out halfway through the question, but I couldn't say I minded that. I had no idea exactly where the question was headed anyway.

He gestured toward the nightstand. "There's water beside you—should help with the throat issue. Rosalind controls air—hot, dry air, to be specific. So when she uses it like that, it can not only push people, but she can suffocate them. Plus, it's hell on the skin, so make sure to moisturize."

I found myself reaching for the glass he'd indicated, caught off guard by his words as usual. If he ever made sense, it might make me more suspicious. Somehow, his nonsense made it impossible to think straight, to recognize that he was a complete lunatic.

But I didn't see what I thought I did, right?

There was no way. Eyes like that would mean standing on the brink of corruption, dancing just breaths away from absolute ruin. No esper could survive in that condition for more than a few minutes— *maybe.*

And looking at him now, I couldn't imagine that. An esper that far gone couldn't ever pretend to be normal.

Impossible.

The water helped my parched throat, and three gulps of it made me feel ready to ask again. "What happened to her?"

Carter tilted his head. "She attacked a guide. That's a death sentence."

I sat up straighter, clutching the glass tightly in my hands. Even if she was a bitch—which clearly she was—I didn't want her to die. I didn't want *anyone* to die, and certainly didn't want that on my hands. "She didn't mean to."

"Of course she did. Come on, Yun, you should know better than most that we need to set an example, make it clear that people can't do that. Otherwise, it could happen again."

"I don't care. I don't want her dead."

The word *dead* stuck in my throat as though I hadn't drank any water at all. It terrified me.

People didn't give *dead* the respect it deserved.

The truth was that it wasn't death that scared me, but the moments that came before. The fear, the pain — I'd seen them all on the faces of others.

Even more terrifying than dying was the idea of others dying while I could do nothing. It was loneliness, the darkness, being isolated and without others because I'd lived while they'd died.

My breathing sped, turning shallow, making my chest burn.

"She isn't dead," Carter offered, his tone softening a hair. "I didn't even report her, so she's not going to get any additional punishments."

Additional?

The word stuck out to me, but I refused to pick at it. If she hadn't gotten turned over and she was alive, that was enough, right?

"She'll know better than to try that again, though. I don't like to repeat myself." An undercurrent of threat rested in that statement, like a warning to me as well.

I shuddered, the memory of how he'd looked coming back to me, one I still refused to believe.

"Did she say anything?"

"Oh, she said a lot. People tend to run their mouths when they're scared, after all. It doesn't really do anyone any favors, but it's still human nature, I guess."

"About me."

"Oh, you mean why they call you Blizzard? Well, I already knew that, so it wasn't exactly new information."

I pulled my legs up and wrapped my arms around them, setting my chin on top of my knees. Sure, I'd known I had a reputation, but most of the details had stayed quiet because the Guild hadn't wanted anyone to know about the unstable guide they kept shuffling around from squad to squad. They wanted that to stay hidden, to keep looking just as pristine as ever.

I was their dirty little secret, too potentially useful to get rid of but too unpredictable to be let off the leash.

He turned more fully to face me, one of his legs cocked at the knee on the bed. "How dumb do you take me for? You were called Blizzard, you've put espers in the hospital and you refuse to do physical guiding. Do you *really* think I couldn't have worked that out on my own? It's like a three-piece puzzle, Yun, I already had a pretty good idea how they fit together. Besides, if the esper you put in the hospital broke that boundary..." He shrugged. "I think he probably had it coming then."

That was unexpected. So far, I'd gotten nothing like that as a response, not from an esper especially. Most of them explained that the attraction between guide and esper was normal, that neither could really be expected to keep their hands to themselves in the heat of the moment, that guiding was an *intimate* exchange and contact should be expected.

In short?

This had always been a *me* problem.

So hearing Carter say that startled me.

"But—"

"But nothing," he cut me off. "Boundaries are boundaries. Same goes here. If anyone on our squad gets handsy and ends up with their brain scrambled, well, that's on us. It's a good lesson about consent, I figure. Now, go ahead and rest up. Maybe wash your face first? You've got drool—" He gestured first in a line at my cheek, then opened his hand and indicated the entire side of my face. "Pretty much all over there."

He turned to walk away, his back looking even larger than usual, but the memory of what I'd seen wouldn't go away.

"Was that just my imagination?" I asked without context.

Was that my way of giving him an out? Because I didn't really want to know?

Probably.

Still, I offered it for us both.

He could say he had no idea what I was talking about, or laugh and tell me my imagination had gotten the best of me, or even ask me just what sort of fantasies I was having about him.

Instead, he paused by the door and spoke without turning back my way. "Instead, I'll give you some advice. It's good not to ask questions you really don't want the answer to."

Which was an answer all its own, wasn't it?

Chapter Eight

Kenyon

Good enough.

I balanced the plates on my palms, thumbs tucked over the top, hurrying up the stairs, my long legs taking them two at a time.

It was nearly nine in the morning, and everyone else had left for some planning meeting with another squad. Normally, I hated getting left behind — I'd never been good at entertaining myself.

This time, though, I accepted it as a win.

Why?

I moved the plates to one hand, then rapped my knuckles on the door to Yun's room.

Because I get to spend the day alone with her.

No answer came back, but after a few seconds and the clicking of a latch undoing, the door swung open to reveal the very guide I'd been thinking about.

Of course, she didn't look at me with the same happiness I felt. That would take time, I figured.

Carter had sat me down—all of us, I think—and reminded us that she needed time and space, not to push her.

I was pretty sure he'd break my legs if I screwed this up, which meant I'd be on my best behavior.

Thus, the food.

Yun frowned as she looked at the plates. "What's this?"

"Scrambled eggs."

Her expression didn't suggest she agreed.

"You didn't eat last night, and you haven't eaten today yet, so I figured we'd have breakfast."

"And you're bringing it to me because...?"

"Because you weren't going to come down. I thought we'd eat on the balcony." I gestured with a jerk of my chin toward the slider at the back of the room. "It's got a view of the ocean."

She sighed but, in the end, agreed by moving out of the doorway to allow me in.

"I'll set it up out there." I went past her, trying to keep my gaze off her so I didn't make her uncomfortable.

I'd been in this room before, since it functioned as a guest room when we needed it. Sometimes that meant for family, for friends, for guides who had to stay over. It never felt like *this* before, though.

It took me back to when I'd first stepped into a girl's room as a teenager, when just being there felt forbidden, when the sight of their bed and dresser and all the strange things they used had captivated me. It had seemed like they were entirely different creatures, something I knew I couldn't really have or understand but wanted so badly.

Somehow, this empty room had turned into that same thing, making me want to explore, to bury my face in her blankets and just drink in her scent.

Which was probably *exactly* the sort of thing that Carter had specifically told me not to do.

I took the plates to the slider, then opened it with my elbow before slipping out. There was a swing to the side, then a small table with four chairs. It overlooked the ocean, and those playing around on the beach.

I set the plates on the table, the forks already on top.

At least I hadn't dropped anything on the way up.

Yun placed two glasses of water beside the plates, along with a paper towel for each. It meant that she'd gone downstairs to grab them while I'd been setting it all up.

The fact that I'd missed something so obvious should have embarrassed me, but if I got embarrassed about every little thing I did wrong, I'd never do anything at all.

Instead, I smiled and pulled her chair out.

She eyed me as though she didn't at all trust me, so I left it pulled out and sat in my own, giving her space.

Dealing with her felt like trying to befriend a feral cat, where I just had to keep doing my own thing and hope she eventually realized I wasn't going to hurt her.

Except, I'd never given a damn about a cat the way I did about Yun.

She sat, though she didn't eat right away. Instead, she waited for me.

"I didn't do anything to it," I muttered, and took a bite from her plate first to prove it.

"I just wanted to make sure it was edible."

"My food doesn't look that good, but it always tastes good." I swallowed down the scrambled eggs, then grinned. "See, I'm a bit clumsy, so things like plating? I can't manage it. But trust me when I say it's always delicious. Sometimes Carter plates for me to make it look a little better. He likes to say that how it looks is as important as how it tastes, but I don't really get that. Maybe it's because I grew up eating whatever I could find — how it looks doesn't change if it'll keep you alive or not."

"But he didn't do that today?"

Did she not know they'd left? "Carter's gone, along with Shear and Ingram. They had to meet up with another squad."

Was she going to feel uncomfortable with just her and me here? If so, I couldn't blame her, really. I'd leave her be, give her space.

I glanced down at my hand, frowning at the size of it. I'd always been large, even bigger than Carter, and people had specific ideas because of that. They figured I was scary, that I was mean, that I was a bully. How many times had people stepped up to me just because of my size?

Then I'd ended up an esper, and everyone assumed I'd be combat.

Instead, I'd turned out to be a healer, even looking the way I did.

It was hard to think she was wrong to be uncomfortable.

"I can eat downstairs," I said, grabbing my plate, ready to head out and give her space.

"Why?"

Her question caused me to pause, half out of the seat, to stare across the table at her. Her expression wasn't full of pity, not even confusion. It felt like a challenge.

"Because you might not feel safe with just me," I explained.

She laughed, but the sound didn't strike me as all that happy. "One esper or four doesn't really make a difference, does it? In my experience, one esper isn't going to stop another, and at the end of the day, it doesn't change anything. So, no, I'm not worried about being here with just you."

Her words sank in, and I struggled with them. They sounded pained, almost hopeless. It wasn't fear, and that felt worse. Fear said a person still believed in good things, but acceptance like that happened when they thought nothing better would come, when they expected the worst.

Which meant she was saying that she fully expected us to hurt her eventually, that she didn't care if there were one or more of us, because she felt sure it would happen, regardless.

I considered all the times she'd been moved from one place to another, from one squad to another, as though she were the problem, as though she were failing others. Each time the system had told her it was *her* fault, and that lesson had stuck, given her tone.

I lowered myself back into the chair, unsure how to continue.

Hearing her speak, though, the bottomless despair in those words, the absolute certainty of them, made me wonder if there was anything we could do to convince her otherwise.

So we ate in silence, because I doubted anything I could say would help. If all I could do was make some food and keep her safe, well, sometimes that was the best a person could do.

Sometimes there was no fixing someone else, no making things better, no healing. If anyone understood that, it was a healer.

I recalled an esper, years ago, who had taught me that lesson. They'd gotten gored by the horn of a monster, one that had run them through from the back after breaking clear of a cluster of trees in a dungeon. There had been so much blood, with flesh in big chunks all over the ground beneath him. I'd dropped to my knees beside him, my hands raised above him, pouring as much energy as I could into his failing body.

I'd gone at it for hours as the battle had raged around us, until I couldn't stand anymore, until I was so close to corruption that Carter had had to haul my ass away and to a guide outside the portal.

The esper had died, of course, racked in pain and having been forced to endure for hours longer than he should have.

I learned my lesson then—not everyone could be saved. Since then, I'd realized the fact that for some people, a quick death was better, that for some, when saving and fixing wasn't possible, all a person could do was ease the pain best they could, to make them comfortable until they passed.

And looking at Yun, no matter how much I hated it, I wondered if I wasn't watching such a case right now.

Chapter Nine

Ingram

I fucking hate these pricks.

No doubt that showed on my face as I stared at the other squad, their matching little outfits making me want to throw up on the spot. What the fuck? Were they cheerleaders or espers?

"The Guild said to bring your entire team," Hester, the head of the other squad, complained like a little bitch.

The show of weakness made me want to poke at it, to dig into it, to make use of it.

I leashed those desires, however, reminding myself that they weren't an enemy.

For a person to be an enemy, I had to give a fuck about them, had to fear them. These assholes were entirely inconsequential to me.

"We've recently gotten a new guide. I didn't want to stress her out by bringing her here to what was just a meet and greet." Carter's tone didn't apologize, just stating the fact as though we were already besties with them.

Hester huffed, as though put out by this.

He wasn't, of course. We weren't doing shit here. Just meeting each other?

Bullshit.

The fact was that squads worked best on their own. We trained with the others in our squad — we didn't need those sorts of groups. Didn't need to practice together like some grand dance recital.

It was nothing but a publicity stunt, a game to try to humanize the espers to make them easily digestible for the public.

Fucking bullshit.

We weren't human, and pretending we were just for a bigger paycheck was self-serving and stupid. I could have been doing actually useful things today instead of wasting time with this nonsense.

But Carter had told me to come, so I'd come.

Not because I feared him — even if I did a little. He'd earned my loyalty, though, and as fucking annoying as he was, he rarely led us wrong.

"We have another meeting next week," Hester said, his tone tight. "I expect to see your entire squad there. It's especially important to have healers and guides there, as they're most useful to other squads."

And just like that, the sensation of shadows crawling along my skin took over. I closed my eyes, trying to leash it, because I didn't need to fucking lose my shit here.

However, the idea of them acting like our guide and our healer were some sort of fucking free use public toilet system pissed me the fuck off.

Fuck that.

I didn't mind ending anyone who thought to lay a damn hand on anything that was mine, and those two sure as fuck counted.

Kenyon could handle his own, but he'd healed me enough times that I didn't want to just allow some asshole to think he got access to that.

A sharp look from Shear warned that he sensed my reaction, that he knew damned well I wanted to take a piece of each of these fuckers.

I rolled my eyes and leaned back farther in the seat. I could have worked hard to pull the shadows back, but why?

Let 'em fucking see it. Let 'em know exactly what would happen if they overstepped the boundaries.

Hester looked at me, his eyes widening before he got out of the seat in a jump. "We'll get going." He rushed from the room, his little lackeys following like a line of lemmings, all wanting to get the fuck out of here before they got themselves into trouble.

Carter twisted in his chair to look over at me, then let out a long, drawn-out sigh. "Really?"

"I was bored." I pulled the shadows back, let them rest inside my skin as they usually did. Sure, I hadn't just been bored—I'd been pissed, but I didn't feel like admitting that.

Telling them that would give them a glimpse of something deeper, and I saw no reason to let that happen. I preferred keeping shit close to the chest, not letting anyone get a look at anything that mattered.

Never expose your heart and no one can drive a knife through it.

Good fucking advice, if I did say so myself.

"Are we really going to work with those fuckers?" I asked.

"The Guild says yes." Carter stared at his phone, his words light as though he paid more attention to whatever was on his screen than me.

"And since when do we do what the Guild wants?"

"We always do what they want—at least enough of the time to stay on their good side. No different from now. We do this, we get our good boy stickers, they stay off our backs for a while."

"Yun doesn't want to go." Shear didn't look at either of us, staring instead at his hands as though his fingernails had turned super fucking interesting. The weirdo was always like that, always doing something that made me think he really was as crazy as people said.

"Does anyone? It'd be weirder if she was excited."

Shear shook his head. "Her reaction came when they said *The Pitt*. It is that dungeon that scares her."

I frowned, hating that he had some insight into her I lacked—that any of the rest of us lacked.

Fucking mentalist.

"According to her record, she was there when The Pitt opened the last time. She lived in that area." Carter shrugged, acting as though it didn't matter, but the tightness of his voice betrayed him in a rare show of actual concern. "Her parents died in the attack, and it destroyed her home. She was found six months later, surviving in the ruins. That'll leave a mark on anyone."

I rubbed the center of my chest to clear a sudden heaviness there, the one that made it challenging to draw full breaths. "Maybe she should sit this one out, then?"

"Guild will never go for that. We're just supposed to do mop up, though, so we can set her far enough back that she won't see anything. Probably put her inside a trailer so she doesn't even see the portal itself. We've done worse—I doubt we'll need any guiding, and even if we do, we can use one of the Guild healers."

I pressed my lips together, hating—well, pretty much fucking all of this idea.

I hated that the Guild thought to control us, that they could send us wherever they wanted. I hated that Yun had to be a part of it, that there wasn't any way to keep her from it. I really fucking hated this tension inside of me, like turning a jack-in-the-box crank, hearing the music go around and around as I winced, ready for it to pop, knowing it would, but never fucking knowing exactly when.

It meant no matter what was going on, what any of us wanted, it seemed we all got to face our demons again.

Lucky fucking us.

Carter lifted his gaze from his phone, then peered over at me, a smile sliding across his lips that spelled nothing good. It was that unhinged look he got, and at times like that, I was damn glad we were on the same side.

"An S-Rank dungeon opened a few miles away." He turned his phone to show the alert. It was a small one, hardly a block, and only set to stay open for an hour or two. That meant the Guild probably wouldn't even send a team to address it, figuring it would take care of itself.

"And?" I asked even as I got up, even as I knew what he was saying.

"Well, maybe it's time to blow off a little steam."

And despite our differences, I had to admit, at least we could agree on this.

Nothing like a bit of violence to destress a man.

Chapter Ten

Yun

I woke with a start, bolting upright and looking around, confused about where I was or what had happened. It took a moment to work it all out.

I'd fallen asleep on the couch, and now the television was blaring an infomercial for some detergent that was supposed to get bloodstains out of clothing.

If I had to deal with that many blood stains, I had bigger problems in my life than needing a new laundry detergent.

The lights were off—only the harsh glow of the television illuminated the large space, casting strange shadows that looked like monsters, all reaching to yank me down.

After another nightmare, of course, who could blame me for thinking that those shadows reached for me?

The memory remained with me, fresh in my mind. That voice, twisted and guttural, tattooed so deeply into my psyche that I doubted I'd ever really escape it.

Sweat covered my forehead, my back, made my shirt stick to my skin even as I moved.

Why had I woken?

The answer became clear when I turned my head to find three massive figures in the office, near the door.

I slapped my hand over my mouth to muffle my scream.

Light poured through the office, so bright that I flinched from it at first. When my eyes adjusted, instead of the monsters I'd imagined, three very real ones stood there.

"Sorry to startle you," Carter said. "I figured you'd be in your room, not camping out in the living room, staying up late to watch…" He turned his head toward the TV then chuckled. "Detergent commercials? You going to start doing our laundry?"

"You wish," I muttered when I pulled my hand from my mouth, angry with myself for showing such weakness. The barb lacked any real bite, but it was the best I had at the moment. Sometimes the most a person could do was move forward, bury insecurities beneath a mountain of snark and lies and false bravery.

The thing that shook me from the distraction was taking a better look at the three of them.

They'd been out far later than they were supposed to be, and seeing them right now gave me a pretty good idea as to why.

Fresh wounds and bruises covered each of them, and in addition? A neon purple that I easily recognized, the scent of it choking and playing havoc with my already fragile mindset.

Monster blood.

There was something about it that nothing could replicate, as though I could smell the very corruption of it, down to some impossibly deep level. Other guides didn't react as I did to the scent, but other guides hadn't gone through what I had.

At least, if they ever did, none spoke of it.

"You were in a dungeon," I said.

Carter smiled broadly, as though to tell me not to worry, to reassure me that this was nothing. "It was a quick one, in and out. Not a big deal."

"You're hurt."

He gestured at himself and waved the concern away. "It'll all be healed up by morning. It was a small dungeon, and we figured it'd clear in a matter of minutes."

"*You* said that," Shear pointed out.

"Yeah, don't put this bullshit on us. You were the one who decided to run fucking headlong into a pack of monsters." Ingram picked a bloody chunk of something from his hair and flicked it off.

"You what?" I knew my tone came out like a scolding mother, but I couldn't help it. "You just headed into one? Just like that?"

Carter laughed and rubbed the back of his neck. "Well, sure. We're espers, aren't we?"

The light gave me a better look at him, the ability to see that his eyes had tinted purple, to see the black lines that bled from his eyes, over his face, his throat, as though blackness ran through his veins instead of normal blood.

"You need guiding," I whispered.

He shook his head. "I'm fine. Like I said, not a problem."

Ingram shoved him hard enough that he stumbled. "Don't be a fucking idiot. You took on way more than you should have, and you're gonna be feeling worse as you start to heal. This is why we have a guide."

"What about you?" I tried to examine Ingram, but it was too hard to tell anything with all the monster blood.

"I'm fine. Shear and I know how to stay away from the claws. Carter here, he decided to go fucking ham on it all. Serves him right since the little outing was his idea. Just focus on him for tonight." Ingram looked down at himself and clicked his tongue. "I'm gonna go fucking shower."

Shear said nothing, just followed Ingram up the stairs, leaving Carter and me alone.

And fuck did that feel strange.

It hadn't been that long since I'd guided an esper, but it always seemed awkward at first. Even if there was no physical contact, even if it was all professional, there was an inescapable intimacy that occurred during such an exchange.

So doing that with a stranger felt like having to walk up and immediately kiss someone I didn't know a thing about.

Even as difficult as that was, as strange and uncomfortable, I'd done it time and time again over the years. A person could get used to about anything, including something as absurd as guiding strangers.

"You don't have to do this," Carter said, his voice surprisingly gentle given the way he stood there, covered in blood.

"It's why I'm here, isn't it?"

"Sure, but that doesn't mean you've gotta start now—or with me."

I stood, my entire body having grown heavy — probably from stress rather than my impromptu nap — and tried to force a smile. "It's fine. Should we do it here?" I peered around the large room.

"I think I'd better at least shower, don't you think?"

What an oddly considerate gesture...

Few espers thought about that, and honestly, few guides did, either. What did a bit of gore matter? Usually, the drunken sensation from the exchange made little else matter. Even if one of them cared at first, they sure as fuck didn't pretty quickly.

It was why there were so many privacy trailers around for espers, to help prevent them from accidentally banging in the middle of the street.

Which meant Carter — even with those wounds and those signs of corruption — managing to think about something like that, to hold himself back, was even more amazing than I'd realized. Few espers would have been capable of considering it, let alone resisting long enough.

"After my shower, I'll meet you, okay?"

His question was interesting, given he offered it as a real question. If I said no, he'd accept that.

Which made no fucking sense to me.

I nodded, my throat far too tight to manage any response.

Carter headed up the stairs without another word, and I found myself unable to tear my gaze away from the floor where the three had stood. Purple gore sat in piles and fat droplets — some blood and other flesh, all signs of exactly what Carter had done. It remained, forgotten on the tile, and it made me wonder just how much of that had been here before, how many times the floor had been covered from previous fights.

After the portal to a dungeon closed, the beasts would slowly die, disintegrating until nothing was left. It sometimes took a few hours, sometimes a few days or weeks for the bigger dungeons, but eventually, all signs disappeared.

At least, all outward signs.

I knew better than most that those couldn't be fully believed or trusted.

So I turned to head up the stairs, wishing like fuck it was that easy to get rid of the deeper wounds, the things that hid beneath the surface, because ten years hadn't been nearly enough time to wipe that shit clean for me.

Chapter Eleven

Carter

I scrubbed at the blood, amazed at how much it stuck. Human blood dried and turned brittle, flaking off the skin in tiny patches, but monster blood didn't do that. Instead, it congealed until it turned to slime, thick and difficult to remove. It would disappear in a few hours, of course, dissipating, fizzling out of existence, but that wouldn't help us right now.

I wasn't the type to give a damn about putting on a good front for a guide. It wasn't like I felt the need to woo them, to romance them in some strange way. It was a business transaction at best, a physical need at worst, but either way, I didn't care to dress up and make a good impression.

It wasn't about making a good impression with Yun, either. Instead, her gaze had locked on the blood that had covered me, and each inhalation through her nose had made her flinch. I could almost see the bile rising up her throat, telling me she had a guttural reaction to the scent and sight of monster blood.

I told myself the shower was about efficient guiding. She couldn't do the job right if she were nearly throwing up, could she?

I nearly choked on the stupid lie.

Still, the sight of her did…something to me. It was something uncomfortable, something I could neither control nor understand, and I both cherished and hated it. Even the subtle proximity guiding she did naturally felt different from anything I'd experienced before.

It wasn't gentle, not sweet, but almost feral. It was wild, rough, like someone who had just discovered the skill and couldn't control it.

And why the hell did I like that?

I lacked an answer, but that didn't change my response. A glance down at my hard cock proved that much, at least. I couldn't walk out of there in this state, could I?

I chuckled as I closed my eyes and pictured her reaction. She'd recoil, and maybe I'd learn exactly why they called her Blizzard.

It might just be worth it. It had been a long time since anyone had put me on my ass.

However, I didn't want her running away for some reason, so it was a better option to take care of this myself beforehand. Better I not show up at her room sporting a baton in my pajamas.

My face already looked a mess, the black veins stark against my tanned skin, a sign to anyone that they should keep their distance. I could go without guiding, had plenty of other times, but it was better not to balance on that edge for too long. Besides, if she was here, why not?

I pictured how she'd look if we did this the way instinct demanded. I could stretch her down on the bed, beneath me, run my hands up her sides. I wanted to hear the sounds she'd make, to press my lips to hers and taste her moans.

I wrapped my hand around my cock, gripping tightly. This wasn't some date with myself, where I took my time and enjoyed the fantasy. Instead, I needed to finish it up as quickly as possible, to get out there and finish this. Who knew if she'd lose her nerve, or just fucking fall asleep, given the way we'd found her?

It didn't seem like she slept all that well, judging from the constant dark circles beneath her eyes.

My breath came out faster as I rested my other hand against the wall to brace myself, leaning forward so the water sprayed down the back of my neck.

It was hot, probably reddening my skin, given the steam that filled the glass-enclosed shower.

I stroked my cock with quick, rough movements, my hips thrusting forward with each one as though my body knew exactly what it would much rather be doing.

Which was the guide probably fretting in her room right now.

A spark of guilt threatened to take hold, that I was in here jerking off when she was no doubt biting her bottom lip and stressing about what was to come.

Of course, I did this for that exact reason, so I didn't have to worry about getting out of hand with her.

Plus, too much had happened in my life for guilt to mean much anymore, so I focused on my cock, on the way I'd glimpsed the sexy curve of Yun's ass through her slacks, on chasing the pleasure that grew inside me. I gave myself over to the fantasy, to the sensations, needing to finish this as quickly as possible.

What got me over that edge was a final picture in my head, of Yun digging those dull little nails of hers into my back as she grabbed onto me, as she held tight. Why the fuck *that* was hotter than stripping her down or spreading her pretty thighs, I had no idea, but who could account for the perverse nature of men?

I came hard, my hand on the wall curling into a fist to help prevent me from doing any damage. Fuck knew I'd screwed up enough other furniture and house fixtures—I didn't need to have to call someone in to fix the shower wall.

I leaned my forehead against the cool tile, panting hard, working to catch my breath. The worst was when getting myself off didn't refresh me, when I didn't get that wonderful, drowsy, ready to take a nap feeling.

This time had just managed to take the edge off.

Just barely. As an esper—especially a physical combat specialist—my stamina was far better than most others. Just once hardly served as an appetizer. Still, it would hopefully keep my cock in check during guiding.

I turned off the water, wondering if I shouldn't have taken a cold shower—or fuck, even an ice bath.

Too late for that now. Instead, I got out of the shower, the blast of cold air not nearly enough to wipe away the thoughts still fucking with my head. I pulled on a pair of sweats and a T-shirt, just enough to cover what needed covering. Putting more layers on wouldn't make much of a difference. I could fuck her in a parka or a thong.

I was nothing if not inventive.

Still, a layer like this would help put her at ease. It gave the impression I wasn't going to jump on her.

And I wasn't, but I could see why she might not believe it. Espers weren't all that trustworthy, after all.

The steam flowed out from the bathroom when I opened the door, like rolling fog, and I walked into my bedroom, my gaze down, a towel still over my head as I dried my hair.

Something pricked at my senses, and I paused, jerking my head up.

Instead of the empty room I'd expected, I found a certain guide sitting on my bed.

And fuck did that set off all my fantasies yet again... How the hell could something this innocent rile me up so much? I wasn't a fucking teenage boy, so how did a fully dressed woman just sitting on my bed make it so the whole taking care of myself in the shower didn't matter a bit?

Again, it felt like it was her personally, and not a me problem. Something about this guide just stripped away every logical thought in my head.

It felt rather fucking dangerous, to be honest. The way that she got me to react even when I didn't want to, when nothing else would get that from me.

She wore the same clothes as before, a basic pair of leggings and a shirt long and loose enough to not show her body and to cover her ass. I wouldn't call it all that alluring, not sexy or seductive, but it didn't seem to matter with how I reacted to it—and her.

She didn't look at me—instead her gaze was on her hands as she fidgeted with the bottom hem of her shirt. The action spoke volumes about her feelings.

If she was this nervous, why the hell was she in here, in *my* room? Most guides would much rather use their own space, to feel the safety of their own room, to feel in control.

"I thought you were going to wait for me in your room?" I asked. "We don't have to do it here."

She shook her head, the action causing her hair to fall into her face, at which point she brushed it back again with a huff. "It's fine."

It sure doesn't seem fine.

Yet she wanted to do it here?

The answer hit me quickly, when I recalled what I'd said to her. I'd told her that the room was hers, that we wouldn't enter it without permission.

Was that why she'd come here? Because she didn't want me in her space?

The idea had me holding back a laugh. She was willing to come into my space, into my room, even understanding what guiding was like, the risk, all because she wanted to keep her space sacred somehow?

Again, she surprised me.

I grabbed the chair from the corner of the room, then pulled it closer and sat in it. It placed me just before her, but gave her a bit of space.

"You know, this really isn't efficient," I said as I set my hands on the armrests, palms up.

"I already told you this was all I'd do."

"I'm not trying to get you to change it, just curious how you think it'll work."

"It's worked before."

"Has it, *Blizzard*?"

She narrowed her eyes until just a slit of darkness remained between her pretty lashes. I had to admit I liked the way she glared. It was sexy as hell, even if it had no good reason to be. "Is it smart to piss your guide off?"

"About as smart as pissing off a date, but still, I do it every time. What can I say? I've never been good at following standard social rules."

"That seems to be a problem for your entire squad." She kept her legs folded and leaned forward, the position rather precarious, but it seemed she didn't want to risk any potential accidental contact. Of course, if she wasn't careful, she'd topple right the fuck off the end. "None of you do what you're supposed to."

"Kenyon is pretty good. He's stupid as the day is long, don't get me wrong, but he's friendly at least." I paused, as though thinking. "Too friendly, maybe. I remember one time he was late for a dungeon and it turned out he was moving someone's goods because he'd walked by and they were carrying heavy things. Of course, he ended up even later because it turned out that the people were robbing the house." I shrugged. "So maybe he isn't the best example."

Yun said nothing back, just stared at me with her cute little mouth agape. It brought back a few of those little fantasies I'd just indulged in. Fuck knew an open mouth featured in plenty of them, though hers was so small I wondered what good it could be.

"Stop it," she snapped. She went on when I looked into her eyes. "I'm not stupid, you know? Especially when guiding like this—I can tell what you're thinking."

"You're not guiding yet."

"Yeah, I am."

I frowned and looked down to spot the maroon mist swirling from my palms up to hers, the sensation so comfortable that I had nearly missed it.

Guiding had always been a necessity to me—unpleasant at the best of times and painful at worst. I'd resisted it, hating the feeling, putting it off because of that clawing discomfort.

This was different, though. It was so easy that I hadn't even felt it. Now that I focused, though, now that I paid attention, I could study it.

The corruption slipped out of me so easily that it made me shiver. Normally, that twisted energy clawed on the way out, left gouges inside me, fighting to stay put. This was entirely different, however. It flowed out of me without struggle.

It stunned me into silence as my mind tried to make sense of it, of how this was possible. I'd been guided for years, rare though it might have been, and never once had it ever felt like this.

"What are you?" I asked when I couldn't come up with anything.

"A guide."

I shook my head. "I'm serious. What *are* you? How are you different?"

"Different?" The flow of corruption slowed, her gaze darting side to side, avoiding mine. "I don't know what you're talking about."

Her expression said she knew *exactly* what I was talking about. No one got this uncomfortable if they were truly clueless over an accusation — they got evasive when they didn't want to get caught, when they felt cornered.

Which meant she had something to hide, something to protect.

What was it?

I got off the chair, leaning forward without making contact. The action drew her backward, until she stretched out on the bed, trying to avoid me, leaving her beneath me. It again reminded me of the fantasies I'd had while getting off earlier.

Still, I made no contact. I didn't touch her, bracing my weight instead against the bed, staring down into her face.

She was pretty, but that didn't mean much. Other than her skills as an S-Rank guide, she didn't appear to have anything special about her. Her history showed a pretty normal lower-class upbringing until the age of fifteen, when she got caught up in The Pitt appearance. She'd ended up among the casualties left behind in San Diego, the ones who'd had to scramble and fight to make it in the fucked-up wreckage—in her case, without parents.

She was located six months later, at sixteen, after an apparent attack in the ruins that used to be San Diego. The hospital identified her as a guide and handed her over to the Guild.

After that, she underwent training and moved from squad to squad, earning herself her nickname until she landed with us.

None of that told me anything useful, though. Judging from her reaction to us — and to others before — something dark rested at the center of all that fear and trauma.

What was it?

Was it connected to why her guiding felt so different?

So fucking good…

She didn't look like some little broken puppy beneath me, though. She didn't shiver and shake and cry. If she'd done that, maybe it would have snapped me free of this need to find answers.

Instead, she bared her teeth like a wild animal. "Get off me."

"Then explain what's different about you. Come on, Blizzard, you're here with us because we're your last shot, so why don't you be honest and just let me in on it?"

"The only thing I'll let you in on is how I got my name. If you don't get off me in the next five seconds, you'll get to experience it firsthand, and trust me, you don't want that." The threat rolled off her tongue, a warning there that said she wasn't kidding.

I could see a bluff a mile out, but this girl wasn't bluffing.

Did I want to let her try that? Part of me wondered if it wouldn't be fun. Fuck, if she could scramble my brains like that, maybe I'd just thank her for it.

At least until I spotted a crease there in her cheek. It was subtle, so shallow, I didn't know if I'd notice it any other time, but right now? From this distance?

Fear. Not of me, not exactly. Was it fear of having to follow through?

Fuck, the girl was a bleeding heart, wasn't she? Even when she'd strike to protect herself, she'd suffer for it later.

That got me moving, pushing off the bed and off her.

I glanced behind me at the mirror hung on the back of the closed bedroom door. It hadn't been that long, really, but the black veins had lessened. They hadn't disappeared entirely, though that was hardly surprising. Even Yun wasn't a miracle worker. There was a limit to what could be done in a matter of a few minutes, especially without any physical contact for the guiding.

Still, the fact that even that small amount of time had given me this much relief was a fucking mystery to me.

I turned toward her, eyeing her, desperate for some understanding of how this could be, of what was different, of how this could be the way it was.

She wasn't lying flat anymore, having gotten up and scooted away on the bed until she could stand on the other side. Her eyes were wide now, frantic, darting about as though she needed an escape.

That shook me free of the insanity that had held me. It brought me back to this moment, to the fact that she stood there, frightened, after I'd assured her that she would be safe here.

I took a deep breath and closed my eyes, relishing the lightness of her guiding.

Right. Be grateful.

There was time to discover her secret, to work out what she hid, to explain why I reacted the way I did, to find out what had happened to her before. At least, there would be time to learn if she didn't take off now, if I didn't lose her to this insanity in my head, to the desires raging inside me that I struggled to contain for the first time.

So I pulled tight the control I'd fought for, then smiled at her. "Sorry. It's been a long time since I've had guiding—too long, clearly. You've got to be tired. You should go to sleep."

She didn't move, her body pinned there in the corner, as far away from me as she could get, as though she didn't trust my words.

Smart girl. She shouldn't trust me. She shouldn't trust anyone.

Instead of trying to convince her of anything, I went another route. "I'm going to go brush my teeth, then get some sleep. Goodnight, Yun." Her name hung on my lips, sweeter than it had any right to be.

I used names like a weapon, willing to wield them in whatever way I needed to get what I wanted. That was how it had always worked. Why then was it that hers threatened to manipulate me, to bring me to my knees instead?

When I turned my back, the door opened then slammed shut. The quick steps of someone running told me she'd fled.

Once in the bathroom, I groaned and rubbed my face, trying to get a grip and failing miserably.

I glanced down at my front, then sighed.

Well, looks like I can try that cold shower now...

Chapter Twelve

Yun

Another damned nightmare.

It was easy to tell when they happened because I was always back *there*.

Knowing it was a dream didn't change anything. It still felt real. It still inspired honest terror in me, still forced me to face everything I didn't want to.

Whether it occurred in my mind or out in the real world didn't change the moment.

The black sky rested above, torn through with streaks of purple that shifted like oil in water. Not the black of the normal night sky, dotted with bright stars or lit by the reflection of the sun on the moon. This was a deeper darkness, one that swallowed up the light everywhere else.

I stood in the forest with the twisted, strange trees surrounding me as they had before. Everything smelled sweet and slightly acidic—the scent that turned my stomach, that made me want to run and hide and curl into the smallest ball possible.

"You belong here," the rumbling voice whispered, hot breath against my ear, a threatening promise in those words. It wasn't a human voice, instead deep and dark.

I closed my eyes, trying to shut out this place, this voice. "This isn't real."

"It will be. The time is coming, and I'll get you back."

I crouched, balancing my weight on my feet, my hands around my head, fingers digging against my scalp, speared through my hair, trying to hold myself together. I shook my head, wanting to deny those words.

"You never really left—you'll always be back here."

I trembled, shivering against the chill of this place, the fear that bounced around inside me. It yanked me back to all the nights I'd curled up and hid, the nights when I'd learned how little hiding did. The roars of monsters, the foliage crunching beneath their massive feet, it all warped together into a chorus of horror.

"Yun." That wasn't the hated voice, and it struck me like a rush of water against a burn.

"You think they'll save you?" A dark laugh spread that searing heat across my ear, my cheek, so close and vicious that I tried to curl in more.

I wanted to become a smaller target, to shrink until I didn't exist, until I wasn't *here* anymore.

It took me back to there, to how helpless I'd felt back then, when I'd wanted nothing more than to have it all end. I didn't care how, so long as it stopped.

"Yun!" The shout shook the entire world that time, though I still couldn't identify who it belonged to. It struck me as familiar, but this place warped my brain so that I couldn't figure it out, couldn't work through it.

The dream collapsed in on itself the same way dungeons did, the sky falling, the sides shifting in, all of it shattering apart until my eyes snapped open and I found myself no longer in that dream.

I yanked upright, sudden pain searing through my face.

I covered my throbbing nose with my hands, trying to make sense of, well, everything.

Kenyon's blue eyes met mine, centering me, at least until I spotted the red mark on his forehead.

"Were you screwing with me while I slept?" My hands muffled my words.

Kenyon shook his head in a quick denial. "You were making noises in your sleep, so I tried to wake you up, but you wouldn't come to. I leaned closer, and you jerked upright."

Which explained the pain in my nose, didn't it? As it turned out, Kenyon's head was a lot harder than my nose.

Chalk another point up to the espers.

"Move your hands," he said, reaching for me.

Except the memories inside my brain ran too fresh, the dream having left me too raw even to consider allowing him to touch me.

I shoved myself backward until I struck the headboard, frantic.

He froze, his hulking frame almost comical in the way he hunched forward, seeming to decide how to respond. "I just want to see your nose. I can smell blood."

Right. I scolded myself for my over-the-top reaction. There was no reason to be extra right now, to behave this way. All it did was prove how unstable I was, that I was weak and afraid.

So I removed my hands, finding that, yeah, blood coated my palms.

"You really do have a hard head," I muttered to wrest back some sense of control.

He smiled, though it wasn't as easy as it had been before, almost as though he humored me. "I've heard that before. Can't really deny it. I don't think you broke it, but it's going to bruise. Can I?"

I swallowed down the rejection. Saying no would just prove that I was still out of control. "Sure, just…"

"I won't touch you," he promised and came a little closer, crouching beside the bed.

I snorted — despite the pain — at that. As if crouching was going to make him look much smaller. When I'd tried to make myself small, it had made sense, but it did little for a hulking esper like Kenyon.

The moment his powers touched me, relief poured through the throbbing space around my nose. The pain lessened instantly, reminding me that Kenyon wasn't just a healer, but a high-rank one. This made a joke of the few low-level healers who had tried to work on me. Those had felt like someone resetting a bone, but this? It was more like slipping into a warm, epsom salt bath, the instant relaxation lessening the pain.

I normally avoided healing, having given in only during the few times when it had seemed impossible to refuse it. Once I had gotten into a minor car crash, just a fender bender that had fucked my neck up. Another time, an especially bad virus had left me in bed for a few days. Both times the Guild had sent over a healer, and I hadn't had a way to say no, and given they weren't serious injuries, they'd sent bargain-basement-level espers.

If this was how high-rank healers worked, I could see why people enjoyed using them.

The pain lessened until it disappeared, until I wouldn't have had any idea it had hurt at all. The blood didn't go away, of course, but at least it no longer ached.

Kenyon let out a long breath, as though relieved, then got up and walked into the bathroom. The water splashed from the sink, and he returned with a damp washcloth. He reached out at first, before stopping and simply holding the cloth to me.

I took it, the water warm, then used it to wipe at my face. I hesitated at first, afraid it would hurt, only to find that there was still no pain. I cleaned my face until no itchiness remained, then wiped my hands as well.

"Better?" I asked.

Kenyon nodded and took the washcloth back, tossing it into the laundry in the bathroom.

When he returned, he seemed unsure of what to do. It was like once we had passed the initial problem, once he wasn't focused on fixing my issue, he didn't know what else to say.

Which amused me, given the way he normally spoke.

"Was that a nightmare?" His voice was soft, careful.

I wanted to tell him no, but I saw no point in lying about it. It was pretty obvious, wasn't it?

"Yeah."

"Have you talked to anyone about it?"

"What, like a therapist?" I let out a laugh I wasn't sure actually tricked anyone, that probably screamed, 'I'm almost hysterical' rather than, 'look how casual I am about this,' like I'd been going for. "Nightmares are normal. They happen to everyone."

Kenyon stared back, a rare moment of seriousness that I didn't care for at all from him. "You could see a mentalist. They can sometimes unstick things in the mind."

"Let an esper root around in my brain? I think fucking not." The very idea made me recoil.

"The fact that you react the way you do to touch and then have nightmares like that makes me think there's probably something you need to work through."

I huffed softly. If even Kenyon figured that much out, it said I wasn't doing very well, didn't it? The man had the brains of a golden retriever—and the temperament of one—so if he spotted enough clues to give him that idea, then I'd been shit at keeping myself together.

He rubbed the back of his neck, his gaze lowered. "I know it's easy to think we can deal with stuff ourselves, but it's not a problem to ask for help."

"By letting someone into my brain? No, thanks, that sounds like a horrible idea."

"It really does help."

"You would know?" I shot those words out like a challenge. Men, especially espers, sure didn't like to admit weakness. I'd never heard of any willing to do something like go to therapy, or even the pseudo-therapy of letting another esper help them.

"Yeah, I would. I had some things happen when I first became an esper that I couldn't seem to get past. They kept showing up in my life, and I had an esper help me. It wasn't fun, it wasn't easy, but it was worth it." He shrugged and tucked his hands into the pockets of his pants, looking uncomfortable with the topic but willing to say it.

Which took me entirely by surprise. If he hadn't given a fuck, it wouldn't have impressed me as much. It was pretty obvious this wasn't something he wanted to say, but still chose to.

Still, him putting his wellbeing and gray matter into the hands of an esper didn't mean shit to me.

Plus, he was an idiot. Maybe the whole fucking with his brain thing was part of the reason?

"I've had an esper fuck around in my head once already," I admitted softly. "It's not something I will ever allow to happen again, not if I can prevent it."

Kenyon froze at my words, or rather probably at the venom within them.

Then again, people like Kenyon saw espers as heroes, as the good guys. The idea that anyone might not trust them, or might even actively distrust them, didn't work well for them. They couldn't come to terms with that.

And there really was no good reason to keep needling him. He couldn't help how he saw the world—it was based on his experience, after all. Instead, I pushed forward to change the subject. "Why were you trying to wake me up, anyway? More breakfast?"

He didn't answer right away, as though weighing the pros and cons of letting me get away with the change of subject. He seemed willing to give in, since he nodded. "No breakfast, at least not here. We've got a job."

And just like that, I wasn't sure if my day was going to get better or worse...

Chapter Thirteen

Shear

Well, that girl was more than a bit fucked up. It was pretty obvious to me as she walked, even if anyone else would have missed it.

Her brain sparked up, so many ugly emotions twisting together, feeding off each other, even though her outer appearance gave none of it away. In fact, it impressed me that she could hide the turmoil so well.

Normally people gave away small hints, but she offered little beyond a rapid heartbeat.

It reminded me to be cautious when it came to her — the girl could probably lie very well if she chose to.

Kenyon had mentioned that she'd had a nightmare, but it was hard to believe it would affect her this much. Mental activity like that implied the nightmare had brought up issues already deeply held. It wouldn't happen from just a bad dream, but only when trauma was pricked by reliving it, when it stirred up the past.

I'd thought the same thing after her reaction to The Pitt.

What exactly had she gone through? What was it that she kept locked up in that head of hers?

I wanted to take a spin around it, to dip my toes into her past, into the tangled mess of her thoughts. That was partly because I enjoyed it, because my powers meant it felt comfortable, but this was different.

It felt more personal, as though I somehow needed to understand. I wanted to unwind the mess of her head, to guide her back through it, to fix it so she could at least sleep.

However, none of that was for right now – probably not ever. That sort of work took trust, and I doubted she was planning on giving me any amount of trust.

Not that anyone ever did...

"Ready?" the police officer asked as he came out of the interrogation room, his voice tight.

Law enforcement tended not to trust espers. We were a force greater than them, something they could neither counter nor control. If we wanted to pose a problem, we certainly could.

That would put anyone on edge, even if we proved ourselves useful from time to time.

Times like right now.

I nodded, noting the way the officer refused to meet my gaze. Did he think I couldn't use my powers if he didn't look at me? Silly superstition. That might be true of lower-rank espers, but one of my skill didn't need that. If I wanted to tear into his mind, I could do it without even line of sight, so long as I'd interacted with him in the past month or so.

Knowing that wouldn't make him any more comfortable, though, so I kept the fact to myself and simply nodded.

Speaking rarely helped me.

He gestured for us to follow, so I did, with Yun beside me. The others had stayed in the waiting area, since the police didn't want four espers traipsing around in their department. As if that mattered. If we wanted to tear this place down to the slab, there was nothing any of them could do to stop us.

The officer held open the door to a conference room, waiting until we entered before he spoke. "I'll go get him." He didn't wait for a response before leaving.

Yun shifted her weight from foot to foot, a sure sign of discomfort. "Why am I here?" she finally asked.

"Policy. When dealing with civilians, they require a guide to be present."

"Why? This isn't even a hard task." As soon as she asked, she let out a soft laugh, as though she'd worked it through herself. "They worry that any esper will get corrupted, huh?"

"A few videos online about what happens and they think it's something to worry about. Don't concern yourself—I won't need guiding. They just require it."

Yun nodded and took a seat near the back corner. Her picking that place suggested that she feared someone behind her. It further drove home her unease, the idea that she was especially untrusting at the moment. "And the job?"

"You're interested now? I would have thought you'd ask on the drive."

She shrugged. "I figured I'd just sit in the car, so I didn't really care. What the job is doesn't change what

I have going on, but I don't usually have to be in the room."

"The suspect they're bringing in has likely abducted a child. The police had searched for the child, but have had no luck in locating him. If they put it off any longer, they fear they won't find the child alive, so they need me to take a look inside his head for the truth."

"Isn't that illegal?"

"It would be if they used that information to convict him, but if it leads only to finding the child? Well, that's a gray area."

"And you don't mind doing that? Prying into someone's mind without consent?" Her question came out with a shakiness that I filed away, that I tried to fit into the rest of the puzzle that she was.

"Not especially. Slipping into someone's mind is hardly intimate in the way you imagine. It's no different to me than reading a person's expression or their body language."

She frowned, as though she didn't agree but couldn't—or wouldn't—argue directly with that assertion.

We didn't need to discuss it any further when the door opened and the officer walked in with a man behind him.

The sight of the man made me want to pull back.

People said you couldn't spot a monster just by looking at them, but those people weren't espers. They didn't have the information I did. The truth was that causing harm to others destroyed the mental faculties of the person doing it. That sort of damage was like a form of self-harm, and the person carried those scars. It was easy for someone like me, someone who could see deeper than most, to spot them.

This man was such an example. The damage to his psyche proved just how much pain he had willingly inflicted on others, and each wound there festered.

It honestly made me want nothing to do with him. I'd told Yun I didn't care about doing my job, and while that was true for the most part, there were some minds I'd rather not touch. It was like a nurse having to help a bloated, diseased, rotten corpse. A strong stomach went a long way, but that didn't mean they enjoyed it.

The paperwork I'd read on the way over, however, played in my mind, a reminder of why I had to do this.

The child was only six, and they had no leads. The child had already been missing for two days— there was nothing to say that he would survive at all, and any delay only reduced those chances and gave this monster time to inflict more pain.

"These are the notaries that will handle taking your statement. Just give them your ID and sign the statement in their presence."

Ah, that's the ruse?

I didn't much care what lie they told the suspect to get him in the room with me—I only needed a few moments.

"Can we hurry this up?" the man muttered as though we were wasting his time, as though we were the problem here. He pulled his wallet out and tossed the ID on the table in front of me, then slammed the page on the table, a pen in his hand. He went about signing it, motions quick.

Which gave me the chance to focus entirely on him. The sensation of his twisted mind made me want to recoil from the ugliness, but I pushed through.

I slid into his thoughts, so subtle he would never notice it. It was the skill of my rank, the ability to spark thoughts in his own mind in a way that made him think he had caused them, allowing me to observe his reaction, his thoughts like a string of statements.

Fucking idiots. Always think they're so fucking smart. Not that smart, huh? They thought they had me, but they don't have shit.

The man went through his little tirade, so sure of his own intelligence. I directed his thoughts with easy skill, making him think about the boy, about where he was.

The images that hit me made me worry I'd lose my breakfast. The boy, dirty, scared, crying.

I didn't follow that further, not wanting it to cling in my mind forever. Instead, I pressed for details, for the location.

4925 Oak Dr. Basement.

Exactly what I needed. I reached out to Carter, the process easy after years of dealing with each other. I told him what he needed to know.

The man finished signing, then tossed the pen on the table with a self-assured smirk. He took his license. "We done here?"

The officer looked my way, and I nodded. He opened the door for the man, explaining directions to leave, then closed the door again for privacy. "What did you get?"

I repeated the address. "Basement, under the garage. It's an abandoned house he's done work on. The boy was alive as of this morning, and the suspect believes he still is. He won't go straight there, though, so you'll have time to retrieve the child first."

The officer didn't so much as give me a thank you before he was off. I sat, more of a collapse than a well thought out motion, but at least I'd gotten myself in front of one of the chairs, first

"Are you okay?" Yun's voice surprised me at first, since I'd been so consumed by the work that I'd entirely forgotten her presence. I hadn't intended for her to see that.

"Yes. It's just never a welcome experience dealing with certain minds. They feel like rooting around in refuse, like digging my hands through maggots." I shuddered, trying to rid myself of the memory.

"But you saved the kid."

"I did a job — nothing more."

She frowned, as though she wasn't sure why I would make a distinction. "Because of you, they're going to help the kid. That's good."

I turned my head to look at her, hating having to burst her bubble but driven to do so. "They paid me to do a job — that's it. What happens next, that's up to the police." I paused, then added on, "Besides, I didn't save anyone. Even if that kid gets rescued, even if they get him out of that basement, he isn't saved. He still will have the memories of what happened in his head forever."

She shifted in her chair, my words seeming to trouble her. Or perhaps it was trouble with understanding how she felt about it. Finally, she spoke softly. "That kid wouldn't agree. Even if there are scars left, getting out of that situation is still worth it."

The way she spoke drew me short. I'd already known she had something in her past, but the truth of those words, the conviction, showed just how much she understood.

"Tell me," I said, a command in my voice.

"Tell you what?"

"Whatever it is that you went through."

That shut down any chance I had. It had been stupid, and the moment I'd uttered the words, I'd wondered what the hell I was doing, what I was thinking.

I knew better than to push a person who wasn't ready to be pushed. I'd seen her mental state, should have known that it wouldn't matter what I wanted to know. Applying pressure would only cause her to retreat, for her to pull back and refuse to answer anything.

Yet I'd done it because in that moment, I couldn't *not* do it. Perhaps it was from seeing the boy, from the way my brain still rejected the touch of that other twisted mind, but the idea of Yun in such a situation drove rational thought right out of my mind.

Worse, it made me want to crawl into hers, to see how it felt to curl up there, if it would be as calming as I suspected, as welcoming.

Well, not welcoming right now.

"I have nothing to say," she snapped. "And don't even think about trying to force your way into my mind. I'll know."

She would, of course. As an S-Rank guide, she'd be able to feel it, unlike most. That wasn't the biggest reason I resisted, though. Instead, it was because some part of me I hardly recognized didn't want to do so. I wanted her to welcome me in, to ask me for it, to have her trust. Doing it without that wouldn't give me what I really wanted, so I didn't give into the desire.

"You'll tell me eventually," I said, more hopeful than certain.

"Don't hold your breath."

But I couldn't let go of the idea, of the fear, of the curiosity of what could have fractured the little guide's mind so much.

Nor could I ignore the desire to watch someone burn for it.

Chapter Fourteen

Yun

I ended up driving back to the house with just Shear as the others had already left when we'd gotten back to the waiting room. Shear had claimed they'd had an errand to run and would meet us back at the house.

The nice thing about Shear was that he didn't talk much. He didn't force conversation, which let me sit there in silence on the ride. We had taken a rideshare since it seemed whatever errand the others had gone on had required use of the car, leaving us stranded there.

It was afternoon by the time we got back, and given my lack of good sleep, I figured something to eat would help wake me up at least.

I stood at the stove, water in the pot boiling, steam escaping the top and sucked into the fan hanging above.

Guilt pricked at me as I recalled the way Shear had sat in the chair, the move so sudden it had taken me by surprise. It was like his energy had run out, more of a collapse than anything I'd seen from him. Worse was paleness of his skin, the way the color had drained from his face. I didn't know what he'd seen, but the loud gulp he'd made, the way he'd reacted, all suggested it hadn't been good.

I couldn't stop myself from adding two servings of pasta to the boiling water, ignoring my actions as I did it. It was just because he'd looked tired—that was it. Nothing more than that, nothing deeper. In another pot, I heated up marinara sauce, then mixed the sauce with the drained noodles and served it into two bowls.

I hadn't eaten, and I hadn't seen him eat. He had to be hungry as well.

I carried the bowls up, set his outside his door, knocked, then hurried away before he answered.

Was it childish?

Sure was.

Did I care?

Not even a little.

I wanted him to eat, but that didn't mean I wanted to actually face him.

Seeing him pry into a stranger's head so easily had thrown me off—though I hadn't been all that steady beforehand.

The reality was that I knew exactly what a mentalist could do, the damage they left behind. How could he do that and not care, not seem to even notice what those actions could mean?

It meant I didn't want to look at him, to think about what had happened or, worse, what he could do if he wanted. If he were that powerful, if he could so easily pluck information from that man's mind, what could he do if he truly wanted to hurt me?

The door opening then closing again from down the hallway made its way through the walls, letting me know he'd taken the food once I was safely in my own room.

The sight of the phone, still on the desk, caught my attention. I sat there, not wanting to make a mess by trying to eat pasta on the bed.

How long had it been since I had a good phone? A place to call my own?

A part of me struggled to believe this was possible. I kept waiting for life to snatch it all away from me, as it always did.

The best example of that feeling was my still-packed bag. I washed my clothes then returned them to that bag, never willing to leave things out of it because I didn't want to have to repack it.

That fear had been with me for years, of course, but had it ever bothered me as much as it did now? The idea of getting kicked out of here pricked at me more than it had at other places, with other squads.

Why? What did it matter? Maybe because this was the first time my boundaries hadn't gotten pushed? It was the first time I could breathe because I wasn't constantly defending myself.

I picked up my phone and dialed a number known by heart, one I never actually saved, that I never needed to save.

It rang only once before a man's smooth voice answered, the closest thing I had to a friend. "Hey there, little kitten."

I rolled my eyes at the nickname Kaidan had given me years ago. "I told you to stop calling me that."

"Why? It fits." He let out a soft laugh. "I heard you moved again. Another problem?"

I didn't flinch at that, as I might have from anyone else. When he said it, it was with a lot of history, with knowing more about me than about anyone else. He understood me in a way no one else did, which meant it hurt less when he brought up things about me I didn't love.

"Yeah."

"What happened?"

I stirred the pasta in the bowl, the food not appearing as appetizing as it had when I'd cooked it. "Same thing as always."

Four words that meant *so much more.* It was funny how that worked, how easy it was to say something in just a few words, as though it were simple when it was actually far from it.

His sigh was loud, speaking volumes.

Still, I went on since I didn't want to dwell on that. "How are you doing? Where are you now?"

"Korea."

"Settled down yet?"

"Me? Never. I'm not that type."

The way he said it made me laugh, the opposite of me. I wanted to settle down, but fear held me back, an inability to find people trustworthy enough to make it happen. For him, the idea of getting tied down, of being bound to anyone, terrified him. So instead, he enjoyed his life as a party boy, as the apple of the world's eye, ready to play that part.

It took me back to when I'd met him, back when I'd first gotten to the Guild and needed a mentor.

I knew him better than most people, just like he knew me. Two fucked-up peas in a fucked-up pod. They hadn't paired us because of that, of course, but it didn't change the truth of it. It felt like a strange twist of fate that we'd worked together.

"How are you doing now?" Kaidan asked. "I've heard some rumors."

"Yeah, I'm with Reject Squad," I admitted.

Silence met me, something thick and uncomfortable. It said more than words could have.

"You watch yourself with them."

"I always do, but why?"

"You really don't know?"

"I know they're low-ranked."

"They weren't *always* low-ranked. In fact, they used to be the top squad in the country."

That took me by surprise. I thought about all I knew about them, the way they acted, the childish behavior I'd seen, and I struggled to comprehend that. It made no sense. *These* men were considered the best in the country?

"You're lying."

"I'm not, little summer child. I was there — I remember. They rose fast, getting to the top of the charts, the toast of the town, all that. Then they ended up having…an issue." The way he said that at the end, the hesitation said it wasn't a good thing.

"What sort of issue? Were they filmed kicking puppies or something?" I let out a laugh to lighten to conversation.

"No — they failed a mission where they were supposed to save people in a dungeon. They ran the other way, and the people died."

Chapter Fifteen

Kenyon

The cool air of the early morning held a chill, with droplets sticking to the leaves of the shrubs out front. We didn't have a lot of plants, given that our place was so close to those on either side, meaning we didn't have room for much in the way of gardening. Still, as soon as we'd moved in years before, I'd put pots along the steps out front, lining the walkway with terracotta containers of herbs and veggies.

I'd have loved to have an entire yard worth of plants, but because of the way the others felt about even camping, I didn't think my future included homesteading. I still recalled the time we'd gone to find a monster hidden in a national park, when we'd tracked it long enough that we'd had to spend the night out there.

I'd never forget the way Ingram bitched, having grown up as a city boy, used to having access to all the niceties there. Even Carter had complained about the lack of a comfy bed.

Shear hadn't said anything, but it didn't take a mentalist to read his unhappiness.

That was okay, though. I'd accepted that being part of a squad like this would require sacrifices, would mean trying to work together to form a future.

Maybe I was better than others at accepting that because of my position, because my entire power had to do with taking care of others. I could put some of my own wants aside for general peace. That meant rushing into a fight with few offensive skills, trusting the others to protect me as I tried my best to keep them alive. It also meant putting plants on the front steps of our place because we weren't going to get fifty acres and a bunch of chickens.

If it was Ingram or Carter saying anything, they'd say I was too stupid to be unhappy.

Maybe there was some truth to that, as well. I just never saw a reason to think about things too deeply. It never got me anywhere good.

"How are the kiddos?" Carter's voice had me looking up and smiling.

He could get under my skin, of course, but he was a brother to me, someone who had gone through hell right by my side. It meant I didn't mind being around him.

"Good." I touched one of the leaves. "I think it's going to get cold early this year, though, so we might lose a couple of them."

He came over and sat on the top step beside me. He was usually smiling, which made it challenging to identify what he actually thought about beneath that false exterior. Still, he'd gained my trust enough that I didn't worry. He'd tell me what he wanted to tell me, eventually. "We've got a dungeon we're going to have to do in a few days."

"Rank A, right?"

He nodded, his gaze on one of the hot burrito pepper plants I grew every year, a few green peppers hanging there, white petals from the flowers still clinging to the fruit. "We'll be going in with the other squad, so we need to make sure we're all good."

And just like that, I got the point he was angling for. "So guiding, huh?"

He snorted softly. "That's the plan."

I peered over my shoulder at the house, as though I could see the woman we spoke of even through the walls. "She's different."

"Yeah, she is. It's one reason I was making sure we're all on the same page. Her guiding...it's something else."

"Yeah?" I wasn't sure what he meant by that. I'd had guiding by the lowest ranks and the highest, and other than the amount they could do, I hadn't felt much difference between them. It was like eating the same candy, just more or less of it. "How so?"

"I don't know. It feels different, like the corruption just pulls out, like it rushes to leave. It's intoxicating."

That got my attention.

Corruption tore at the esper it rested inside, growing and clawing and fighting to take over. There wasn't a moment in an esper's life — after becoming one — when they got a full reprieve from those feelings. Even guiding, which felt good, didn't fully remove the problem and often, the corruption seemed to fight first, like draining an abscess. It hurt, but there was a relief to it as well.

The way Carter talked about it felt different, though, like it was the best sensation he'd ever experienced.

And I really wanted to feel it myself. Even though I didn't fight people for the most part, that didn't change the way the corruption accumulated inside of me, the way it took over and festered. Getting a break from that sounded fantastic.

Then I recalled the way she pulled back, the distrust in her eyes when she looked at any of us.

Right.

No matter how good we thought the guiding was, it didn't matter if she put the brakes on like that.

"Do you think she'll make it long?" I asked, hating the question as soon as I uttered it. I didn't like the idea of her leaving, as though she'd already worked her way into my life.

"She's flighty, but she's stubborn, too. It's normally not a great combination—tends to be pretty annoying—but somehow she pulls it off. The better question is whether we *want* her to make it long."

I turned my head to give him a side-eye. "Why wouldn't we? If her guiding is that good, and she's an S-Rank who will work with us, what's the problem?"

Carter scooted down two steps, then leaned back, placing his elbows on the top step. It was the sort of time he was deceptively casual, as though none of this meant a thing to him. "We've stayed out of the way for a long time, and taking in a guide with the problems she has? Seems pretty complicated."

I swallowed hard, knowing exactly what he meant and not liking it one bit. He wanted me to understand that we'd sworn off connections like that, didn't want to become responsible for anything, and taking on a full-time guide with the problems she had was taking on one hell of a connection.

I knew that, understood exactly what he meant, but it didn't stop me from disliking it. Agreeing to something was one thing, but having to accept the reality of the choice was another.

Even I could think logically from time to time, and I knew the dangers of having someone with us all the time.

"You know what happened last time," Carter said, his voice soft. "Come on, Ken, didn't you learn your lesson then? Remember what happened? All the backlash?"

I blew out a long breath, that old pain coming back.

Yeah, I sure as hell remembered. Usually, I worked hard to ignore press, never gave a damn about what people said. I'd never craved fame, never wanted accolades or people talking about me. The work was reward enough, so those things hadn't mattered.

Not mattering when they were absent was a lot different from what happened when they turned on you, though.

"So what are you suggesting? Because we need her to stay on the Guild's good side."

"I'm not suggesting anything. Just pointing out facts."

I narrowed my eyes. A few things always proved true, and one of them was that Carter always had a plan. He never did or said anything without good reason. He liked to pretend he was an idiot, that he went with the flow, but after so many years together, I knew better.

"You *always* have a plan."

Carter smirked, that look an answer all its own. "Tonight, Yun will guide the three of you."

"Not you?"

"I've already had my turn. Three might be too much for her already, so we'll keep it easy."

"Does she know about this?"

Something shattered upstairs, drawing my focus that way.

"Pretty sure Ingram just told her."

Wonderful.

Chapter Sixteen

Yun

Dinner had looked delicious, but I couldn't say whether it was or not. I couldn't taste a single bite, and I hadn't shoved much down my throat, not with how my stomach rolled.

At least they hadn't made me eat with them. That was one of the few blessings as far as I saw it. I'd scrolled on my phone, looking at random nonsense to ignore the coming evening.

I could have said no, of course. It was my choice whether I guided, whether I even stayed here. They weren't wrong, either. Given the dungeon they had coming up, guiding was smart. Sending an esper into a dangerous situation with their corruption levels too high was stupid. The last thing we needed was one of our squad ending up corrupted.

The thought chilled me, winding its way through my veins the way ice crystals formed when a water bottle was opened at the right temperature, when it turned icy all at once.

I never wanted to encounter a corrupted again, and if that meant guiding — even if I hated it — then it was what it was.

Of course, that was if I could even handle it. It was easy to think I had to do something — another to do it. I could know I had to fly to get out of a situation, but knowing it wouldn't sprout me any wings. Guiding three S-Rank espers without any physical contact was a tall fucking order.

I had confidence in my powers, but I'd never tried that.

And worse, they were giving me time to 'get ready',' which meant I was just stewing in my own thoughts, having to deal with the fears that filled me. They were probably trying to be nice, but it only made it all worse. It let my mind run down every path it didn't need to go down, focusing on all the ways this could go wrong, on all the other things I could be doing instead, on the parts of my memories that I didn't want to address.

I sat in a chair in the living room, preferring the space outside my own room, nothing personal. That worked far better for me.

Plus, being far away from any bed-like surface helped remind us all that guiding would *not* end up there.

Though…

Just that brought me back to when I'd guided Carter, to the way it had terrified and excited me in equal measure. Even thinking about it caused my pussy to grow wet, as though it really wanted to give that a try.

Keep it in your pants!

I scolded myself, but what was the point? I never fucking listened, and I doubted it would work this time, either.

A water bottle appeared from behind me, and I fought the urge to jump away. That would be too embarrassing.

"It's cold," Kenyon said, his mothering as sweet and stupid as ever. As if some cold water would make any sort of difference.

Still, it was nice to have someone thinking about me, so I undid the cap and took a drink, surprised to find it helped. The coolness of the water washed away the layer of discomfort that had thickened in my throat.

"You're good with this?" he asked as he took a seat on the couch. He had his hair pulled back into a man bun, something I would have thought I'd laugh at if I ever saw in person.

How could it somehow look charming on him?

"I have to be, right?"

"No, you don't." At my look, he went on. "You don't have to do anything you don't want to. We're not about to force you, after all."

"I'm here to guide. If I don't do that, I'll get fired." The unspoken *again* hung in the air.

Kenyon tilted his head, and for once, he didn't look quite as dumb as he usually did. "That's not true. First of all, you can always say an idea is too much. You don't have to do whatever we say, and even if you wanted to help, you don't have to do it the way anyone says—not even Carter."

"Rude." The familiar voice cut into our conversation, and I turned my gaze to find Carter breezing in as though nothing had happened.

He looked far too nice for this time in the evening. He wore a three-piece suit, and he wore it well. It showed off the way his waist narrowed, the wider set of his back and shoulders.

This was what women meant when they said they liked men in suits.

Bastard.

Why had he dressed up so much? As though this were some date? It wasn't even like I would guide him today, so was he just showing off?

Part of me wondered if he was just being respectful in some weird way.

That didn't seem like this man, though.

"It's true," Kenyon said. "Even you wouldn't force her to do this if she said she couldn't."

"You think I'm way nicer than I am." He undid his jacket and removed it, slinging it over the back of the couch. It showed off the way the fastening at the back of his vest pulled in at his waist, and his wrists had cuff links with pearls in them.

I'd never thought a man could pull off pearls, but here we were.

"You want a drink?" Ingram carried a bottle of alcohol in his hand, but he stood too far away for me to identify it.

"Is drinking a good idea?" Kenyon asked.

"It helps relax people, and she looks like she could fucking use some relaxing." Ingram unscrewed the top, then tipped it up and dumped a gulp into his mouth. He didn't so much as grimace afterward, like he'd just swallowed a mouthful of water rather than hard liquor.

"She's fried espers before. Perhaps we shouldn't have her in a condition likely to cause that." Shear snatched the bottle from Ingram's hand, getting a glare in response. Not that Shear gave any reaction, as though he either didn't notice the look or didn't care.

Then again, none of these men seemed afraid of each other, none watched their backs. No matter what others said or thought about them, it was pretty clear they trusted each other.

"Drunk people are happy," Ingram argued.

"Have you never heard of a mean drunk?" Kenyon pointed out. "For all we know, she gets extra feisty when she drinks. Not everyone gets cuddly like you do."

Ingram shrugged and plopped onto the couch, his legs stretched out, his body slouched down. "Let's be clear—I don't cuddle."

"Tell me again why you ended up spooning me the last time you drank yourself into oblivion?" Carter asked, crossing his arms.

"I never!"

"Wait, *your* bed? But he crawled into mine later." Kenyon twisted to move his gaze between Carter and Ingram as though he couldn't quite believe it, like some scorned lover who found out he'd been cheated on.

"You left mine for his?" Carter played right along.

And for a moment, I forgot about my nerves, about anything except the absolute spectacle these men made.

It made me wonder what anyone would think if they saw them like this. These men were espers, some of the most feared and celebrated people in the world—even if these specific specimens weren't thought of so kindly—and no would believe that they acted in this way.

"He's more cozy to spoon," Ingram said with a shrug.

"He's saying you're fat," Carter added on.

"I am *not* fat." Kenyon crossed his arms, and I had to admit, I'd seen no sign of fat.

"You're in the overweight category for BMI." Shear set the bottle of alcohol on the coffee table.

"They don't take into account muscle!" Kenyon huffed.

The exchange struck me as so absurd, I couldn't help the laugh that left me. It stole the strain that had rested on me, turned the men from terrifying, powerful espers to idiots.

Sure, idiots could still hurt me, but it made them far less scary.

Kenyon offered me a smile, a gentle one full of kindness, telling me he'd known *exactly* what he was doing.

"Well, fatty should go first," Carter said with an exaggerated sigh, as though he hated the idea. "He got her to smile, so he's earned it."

Ingram and Shear both muttered, their words so low I couldn't catch them, only the soft buzz of discontentment making its way to me.

Even so, neither spoke up directly, seeming to accept the choice.

Kenyon didn't look around, though. He didn't seek permission from Carter, from the others, instead staring at me. He remained still, seeming to wait.

For what?

For me. He wanted permission from me, to make sure I was okay with it.

It made it all the clearer that Kenyon was the absolute best choice to start with. He enabled me to relax in a way that the others didn't.

He was a healer, after all, and maybe that was part of it? He wasn't crafted to do harm, to hurt others, to cause them pain. He could, of course — we all could — but his powers didn't lean toward it. Likewise, his personality tended to ease me, not to set off the warnings inside me. He wasn't playing that game to try to come out on top. I didn't have to worry about him in that way.

Even after everything that happened, even after learning my place as a guide, my interactions with espers hadn't been great. Something about Kenyon, the casual way he addressed everything, helped lower my guard.

I scooted my chair closer to Kenyon until I sat just in front of him. I didn't want to touch, but the less distance between us, the easier the process.

Guiding three espers wasn't going to be easy no matter what, so making each session as efficient as possible — given the parameters I'd set — was best.

I focused on him, on feeling for the corruption inside him, that hated, dark, wriggling energy that infected him, that infected *all* espers. It was higher than it should have been, higher than most espers allowed it to get.

It had to be uncomfortable, a clawing sensation he could never escape, but he hadn't let on about it. He'd never said a word.

An uneasy knot formed in my lower stomach. Something inside me didn't like that for him. Normally, I didn't give a damn about how espers suffered. They were well paid by the world for what they did, so who gave a damn if they had problems? Everyone had problems, after all.

However, thinking about Kenyon awake at night, sweat beading on his forehead, an aching, gnawing pain that he couldn't escape, it didn't sit right. His easy smile, the way he always worried about me, those made it more difficult to accept that he hurt for no good reason, for something that I could easily resolve.

Those thoughts would do me no good at the moment, though, so I pushed them aside and focused on the task at hand. I grasped the corruption within him and allowed it to flow into me. It filled me, though with the distance, without physical contact, I had to pull it on purpose. The space it had to flow through made it more difficult.

That unwanted, hated heat started inside me, my treacherous body betraying me as it always did. It was like it couldn't understand the danger, like I was desperate for a drug I knew damn well would destroy me, but my addiction craved it anyway.

It made me wonder what it would be like with Kenyon...

He scared me less than the others, was less overwhelming. In fact, whereas the idea of sex with the others terrified me, with him, curiosity outweighed fear. I imagined he'd be sweet, gentle, slow and careful. It was how he was in regular life, so I had to guess he approached sex the same way.

I could almost imagine I might even enjoy it, that his gentle kisses, his large hands and solid body might actually please me.

I shook my head to dislodge that idea before it could take hold any deeper. It didn't matter how tempting the idea might have been right then, I knew better than to give in.

So instead, I focused entirely on pulling the corruption from him, on alleviating his burden. My eyes slid closed, everything locked on tearing free that sickness inside him.

"Enough." The voice shook me out of the action, causing me to snap my eyes open to find Carter kneeling before me but not touching me. His expression implied he'd said my name a time or two before, that he might have even considered touching me to wake me from that trance. When my gaze met his, when he seemed to notice that I'd come back to myself, he smiled. "You went a little deep there, didn't you?"

I blinked slowly, not sure what he meant until I looked back over at Kenyon.

I didn't sense a speck of corruption, as though I'd dragged every last bit of it out. It was an exceedingly difficult task, something that only the most powerful or most in-tune guides could do. I'd never done it because I'd never wanted to, because I'd always wanted guiding to end as fast as possible. I'd never given enough of a damn to do that sort of work, but I'd done it just now without even meaning to?

"That's amazing," Kenyon whispered, voice full of a strange awe. Then again, who knew how long it had been since he'd been free of this? He stared at me with a fondness that made me entirely uncomfortable. I was pretty sure he'd have reached across the space and wrapped his arms around me if it hadn't been for the whole risk of getting fried if he tried it.

"Me next." Ingram shoved Kenyon's arm until he moved from the couch, taking the spot he'd just vacated.

And boy did this show me the difference.

Where Kenyon was soft and gentle, Ingram was all hard lines. The tattoos that covered him proved that point, along with the black gauges in his ears, his hair slicked back. It all made him unapproachable. All the ways in which I relaxed with Kenyon closed right back up when it came to Ingram.

Worse, where Kenyon was so open with everything, where he seemed without guile, Ingram served as an exact foil. He was all secrets and shadows and hidden danger. Even his skills as an esper played into that, him making use of the shaded, the hidden to gain an advantage.

He didn't soften his gaze as he stared at me, as though daring me to give up. It almost seemed like he wanted me to surrender, to admit defeat. I had a feeling everything was a contest to him. His lips curled up on one side, as though he could read my loss already, and it amused him.

That pushed me onward, made me unwilling to give in. I didn't want to appear weak. I *was* weak in a lot of ways compared to them, but the idea of looking that way infuriated me. It felt like lighting a signal to predators, a way of making myself a target — which was foolish, given my current position.

So I focused instead of giving into my worries, identifying the corruption inside Ingram. Just like Kenyon, it was higher than it should have been.

I wasn't about to back down, not from him…

Chapter Seventeen

Ingram

Fuck.

That was all I could think as Yun began guiding, as the corruption moved from me to her. It was like nothing I had ever experienced before.

That clawing, desperate need inside me lessened, and for a moment I actually felt an entirely foreign sense of contentment.

That darkness had quieted, lulled to peace, tamed by this little spit of a guide?

And with that silence, with that peace, another hunger woke.

But this was different.

Normally, when I wanted to indulge in another person, it was to lose myself, to bury myself in their warmth since I had none of my own. It was a craving I couldn't ignore, a way to rid myself of everything about me I hated. It was to silence that gnawing, growing darkness that prowled beneath my skin.

However, this felt different.

It was a strangely natural pull, almost teasing, oddly seductive.

Was this what normal people felt? This sort of desire? Was this the sort of typical back and forth that couples experienced? It was nice in a way I couldn't identify with.

I opened my eyes, staring at her, trying to gain some understanding of this woman who confounded me constantly. She was braver than she appeared, willing to do this, even when everything about her said she didn't want to.

Why?

I couldn't help but wonder about the reasoning behind it. What caused the fear that swarmed her? Why did she act that way? Why didn't she let it take over, either?

She was like one big enigma, and worse? I lacked Shear's powers, the ability to crawl right into her head. I was death—something crafted for the singular purpose of ending life. I could get in close and pull the living force of any creature—monster, human, esper— nothing more.

It meant I had no way of working out why she was different, why this felt so strange. And for the first time, I really *wanted* to understand.

That hunger inside me, though, the one that couldn't help but crave more, always more, eased for this short time.

What would it feel like to get closer? If guiding felt this amazing just like this, what if I sought more? What if I grasped her hips and pulled her against me, got her to spread those pretty legs of hers around my hips?

She was tough, even if she didn't look it, so would she pull back? Would she go rigid? Or would she melt against me, give in to me, go along with anything I wanted?

"Stop it," she whispered, voice low enough I wasn't sure it carried any farther than me.

At least, it might not have in a group of humans, but with espers? She might as well have used a bullhorn to announce it.

Not that I gave a fuck. I had no shame anymore, so I'd have happily fucked her in the middle of this room with a full audience without a second thought. I'd done worse, after all, and if there was anyone I didn't give a damn about seeing my bare ass, it was the other men in my squad. We'd seen each other at far lower points than this.

However, it was almost adorable the way she tried, made me want to tease her. "Stop what?" I asked, mirroring my voice to hers, matching her tone.

"You *know* what. You think I can't tell what you're thinking?"

A bond formed when guiding, no matter how limited or transient. It caused the two to react to each other, and for some, it allowed a certain level of information exchange, a general sense of the other and their emotions.

Some guides were more sensitive to it, and the fact that Yun picked it up said she was likely one of them.

Or maybe it's just me?

I didn't mind that idea one bit. It was fucking nice to think that she gave a damn about me, that she felt a pull toward me.

Her cheeks flushed, and it made me wonder where else her skin would turn pink. Would it extend down her neck, her chest? Some women got red damn near all over, and I wanted to see that with her, to put it to the test. I was pretty sure that even if she didn't naturally turn that pretty shade, I could bring up some color over the curve of her ass with my palm.

Which had me groaning as my cock ached, rigid against the metal teeth of my zipper.

Carter would kick my ass if I tried to take it out right now, to stroke myself as she guided me, but fuck, I wanted to. Carter had given me enough talks about when my dick could make an appearance, and I was pretty sure now was not one of the acceptable times.

Instead, I focused on her, on the way she pulled air in through her nose with breaths shorter than normal, a sure sign of her own reaction. I couldn't quite tell if she reacted directly to me or not, but I didn't think I cared that much.

Whether it was because of me or just the guiding, she was getting off on it.

I dropped my gaze to find her nipples pebbled against her shirt like the prettiest lures I'd ever seen.

Well, well…

"You don't want me thinking that because you got some interest?" I made a show of letting my gaze linger there.

She didn't cross her arms, didn't hide the evidence. She was probably too smart, knew damn well that it wouldn't make a bit of difference. It was adorable for her to think she could hide shit from me, at least when it came to this.

Anything deeper?

Fuck, I didn't have a clue.

But the way her leg trembled, just a bit, the hitch in her breath now and then, it all was a language I'd spent a lifetime getting fluent in.

"You don't know anything," she answered.

"Pretty fucking sure I do. Bet you if I slid right down between those thighs of yours, if I took off those god-awful pants you're wearing, I'd find you drenched."

Even as we spoke, the guiding never stopped, never slowed. In fact, it amazed me that she seemed to not even have to concentrate on it. It flowed into her without thought or effort.

Normally, back and forth like ours would cause a slowdown, even a break, but the corruption left me and entered her at the same rate — picking up speed slightly, if anything.

"Well, it's not like you'll ever find out."

Not denying it, huh? Interesting.

"You sure about that? Come on, Flicker, I promise I'm good at it. Fuck knows, you'll enjoy it."

"Flicker?"

"You don't like it?" I smirked at the nickname, at how perfectly it fit her. That's what she was, just a tiny little spark in the darkness, just a flicker of something in the endless blackness that existed. So easy to catch, so easy to see, to find, to snuff out.

The press of her lips into a thin, flat line told me her opinion.

Not that I gave a fuck. A nickname wasn't about pleasing the other person, it was about a name that fit whether or not they found it appealing.

"Do you think of nothing but sex?" she asked me.

"I think about killing, too."

Something like that would scare off most women — except the ones who said yes to me out of some weird fucking fetish, the sort who would have loved if I'd shown up with glowing eyes and covered in monster blood. Yun, however, didn't so much as flinch.

"So you're just a pervert, then?"

"Basically. Still, it's not so bad. Think about it. You want to go skydiving? You want an expert. You want a fun time, you go find yourself a willing pervert—and, Flicker, I'm really fucking willing."

She rolled her eyes, but that didn't hide the reaction her body screamed loud and fucking clear. Every bit of her was a lewd come-and-get-it, even if she didn't mean it to be. She leaned in, her tongue wetting her bottom lip, batting those long, pretty lashes of hers. Even her scent drew me in, promising something exquisite. Fuck, I wanted to lap at her cunt until we were both too tired to give a damn about anything else. I wanted her fingers wrapped in my hair, urging me forward, my arms curled around her thighs, around her hips, holding her still for my meal.

I'd *never* felt like this.

Lust? Sure. Usually because it was a way to quiet that unending hunger inside of me, but it was like wanting saltines because I didn't want to throw up. This was deeper, more pointed, a ravenous need for *her*.

And just as my body moved, as I shifted forward to do what I was pretty fucking sure we both wanted, a hand came to rest on my shoulder, breaking the spell.

Fucking Carter.

If it were anyone else, I might have ignored them, but not Carter. That fucker was one of the few who could stop me—permanently—if I didn't listen and fall in line.

I shuddered, wrangling control back from that precarious edge I teetered on. Right, I needed to stay focused. This was a long game, not a short one.

And given the way Yun stared at me, the way desire flickered in her eyes just like her new nickname, I knew the game would get me where I wanted, eventually.

Chapter Eighteen

Shear

I found the lust that poured from Ingram as repugnant as usual. He behaved like a bitch in heat, content to spend his life sniffing the asses of others just to pass the time.

After all these years by his side, however, I'd grown used to it. In fact, I had done far more than grown used to it, helping him at times when he was too far gone to seek out companionship. We all had our quirks, after all, and I had to admit to my own. If he put up with mine, I could ignore the way he eye-fucked everything that walked.

At least, I could because Carter had stepped in before he'd done anything more, before he'd crossed that line.

With my powers, I could sense the lust in Yun as well, as though written in scrawling letters across her face.

Ingram was always searching for the hidden, for the darkness inside people, but for me? There was no search.

I could read it, every emotion so plain, like a label on a bottle, telling me all I needed to know.

Without physical touch or eye contact or true effort, I couldn't go deeper, couldn't gain previous memories, couldn't dig around, but those things required effort and energy. They exhausted me.

And more often than not, I'd rather avoid it anyway. I didn't see any real reason to concern myself with the feelings or thoughts or memories of most people. Who cared what the cashier at the store had for breakfast or why the crossing guard hated the dark or any of the mundane nonsense that formed people's fractured psyches?

It bored me.

Still, when I looked at Yun, I didn't experience that nagging boredom. I didn't want to retreat, to pull away, to get as far from this and her as possible. In fact, an odd desire urged me forward.

"Your turn," Carter said after he got Ingram out of the seat—no small task, given the man's reluctance.

The way all three had reacted so far had me curious about Yun's guiding.

We'd experienced guiding plenty of times, and it had never mattered. It was much the same no matter who did it.

So why did Ingram and Kenyon act as though this were somehow special?

It felt like watching someone eat a chocolate chip cookie and marvel over how amazing it was, and me wondering how that version of someone so common could be that amazing.

How could it be unique?

It made no sense to me, but I'd learned to never take things for granted, that nothing was ever quite as it seemed.

I eyed the spot that Ingram had been, unsure about it, as though something from him would get on me.

"Don't be like that," Ingram said from across the room, amusement coloring the words. "Ain't like you haven't had my cum on you before."

He wasn't wrong, so I refused to give him the satisfaction of getting a rise out of me. Ingram enjoyed that far too much. Instead, I took a seat, the position placing me close enough to Yun for guiding to take place without contact.

Her gaze shifted between Ingram and myself, the back and forth like she watched a match and followed the ball from player to player. Curiosity rested in those dark eyes of hers, questions that she desperately wanted to know but didn't dare ask.

And I had to say, I didn't mind her curiosity. I normally loathed when people wanted to dig into my privacy, when they wanted a glimpse beyond the placid façade I'd built, but Yun?

She somehow proved immune to that reaction.

However, I wasn't sure how to explain my relationship with Ingram, so I ignored the unasked questions and focused on her.

Her irises were dimmer than before, a darkening shadow in the soft valley beneath each eye. Even without my powers, the exhaustion that hung on her was easy to see.

"She's done," I said, hiding my disappointment beneath a blanket of indifference.

"We said she'd guide each of you," Carter argued.

"Look at her. She is exhausted and needs rest. I can do without."

"I'm fine," she said, voice soft and unsure.

I refused to break eye contact, instead staring right into the darkness, bridging that gap with her.

I spoke—not aloud, but inside her head.

"You've done enough."

"I can do it. Stop doubting me."

"I'm not doubting you—I am saying you don't have to push yourself. I can manage."

And I could. The truth was that for me—for most of us—corruption was so constant a companion that it hardly bore the worth of noticing. It was like owning a tiger that snarled and lunged at the cage and occasionally managed to swipe when you ventured too close. Live with it long enough and most stop noticing it, stop thinking about it, stop worrying about the bit of blood it draws.

"If you don't get guiding, you sit this dungeon out," Carter said, a stern voice full of no humor.

The worst part was that I knew him well enough to identify his little plans. I couldn't always see what he was after, where he was headed, but I always knew when he moved us around like game pieces.

He didn't care about my guiding—he knew I could handle this. Instead, he cared about the connection with her, that we forge some bond, and had likely planned for me to go last on purpose.

Her guard would be down after guiding the others, making it easier for me to slip into her mind and take her unaware.

The bastard.

It wasn't that I disagreed with his plan, but I never cared for feeling manipulated, not even by Carter.

"It's really okay," Yun pressed, her voice stronger. That was likely all stubbornness, but I had to respect the backbone all the same.

"Fine. Only guide as much as you feel able to, though. You do not need to do a full session." I added weight to my words, wanting her to understand the meaning.

This was not a battlefield issue, where guiding me could be the difference between losing myself and not. She didn't need to bring me down from that edge so I could save lives, so I could keep her and others safe.

She nodded, but the set of her lips suggested that she would do as she pleased — and I begrudgingly had to respect that.

She took a deep breath, her chest rising and falling beneath her shirt, a moment before a gentle pull against the corruption that spanned inside me. She didn't yank, didn't pull hard, but offered an almost sweet acceptance that had the corruption snaking out of me, vacating me in a way I'd never felt before.

It surprised me so much that at first, I forgot the rest of my job.

No matter how pleasant this seemed, I couldn't forget the plan or the opportunity.

It meant that I used her distraction, the unavoidable closeness that came from guiding, to slip past any natural defenses she might have had and into her mind.

And fuck, was it a mess.

I'd known it from a few of the sparks I'd spotted before, the times when her entire psyche lit up in pain and fear and anguish. That sort of thing only happened with deep-rooted trauma, with wounds that went so far into a person they never could fully heal.

I didn't enjoy poking at wounds like that. Trauma was far more common than most believed, and because of the way people experienced it, it was impossible to qualify.

I'd once dealt with a teen boy who had the pattern of someone who had been abused and tortured. I'd been asked as a favor from a family member to look into it, as he had struggled, and I had prepared myself for the worst. I'd readied myself to relive sexual abuse, to find rape or severe physical assault.

Instead, I'd found a spoiled rich boy whose largest problem had been that his mother had taken away his gaming console.

The truth was that minds were horribly unreliable. Add that individuals experience things through relativity, and what was traumatic to one was a Tuesday to another.

It meant that even though I felt certain Yun had suffered *something* to cause such a reaction in her mind, I couldn't know how significant it truly had been from the outside.

Still, stepping in, there was no doubt of her suffering. Her mind resembled a funhouse full of cracked and splintered mirrors, something twisting and impossible to navigate.

Her thoughts were jumbled, passing her by as she focused on the guiding rather than any specific line of thought.

Almost done. Hold on, just a little longer.

Was she hyping herself up? I nearly smiled at the thought, at how she'd so confidently told me she could do this and how much less sure she was in her mind.

I turned, taking in the space, the snaking darkness inside of her. It almost seemed as though some of it were the deep purple of corruption, as though somewhere along the way, she'd taken in too much, as though her body had been unable to rid itself of the damaging substance as it should have.

But that made no sense. Guides could take corruption in as they did because their bodies converted it to normal energy, they dissipated it until it turned harmless. If they took in too much, it would only cause them to pass out, not do any long-term harm.

Which meant the corruption I spied could have only been a mirage, a mirror of trauma and fear and the doubts inside her.

That made sense, given her life as a guide. Her worries had to revolve around espers and corruption, didn't they?

I raised my hand, easing her mind more, relaxing any hold she had on it. This would allow her thoughts to pass more easily, to slip from one to another. It was like being in a meditative trance, and due to our bond and the guiding, she wouldn't be able to tell I'd done anything.

The memories played across the space, above me, like holographic movies, all first person from her point of view.

She recalled walking into our office just days ago. I hadn't been there at the time, but her thoughts whispered as she relived it.

The thoughts were hardly positive, but who could blame her? She hadn't wanted to be there anymore than we'd wanted her there—just misfits forced to work together for our mutual good.

From there, it slid backward…to a hospital? An esper lay in the bed, eyes closed, the soft whir of machines and the beeping of monitors loud in the silence.

This is my fault... Guilt assailed her, piling up so heavy that I was amazed she could stand.

Ah, so that had to be one of the espers she had shocked. I'd heard about it, but I had hardly been able to believe the truth of it. What guide could do that? It was so unheard of, I couldn't bring myself to accept it.

At least, until I saw this, until I watched the esper there, helpless. If I were truly there myself, I might have been able to sense whether the esper had any brain activity at all, whether he would recover, but like this? I was as helpless as her.

Again, it all changed around me, this time to that same esper awake, standing, the pinnacle of life.

I didn't recognize him, but I usually tried not to know anyone well enough for that. He stood so close to Yun that he towered over her.

Were his hands on the wall to either side of her? Caging her in?

Their conversation was muted, soft, but I could catch it.

"You'll like it."

"You know my rule. No touching."

"Come on—I know you want me, too. All guides do. You're going to try to tell me you don't feel that?"

"Please, stop."

Her heart hammered so loudly that I struggled to hear their conversation over it. Inside her?

Lust? Maybe, but it was muted and distant and unwanted.

Instead, fear had a full front seat, controlling her actions, sending her mind into fight or flight. I could *feel* her beg him to stay back, but the arrogant prick couldn't see beyond the tip of his own hard cock.

He reached out and cupped the back of her neck, then pulled her in and all but slammed his lips to hers in a crushing, domineering kiss.

It lit the parts of her brain that had suffered whatever trauma had caused this, sparking them to life until that current of power rushed over her skin.

Normally it would only be enough to startle an esper, perhaps to drive them back, like a static electricity charge, but this?

It was so overpowered, so far past that that it flung the esper backward, crashing him into a table and leaving him unmoving on the floor.

Before I could gain anything else, the scene changed again.

It was the good and bad thing about this method of insight. The good was that the subject knew nothing about it, that the information gained was more natural, but often things went unanswered. I couldn't control the direction, couldn't stay with something for more information, so I could only glean what I could from the flashes she relived. I got only part of the story, and was left to fit together pieces and make guesses for all I didn't see or know.

Everything went dark around me, and for a moment, I wondered if the bond had broken.

Black streaked with dark purple filled the sky above the memory, and I knew the sight instantly.

Some things burned themselves into memory. They dug so deeply that nothing could free them, nothing could pry them loose, and the sky of a dungeon was one such thing.

The lower levels had less purple, appeared more similar to the real world, but the higher-level dungeons? They looked exactly like this.

How had she seen this?

The question confused me all the more when the memory turned, and a monster leapt at her, with huge fangs inside its wide open mouth, its massive body barreling through the air at her.

She didn't even have time to scream before the memory shut off and I found myself thrown back to my own body, back to my own mind, the connection severed.

It happened so fast that I struggled to regain my senses, to work out where I was, the memory so real and so fresh that I wanted nothing more than to feel a blade in my hand.

Except, there was nothing here to fight.

Across from me, Yun was slumped over in the chair, having passed out. From guiding? The exhaustion from guiding three of us must have proven too much, especially when faced with that memory.

It left me sitting there, staring at her, unable to avoid considering the only possible meaning, even if it made no damn sense at all.

At some point, Yun, a guide, had been the one place she should have never been...

A dungeon.

Chapter Nineteen

Carter

I let the beer sit in my mouth longer than it should have, until it was lukewarm and flat. I swallowed it down as though having just realized it still lingered there.

Yun slept in her room, with Kenyon having risked picking her up to take her to bed.

And it *was* a risk, given her history and reputation. It seemed the nickname Blizzard sure suited her, after all.

Kenyon had assured us that she was healthy—just overwhelmed and exhausted. It seemed the girl truly had no sense of her limits, having guided until she could no longer keep her eyes open.

The fool.

"We need to keep her." Ingram spoke that as though it were an obvious and forgone conclusion.

Which I struggled to argue against.

Still, devil's advocate and all… "She's not a thing to be owned. She'll stay or not—it's up to her."

He shook his head, already on his third beer. Alcohol didn't affect espers as much as humans, so that wasn't enough to loosen his tongue. "You've felt it. Her guiding's like nothing else. I've never felt this good, not once in my whole fucking life. Whatever it takes, we gotta keep her."

"She's good," Kenyon offered, a soda in his hands. He didn't like drinking much, so usually went for something without alcohol. "It feels like back when I first became an esper, before the corruption started to build. I've never even heard of this being possible."

"None of the other squads reported anything like this," I pointed out. "Why is it like this now but not before? If she guided like this, do you really think the other squads would have let her go?"

"Maybe we're different," Ingram said. "Fuck, I don't know, but isn't like, compatibility a thing? What if she just fits with us?"

I offered him a chiding look. "That sounds like some romantic bullshit that little girls believe."

"Yeah, well, argue with the results, then. *You* explain it."

I leaned back on the picnic table, staring out at the dark ocean. The beach was closed this time of night, but that didn't stop us.

Espers didn't really follow the normal laws, and cops around here knew us on sight. They pretty much let us be.

What human was stupid enough to want to take on an esper, especially for something as trivial as enjoying the beach after hours?

Not one who lived very long, that was for sure.

"She won't let you touch her," I pointed out.

"She'll change her mind." Ingram reached down and grabbed his groin, adjusting himself, his erection *still* there. I nearly reminded him that after four hours he should go to the ER, but why?

That man lived with a hard-on. If it hadn't fallen off by now, he was probably fine.

Besides, worrying over his cock was hardly my job.

"What if she doesn't? You okay with having a guide long term who you can't fuck?"

Ingram waved off the concern, the beer bottle hanging between his fingers, the liquid inside sloshing but not spilling. "So she's a little gun-shy? I've dealt with virgins before. Trust me, that girl'll warm right up with a little time."

I opened my mouth to argue, but couldn't get the words out before Shear spoke, him sitting on the table, his legs crossed in front of him, a water in his hand. "She's not going to just get over it."

"Oh, did you maybe take a little trip through her mind?" I asked.

"You say that as though you hadn't expected exactly that."

I didn't bother to deny it—he knew me better than to believe that. Instead, I took a drink of my beer and shrugged.

"She's been inside a dungeon."

That drew all conversation to a rapid and abrupt stop, like slamming a car headfirst into a wall.

It was like saying a kid had been in the middle of a war zone.

It wasn't supposed to happen.

"That isn't in any records," I said, my tone careful. I'd scoured through every file on her I could find — and there hadn't been much—but nothing had hinted at anything like that.

"There haven't been many cases of guides inside dungeons," Kenyon offered. "The few that happened, the guide was killed almost immediately. If she'd been inside one, there'd be a record of it."

"Her history since turning into a guide is well documented. She was found in The Pitt ruins, living there alone, and taken to the Guild for training," I said.

"I saw it in her memories. She was in a high-level dungeon and a monster attacked her." Shear spoke with his usual confidence, the sort that said he knew his skills and trusted them.

"If she was attacked by a monster, she wouldn't *be* here. Certainly not in one piece."

"And yet she was. As I've said before, I can't explain how something happened, but I can tell you it happened."

I frowned as I tried to piece together the things I knew. I didn't doubt Shear—I knew him well enough to believe that if he said it, no matter how unlikely, it was true. That didn't mean everything, though.

If I accepted that she had been inside a dungeon at some point, and further acknowledged that it wasn't feasible for it to have happened after she joined the Guild, it had to be before she turned into a guide, right?

"The Guild keeps track of civilians rescued from dungeons," Ingram said, as though he followed along with my line of thoughts. "So if she'd gotten rescued, it would have been recorded. They offer them therapy and run blood work on 'em. No fucking way that could happen and there wouldn't be a paper trail."

"What if a rogue saved her?" Kenyon asked.

"Rogues aren't known for being that helpful."

Rogues were espers who refused to join the Guild, often ones who hid their skills to fly under the radar. Some worked odd jobs, using the skills for personal gain, while others tried to fit in with humans.

Either way, they weren't the type to rush in and try to save trapped civilians. The cowards left that to us.

"Still, it's the only thing that makes any sense. Civilians don't just escape dungeons on their own. The only logical way that happens is if an esper clears the way and helps them out. If it were someone from the Guild, they'd report it, but there's nothing in her history."

"It was a high-level dungeon. At least A, if not S."

I tapped my finger against the glass of the beer bottle, trying to work that out in a way that made sense.

Dungeons sprang up all the time, but few were high level. Some opened and collapsed so fast that no one ever noticed them.

That had to be it, right?

A small, higher-level dungeon opened, trapped her, and a rogue esper got her out?

It sounded absurd, but still less crazy than any other option. No worthwhile esper would fail to report a rescued civilian, not when we knew what could happen with them. Many took their own lives eventually, both due to corruption infection and because of what they saw and experienced. Human minds weren't designed to come back from that sort of thing, not without extensive help.

"So what does that mean?" Kenyon asked. "We still don't know anything about her, really, so what do we do?"

I wanted to tell them an exact plan, wanted to say that I knew what we needed to do, how to resolve this, but I just didn't have enough information.

"We figure out the truth," I said, hating how vague it was. "Having her around is good for us, right? Well, in that case, we'd do well to get her to admit to whatever happened. It would help us interact with her better and increase the odds that she decides to stick with us."

"With the joint Guild events coming up…" Ingram said.

I waved him off. "I know. Now's not the best time to be trying to work through this, but it's not like we can just ask The Pitt not to open. It's going to happen no matter what we do, and we're not going to be able to just sit it out this time. It means it's best that we get this handled *before* that happens, so we aren't pulled in too many directions."

I turned my gaze to Shear, expecting him to be paying attention to me — he usually was — but instead found his gaze locked elsewhere.

Yun.

He stared at the large glass sliding door to her room, up on the second floor, the night sky reflecting off the sheer surface. I didn't know what went on in his head, but I suspected it was similar to my own, to the chaos there, the desire for a clear understanding, for some sort of path forward among so many unanswered questions.

I told myself we'd been through worse, that we'd handle this as we had so many other things, but I wasn't sure if I actually believed it.

Something about this said it might just end up being our most dangerous battle.

Chapter Twenty

Yun

Darkness engulfed me. I knew it was a nightmare, but that didn't remove the sting or fear. Even if I knew I'd wake up in a safe bed, even if I knew that there weren't actually monsters surrounding me, that didn't stop my physical reaction to a nightmare that felt so real.

I didn't close my eyes, didn't hide from it — hiding never helped.

I'd tried it so many years ago. No matter where I'd hidden, it hadn't changed a thing. Monsters could smell me, were drawn to the scent, to their cure, even if they didn't know directly that was what it was.

So I stood tall, the world shifting around me as the nightmare changed, some of it a memory, some of it an amalgamation of my own fears. Monsters ran around my feet, snapping their teeth breaths away from me, as though to remind me that they were there, that they could tear me apart if they wished.

Or perhaps it was better to say they would if no one was stopping them.

"My dear." The voice of the one who had stopped them came to me, my savior and my tormentor all in one.

He was a shadow, as he always was in the dreams, all details obscured. Sometimes I wondered if I remembered his face at all. Perhaps it had gone away through the years, drifted to distant memory, then forgotten? Or maybe I just refused to confront it anymore, too scared and traumatized by it, unable to face it again.

It meant he was just shadows and darkness and that damned voice.

I cowered, no matter if I'd told myself not to flinch, not to run. I couldn't help it. "You're not real," I said again, like a chant.

"Oh, but I am. It's almost time. I can *feel* it. I miss how you taste and your screams and your begging. You escaped me once, but it won't happen again."

"You're not real."

"Are you sure about that? Maybe I'm just a figment of your imagination, nothing but a spark of memory and terror that you replay over and over again." He came closer, my feet rooted in place, keeping me still. He walked around me as he spoke, humor coloring the words. "Or maybe I planted some bit of me deep inside your brain as I was playing around in there. Maybe it's still there, whispering to you, just a mirror of me that you can't ever dig free."

That terrified me almost more than anything else, the thought of having any of him inside me, any of him still there, forging a bond between us.

"Or maybe this isn't a figment or a fragment or anything else. Maybe it's me, since we're bonded, and I'm talking to you."

"That's not possible," I said.

"Are you sure? You probably didn't think anything that happened was possible, but it still all happened. Maybe we're bonded across realms, and I'm just reminding you to get ready. Get your things in order. Do whatever you have to do because you don't have long before the portal opens again, before I come for you. Make no mistake, Yun, you are *mine*."

He reached out, gripping my chin as he'd done before, his fingers like shards of ice that buried themselves inside me. That old sensation of him slipping into my mind came back to me, the pain of it, the way he'd cracked my brain open and forced his way inside. It was a violation unlike anything I'd known possible, the way he'd taken over my thoughts, guided them, stole my freewill.

It felt so real, just like back then, when he'd done this so many times. I cried out at the way corruption forced itself into me. It wasn't the way it happened with espers, not the way I'd experienced it so many times since, but the difference between taking a drink of water and drowning. The pain overwhelmed me, and only his laugh kept me rooted.

The dream collapsed in on itself, disappearing, causing me to bolt upright, gasping, my throat sore.

Had I been screaming?

The dreams were getting worse night by night, taking more of me, going further. Why? Was it the stress of guiding, or perhaps the anxiety as we approached The Pitt opening again?

That made sense, even if it didn't feel quite right.

The dream had felt so real, like that place had trapped me yet again, like the last decade hadn't passed.

I swallowed down the sick in my throat, past the roughness there, praying no one had heard me, that I'd gotten through this little tiny meltdown with some privacy. I doubted it, since I was in a house full of espers with heightened senses, but I could hope.

The light poured in from outside, telling me that I'd slept through the night. I had no idea who put me into bed, and for once, I didn't give a damn. They'd risked enough to move me, but at least it had given me a good night's sleep—minus the nightmare. I didn't have to worry about guiding for a while. I'd guided them fully, ensured that every last bit of corruption was pulled from their bodies.

I wanted to shake off the dream, to forget everything that had happened. Wanting to do it and having it happen, were totally different matters. No matter what I did, that memory clung to me, threatening to drag me back.

Eventually, I gave up hiding. I headed downstairs to see the others. It was unusual for all of them to be in the house at the same time, so it wasn't a shock that only Carter and Ingram were there.

We had three days until the dungeon opened. Three days before I had to work with another squad. I'd hardly figured out how to deal with these espers, let alone now having to add in extras I didn't even know.

Still, complaining about it wasn't going to do a fucking thing. At least that's what I told myself, since I didn't see a real way out of it.

"Sleep well?"

"Sure," I answered.

It wasn't the truth, but I had a feeling he already knew. No matter how much I wanted to deny it, there was a good chance that he'd heard me screaming, along with the rest of the house. During training, I had once heard that there were no secrets among espers, and I understood why they said that now.

At least he didn't ask me about it. There was no reason to air my dirty laundry or let them see just how fucked up I'd been. If there was one truth to our world, it was that everyone was fucked up. We all had our problems, we all had the things that we just couldn't handle. I saw no reason to air mine out for their perusal.

It did make me wonder about their past, though. What exactly had happened that made them the way they were? I knew the story I'd gotten, but it just didn't fit well with the men that I'd spent time with so far. It wasn't like I thought they were perfect by any means, don't get me wrong. They were selfish and self-centered and difficult at the best of times, but the idea that they'd purposely let people die?

That didn't sound like them. Or maybe I was letting myself get carried away. There was always a chance that this was nothing more than my reaction because I'd found a place that I sort of liked. It was like the times women ignored all the red flags they saw in a man just because his ass looked fantastic in a pair of jeans. The body's reaction did not warrant an actual fact. There was no reason for me to think that these men were anything other than what everybody else saw.

The truth was that people saw me a certain way too, and they weren't entirely wrong. Sure, there might be a reason that I acted the way I did, there might be details that they weren't privy to, but that didn't make them wrong.

The entire idea of calling me Blizzard, for example. It was an apt nickname, no matter how much I hated it. And when it came down to it, it wasn't as bad as a lot of the other names they could have used. They could have called me ice queen or frigid or a million other insults that held some truth. At least Blizzard sounded a little bad ass.

None of that really mattered at the end of the day.

I was here because I didn't have a choice. I was here because everything had led me here and this was my last chance. If I thought life sucked now, all I had to do was think about what life would be like without the Guild.

I wouldn't have a job, no one would want to hire me, rent to me or give me a place to live. I'd have to take jobs that nobody in their right mind wanted to do. What did it really matter if I wanted this to happen or not? What I had to do was accept where I was and keep moving forward. That was all any of us got to do.

So I sat down to have breakfast with the other men. I ignored all my fears, I ignored the way they stared at me as if they knew something. We pretended they hadn't heard me screaming, we pretended that we were one happy little squad, just like the Guild wanted. At the end of the day, that was all that really mattered.

Just playing the game so you could play for another day.

Chapter Twenty-One

Carter

I really hate people.

Sure, dealing with others was a part of life. Maybe I'd never really grown past being an angsty teenager who was always rebellious and wanted to do my own thing. There was some truth to that, after all. I tended to like to do things my own way, to take my own chances, not have to rely on others. Of course, I worked with the squad, so I wasn't fully on my own.

The benefit of staying off the Guild's radar was that we got left alone. We'd gotten used to being able to take the jobs we wanted, skip the jobs we didn't, and keep the Guild the fuck out of our lives.

All good things came to an end however. The other squad, only an A-Rank, sat across from us. We were all here, just like a happy little family.

Well, a family that was about to kill a bunch of things. Then again, maybe all good families did that. Nothing brought people together quite like homicide.

Except maybe funnel cake.

We'd left Yun back at base.

Getting too close to a portal was never a good idea for any civilian or guide. There was no reason to put them in danger like that. Instead, the Guild brought portable trailers and placed them around the entrance to the portal. This offered a mobile command unit for any dungeon expected to last more than twelve hours.

This worked out well because it gave guides a place to rest and wait until they were needed. At times, some of the more powerful guides who worked on rotating schedules would venture somewhat closer, but they'd never be allowed too close.

No one wanted to risk losing a guide to monsters, friendly fire, or the dungeon itself.

"Let's get this shit over with," one of the other espers said.

That wasn't an unusual reaction, all things considered. It wasn't exactly a secret that they didn't want to be here.

And the fact was I agreed with them. I didn't want to be here any more than they did.

The Guild was forcing this on all of us. But that was part of the way of life around here. Whatever tune the Guild wanted to play, we all had to dance to. That was why we'd put as much distance as possible between us and those in charge. All we had to do was get through this mission, clear the dungeon, prove we could work with others, then play cleanup crew on The Pitt.

I didn't love the idea of having to play their game, but I was smart enough to see enough steps ahead and know that there wasn't much of an option.

"You know," Ingram said, "we could kill them."

"You always think killing people is the right answer."

"No, I think killing people is *an* answer." Ingram shrugged as if the point was obvious.

The funny thing about him was that he wasn't kidding. He didn't go around killing people without any thought, of course. That would make him a psycho.

And we were definitely all just slightly over the line on the sane side of psychopathy. We might jump rope with that line occasionally, but we never drifted too far over it.

"We just have to get through this. No reason to make it more difficult than it has to be."

Shear had taken point up on a rocky cliffside not too far away. He worked best when he could oversee the entire battlefield.

This dungeon, despite being an A-Rank, was rather small. A person could stand on one side of it and shout, and someone on the other side could still hear them. I'd seen other dungeons this small, though they weren't that normal when it came to higher ranks. We hadn't run into any monsters yet, and that unnerved me all the more.

Monsters that hid in dungeons like this tended to cause a problem. It wasn't even that I cared about that. I could fight whatever showed up without worry, but I really didn't want this to take long.

The image of Yun, sitting back at that trailer, waiting for us — that was the shit that came back to me. I wanted to finish this up and get back to her, to dig a little deeper under her skin, to get the answers that we still didn't have. This dungeon felt as frustrating as getting a pointless traffic ticket on the way to the most important day of my life. It was just a distraction that I wanted to finish as quickly as possible.

"So, what's the plan?" The esper, Hart, who asked looked at me as if I was supposed to have that answer.

It made me want to fuck with him a bit. After talking so much shit, after having everything in the world to mutter under his stupid little breath, he really was asking me what we were supposed to do?

Pathetic.

Sure, I was higher rank and had been doing this longer, but the Guild didn't worry about how squads dealt with each other. It wasn't a hierarchy, where we had to listen to those above us. Instead, each squad only answered to the Guild, not to one another.

It made his tendency to follow me nothing more than an unwanted annoyance. It wasn't *my* job to keep them alive, after all.

Still, I plastered a smile onto my face, ever the jovial idiot. "I think we're supposed to clear this place."

He didn't look all that pleased with my evaluation. Of course, he tracked it up to my idiocy rather than me being a smartass, which I preferred people to do. I'd always rather they not see me coming, that they doubted my ability and intelligence.

It made it easier to maneuver them exactly where I wanted them.

"I mean, *how* do you want to do that?" He gestured at the mostly cleared space, at the line of trees and cliffs to the edges, surrounding us.

One of the things that had surprised me about the dungeons was how similar they all looked. Often, before anybody entered one, they assumed that they were as unique as the places on earth.

They figured that the trees and monsters would all be unique. The problem was that they seemed to think that dungeons were actual places. They were under the misunderstanding that dungeons were like different states or countries in our realm. Instead, dungeons were simply tiny broken pieces of space. They could have slight variances from one another, but for the most part they resembled the same dark, barren landscape.

In that way, this place was just the same. The trees were spindly, with thin branches that stretched up toward the sky. They were white, with black lines winding through them. Some had leaves, but they were sharp-edged and thin and mostly black. Small veins of purple ran throughout the trees, mirrored in the skyline.

Ingram remained with me, and Kenyon not far behind. We tended to work closely together, when possible. Ingram often took off on his own since he moved fastest by himself. He liked to slip past defenses and go after the most important areas.

At the end of the day, there were two ways to clear a dungeon. The first was to kill every monster within it. Without anything alive inside it, the dungeon would naturally dissipate. The other option was to destroy the heart.

That was usually the preferred method, but it wasn't easy. Dungeons like to protect the hearts, as if they knew it was their lifeblood. This area was always thick with monsters, and even getting the heart was never easy. Only an S-Rank esper could do it, and it was still dangerous. Plenty of espers had died in the attempt. The higher level a dungeon, the more dangerous the heart.

A dungeon like this was probably best served by removing all the monsters. I wasn't looking forward to a fight like that—though it had been a while since I had gotten to go all out—but it was the smartest choice.

I didn't want to leave Yun alone for too long.

"Let's set up a line there." I gestured toward the center of the open space. "If we get near the heart, the monsters will come running."

"Are you serious? That's a terrible idea." Hart stared at me as if I'd lost my ever-loving mind. It was funny, because if he had admitted anything before, he would have probably said I had already gone mad.

Or, perhaps that wasn't fair. They often saw Ingram as a mad dog who would kill anything that crossed his path, but they usually just saw me as an idiot.

"Look, I want to get this done as soon as possible. There's no reason to drag it out, and make it take longer than it has to. Let's just get this over with and get back home."

"This is barely an A-Rank dungeon," Ingram said. "I say we can clear it in twenty minutes, tops."

"Twenty minutes? You used to be able to do this in fifteen. Are you losing your touch in your old age?" I ask with a laugh.

Ingram scowled, a look that might have scared off anyone else. Too bad for him, I'd known him long enough not to really care about his hissy fits. If he was going to kill me, he would have had plenty of chances to do so before.

"A hundred dollars on twenty minutes," Kenyon said.

"Are you seriously betting on how long it takes us to clear this dungeon? Do you not understand how dangerous this is?" Hart spoke to us as if we had never been in a dungeon in our entire lives.

Maybe that was the problem with A-Rank espers. They liked to think they were special. They were way too concerned about things that they didn't need to worry about. This dungeon was hardly an issue — even if our squad had been on its own. Between two squads of our caliber, this thing might as well have been a fly we swatted.

It was something that came with experience, with understanding that none of it really mattered that much. As A-Rank espers, they probably had never been into an S-Rank dungeon. They sure as fuck had never gotten sent to one of the permanent ones. There was no way to explain to a person like that what a stable dungeon was like. It meant they freaked out over little pointless dungeons like this one.

"What are you upset about? Do you want in on the bet?" I asked, as though I didn't understand their point.

He didn't respond, instead just stammering, his mouth opening and closing time and time again as though he thought that action was going to warrant him some sort of understanding. I could have told him that he was probably just an idiot, but I had a feeling that wasn't going to help our situation at all. Instead, I looked up toward Shear, who still stood on the cliff.

I didn't need to say anything, because I was certain he was crawling around in my skull as he normally did. Like many of us, the dungeon amplified his powers. It meant he had a good sense of control over the entire battlefield. I didn't need to speak to him, didn't need to give him any signals. He knew exactly what I wanted to tell him.

Which was that it was time to go.

I didn't bother asking the other squad anything else. They'd just bitch and moan as much as they could, hoping to get out of this entire thing. They still imagined that they were somehow above us. They thought that reputation was what mattered then. They were about to learn they were dead wrong.

If there was anything that I had learned, it was the power mattered at the end of the day. It didn't matter what they thought about us, it didn't matter how useless they thought we were, they were about to see exactly why we had the rank we did.

Enjoy the show, you assholes.

Chapter Twenty-Two

Kenyon

The way Carter moved always put me on edge. I wondered if he didn't enjoy throwing himself into danger just for fun. In fact, I wouldn't even put it past him to do it just to annoy me. I was probably going to die years earlier than I should have, just from the stress of keeping him alive.

Not that he cared. He was probably laughing in that screwed up little head of his. He enjoyed every stress line he put on my face, every hour of sleep I lost, every frantic rush to try to save his useless life.

Well, that probably wasn't fair. As much as I hated the way he did things, I really wasn't sure he thought about much of anything when fighting, which was almost more terrifying.

He proved the point when he sailed forward, toward the pillar at the center of the clearing. That held the heart of the dungeon, the source of power that kept this entire place together. I'd seen them before, of course, as it was common in our line of work to run across them, but they always startled me.

We usually think about important things being large and flashy and somehow obvious. Even things like gems had a shine to them, a draw that made people want to own them. The dungeon hearts were entirely different.

If anything, they resembled pieces of obsidian, but not quite as glassy. They were dull and flat and chipped and ragged, as if broken pieces of concrete. And yet those tiny little chips of rock were responsible for all the damage a dungeon could do, all the lives they stole.

Ingram preferred going for the heart. His hands still carried the marks of hearts that he'd removed and destroyed over the years. Maybe it was a personal challenge for him to get in close, to get rid of the entire dungeon in one swoop.

Carter, on the other hand, much preferred killing everything inside a dungeon. Maybe he saw it as a personal failure if Ingram got all the credit for actually closing a dungeon. In fact, I had a feeling that if Carter left a dungeon not covered in blood, he would view it as a pointless task.

It meant that even though Carter moved toward the central pillar, where the heart sat, I knew he didn't plan to go for it. Instead, it was just an attempt to rile up the monsters. The more that outsiders interfered with the heart, the closer that they got to it, the more vicious the monsters grew.

That meant it was far easier for Carter to gain the upper hand if he set the monsters into a frenzy by threatening the heart first.

Sure enough, before he got anywhere near it, the ground shook. A thundering crack echoed through the entire battlefield, and even I struggled to keep upright.

The terror on the others' faces signaled them as newbies, unused to the violence that bathed a dungeon. They looked young, but that didn't always mean much. Espers often looked far younger than their actual age. It was one of the benefits of being an esper. We didn't live longer. If anything, we rarely made it past fifty or so.

Whether it was a fight with a monster, the corruption, or that we simply decided that we didn't want to keep going until one or the other got us, espers weren't known for being long lived. Still, there was a youthfulness to this squad that said they hadn't had any real taste of battle.

Too often the younger espers would fight a single monster at the entrance to a dungeon and act as though they'd earned their stripes. I had a feeling this was the first exposure to that that this squad had ever gotten.

One of the reasons that they'd been sidelined from the more dangerous situations was probably because they didn't even have a healer. The squad was made up of two combat specialists, a debuffer who could control the weather, and a stealth expert. Without either a mentalist or a healer, there were a lot of dungeons and monsters that they simply couldn't deal with.

That also meant keeping both squads alive rested squarely on me. It was my job to make sure that nothing got them, or if something did, that I kept them from dying.

And fuck knew that wasn't an easy job when it came to my own squad. They put far too much trust in me and didn't value their own lives nearly enough.

The first monster to appear came from the treeline. It was far from the largest or scariest thing that we'd ever encountered, but we'd learned never to underestimate a monster. Doing that almost always led to injury or worse. The thing was large, probably as tall as a horse. It had six legs, and they worked together like an insect's to propel it forward. A short, stocky neck led to its massive wide, flat skull. The head resembled a lizard, with a short snout full of teeth that didn't line up quite right, so a few stuck out from over its lip line and showed even when its mouth was closed.

It headed straight for Carter. That didn't shock me, as Carter knew exactly how to piss anyone off.

Before the thing could reach him, however, Ingram appeared out of nowhere.

It had freaked me out when I'd first met Ingram and learned how quickly he could sneak up on people. In fact, he seemed to revel in jumping out of nowhere and scaring the shit out of me when we were younger.

I think he got off on the control.

I'd gotten used to it, much like Shear's ability to sneak into my head. They were just things that we had to accept about one another. Were they weird? Fuck yes they were. But they were part of us. It was no different from my ability to heal or Carter's uncanny ability and desire to kill anything that annoyed him.

Ingram's shadows engulfed the creature. Some of the time he used a blade, like Carter, but he also had a few skills that Carter lacked. It required significantly higher risk to use shadows, but there was no doubt of their effectiveness.

A frightened, pained screech left the creature, escaping through that cloud of shadows, and when the dark shroud cleared, an emaciated husk remained. Ingram's eyes glowed from the effort, but he hadn't allowed the creature to get anywhere near Carter.

"What the fuck?" Carter held out his arms as though he'd just been personally wronged. "That was mine!"

Ingram smirked, the expression pulling one side of his lips up higher than the other. "Well, you should have been a little faster then, huh?"

Carter reached into his jacket and withdrew two blades, gripping the handles tightly. Each one was about the length of his forearm, incredibly sharp and thin. He had any number of blades on him, but those were his favorites. "So what are we betting on who gets the higher number?"

"First guiding when we get back?"

"But I'm not gonna have any kills!" I shouted at both of them, annoyed to be left out again. They always liked to base everything on kill count, as if that was the only thing that mattered. It felt rather unfair.

"Well, that seems like a you problem," Carter said.

"Maybe we should count every one of your kills for me. I mean, I did save you, so you wouldn't even have any kills if it wasn't for me."

He chuckled, but didn't seem all that inclined to accept my idea. Not that it really mattered—most of these bets never actually went through. No one kept their word at the end of the day. What did it matter when most of our resources were all pulled together? It was just a way to pass the time, to have a little fun in the midst of something that was unquestionably not fun.

Of course, I also had never really wanted to win before. What was a hundred bucks to me?

But getting first guiding from Yun—now that was something worth fighting for.

Even if I thought I had a chance, that belief went away rather fast. One look at the way the others moved around the battlefield reminded me of exactly where I sat. Carter moved like a typhoon, fast and devastating, barreling through the open space. I'd seen him fight countless times before. It wasn't like this time was unique or special in any way, and yet, there was no doubt that it astounded me. Maybe it was some amount of jealousy.

The truth was that I had always fallen short. Despite my size, despite how I looked, I'd never gotten to be that vision of masculinity. Everyone always expected me to be the combat specialist. Anyone who looked between Carter and me would assume that I was the fighter. At my age, by my point in life, I'd think that I would have gotten over questions like that, fears like that, but I guess no one really got over that sort of thing. We moved past it, we made amends with it, we accepted it, but we didn't ever really silence the doubts.

It was why it was ridiculous to me, but I still watched in awe, and a bit of jealousy, as he tore through the monsters that appeared. More and more showed up, causing that slightly acidic scent to fill the space. It was like rot, but more like rotten fruit. It had this fake sweetness to it, something that I had grown accustomed to over our years of fighting monsters. The more and more of them they came out, the more bodies piled up. Despite that however, we kept the upper hand. No matter how many appeared, neither Ingram nor Carter struggled beneath the onslaught.

The other espers fought in the way toddlers helped clean up the house. They usually just made more work, but they still got praise for it. They did their best.

I mean, it wasn't good or anything.

I stayed where I was, monitoring the situation. Since I wasn't that useful in a fight, I tended to try to stay back. Carter and Ingram had no issues with the monsters, so it wasn't like there was anything for me to do.

At least not when it came to my squad.

One of the combat specialists for the other squad, the one who liked to talk a lot, rushed toward a monster, thinking he had the upper hand. It didn't take a genius to see the way the monster whipped its tail back and forth. Too often, people focused only on the teeth and missed every other danger a monster posed. Sure, the teeth *were* a problem, but they were far from the only thing to be aware of. Well, that asshole learned that the hard way when the monster turned, catching him in the ribs with the full force of its tail.

I rushed forward, my body moving out of instinct. Just like Carter and Ingram couldn't help rushing toward monsters, something in their blood wanting them to get into the fight, I couldn't ignore it when somebody was hurt. And judging from the way that he went flying to the side, thrown at least ten feet, there was no way he wasn't hurt. Sharp bits of gravel dug into my knees as I skidded the last foot to where he rested. I set my hands over his midsection, the information rushing into me as though it were printed on him. Was this how Shear saw the world? I could tell when somebody was hurt, when they had an illness or disease, when there was something that I could do to help it. It wasn't always all that helpful, like meeting a stranger and knowing instantly their entire medical history. However, it was made for exactly times like this, when a moment delay in diagnosis could lead to death.

The esper whimpered, pushing my hands away, swatting at them as though I were the problem.

"Just relax. I'll take care of it," I tried to reassure him.

Clearly, this esper hadn't dealt with healers much before. Then again, we were rather rare when it came to the general makeup of the esper population—only mentalists ranked rarer on the levels of regular designations. There were a few types that were so uncommon they didn't even fit into one of the standard types. It wasn't a shock then that this guy wouldn't have a clue how to deal with my powers. However, I'd dealt with plenty of difficult patients in the past. None had been difficult enough to stop me from doing my job.

He gave in to my probing—probably because he didn't want to argue anymore.

Broken ribs, four of them.

A fracture in his spine.

Pulled a muscle in his hip.

No internal injuries.

All that information floated to me, past my conscious mind, just facts that added to my plan. Not a bad injury, at least not for an esper. A civilian would stay down for months from something like this, but for an esper—especially a combat specialist—they'd heal up in a matter of a day and, by tomorrow, he wouldn't even so much as limp.

It meant my job right now was less about saving him and more about getting him back into the fight, back to useful status.

That had been drilled into my mind in training, after all.

It was all about making sure that an esper could still fight, that they could keep holding the line. Nothing else mattered—not the long-term health of the esper, not giving a damn about their future. The Guild didn't really care much about that. Instead, they focused on letting nothing get in the way of clearing and closing dungeons. They wanted to make sure that their army had every ability to save civilians, at least the ones they deemed most important.

I'd learn that lesson just like every other healer trained by the Guild. It didn't mean I always followed it, of course, but it always weighed in my mind.

I patched the esper up quickly. I knitted bones back together, reduced inflammation around the wounds, forced extra adrenaline into the body to ensure that he could get up and moving again. I even had the ability to lessen the pain that he felt by turning off some of the neurons around the injuries. None of this would do any long-term harm, at least nothing that mattered. Since we didn't live all that long compared to humans, it wasn't like he had to worry about his joints once he turned a hundred. The esper took in a deep breath as he sat up, his eyes wide, surprise written across his features.

He patted his own front as though he couldn't quite believe that he could move without pain.

"That's...amazing."

I had to admit, it felt kind of nice to have someone actually impressed by my efforts. Like anything, after spending enough time with people, they stopped noticing the things you did.

He hopped to his feet, spryer than I think he expected, and with barely a thanks thrown over his shoulder, he was back at the fight. Of course, the way he rushed in made me suspect I'd be healing him again before long.

I rose, surveying the battlefield.

Shear remained on the cliff, his focus down on all the moving players. He could transmit information to each of us from his position, and the way the monsters moved—not quite with the purpose they should have had—went to show that he was likely fucking with their heads as well.

With the number of monsters decreasing, it seemed that we were almost through this job. At least, that's what I thought before the ground shook hard enough to knock me off my feet.

A loud cracking echoed, similar to before. Dungeons often settled, making noises that no one could quite identify, but this was different. It was as if something traveled beneath the earth, and I wasn't the only one to lose my balance.

From just ahead of us, beside the pillar that housed the heart, the ground exploded in sharp angles, a rain of dirt. I turned my head and used my arm to shield my face from flying debris, and when I turned back toward it, when the dust settled enough to see, I knew we were far from done.

Chapter Twenty-Three

Yun

"You look way too tense," the woman across the trailer from me said as she examined her long, artificially colored nails.

She reminded me of a bargain basement version of Mercy—poorly dyed blonde hair, clothes that were similar but not quite right, and sure didn't fit her, and a false sense of arrogance that Mercy never had. In short, I got the sense that this was a girl who had grown up watching Mercy on the news, and when she turned into a guide herself, she figured she'd base her entire look on the other woman.

"You don't get nervous? You never know what's happening in there."

"They're *espers*. You don't have to worry about them. They know exactly what they're doing." She held her hand out, examining the gaudy red polish that covered each long nail. It made me wonder how she didn't get them broken off constantly.

I could have responded, told her that espers are hardly gods, but I had a feeling she wouldn't accept any of that. In fact, it was easy to pin her exact type. She saw everything as a fairytale, and she had a part to play in that. If she was the princess, they had to be her knights in shining armor. Anything else would break that fantasy for her, and she couldn't allow that to happen.

The memory of the nightmare, of that thing reaching out for me, of all the things I'd done to escape both the memory, and the reality, came back to me.

Maybe I'm not as different as I want to think.

"How long have you been with them?" I went with a nice, easy line of conversation. The last thing I wanted was to sit here in silence for what could be hours.

The woman smiled brightly, telling me I'd picked the right topic of conversation. "We've worked together for a little over a year." She seemed to have to do some math to work that out. "There were so many other guides who wanted this spot, but I just knew I had to have it. Have you seen them on the magazines? They're moving up so fast, and I knew I wanted in on the ground floor."

Her words caused an uneasiness in my stomach. Did she see them as just a way to scramble to the top? I guess I couldn't blame her that much. The reality was that guides took most of our position from the squad that we worked with. Sure, we had our own ranks, but we were only as good as the espers we served. It was hard to get mad at her for trying to play the game society forced us into.

"I was surprised that Reject Squad got themselves a guide." She didn't say that like a question, and I didn't get the sense that she really needed an answer.

"Why? Don't most squads need a guide?"

"Well sure, ones who actually do things do. Usually, they just use rotating guides. Basically, whoever gets in trouble gets sent there as a punishment to take care of them. It happens like that with a lot of the lower squads. Of course, lower squads usually mean like, Rank C or so."

She left the rest of it unsaid. At least from her lips. Her expression made it perfectly clear what she thought about all of this. It wasn't the first time I'd seen that look, of course, and I'd probably had it myself before.

I couldn't seem to right what I knew about them with what other people said. I just couldn't see the men that I had known thus far turning their back and just not giving a damn about dying civilians.

At least, not all of them.

"What's it like?" she asked with a soft voice, as though afraid of anyone overhearing us.

"What's what like?"

"Well, you know, being with them? There's plenty of stories about all of them. I'm not sure there's anyone that Ingram hasn't been with. Kenyon stays a little quieter, but there's stories about him too. Carter seems like he's just an idiot, but sometimes I don't know if that's true. And Shear? I know espers aren't exactly human, but I'm not sure it's ever been as true as it is with that one."

Every word out of her mouth annoyed me. I wasn't even sure why. She wasn't wrong, and I'd thought the same exact things about them too, hadn't I?

Whether she had a point or not, however, she didn't have the right to say it. It was like hearing someone talk shit about your sibling. It didn't matter if you had thrown a flat-screen TV at them a week ago, no one else got to talk shit about them. These men might be terrible, and they were probably stupid, but at least for right now, they were mine.

And as tempted as I might have been to say that, I press my lips together instead. There was no good reason for me to go and out myself like that.

Thankfully, before I had to come up with something to say back, an alarm signaled inside the trailer.

The portal had started to disintegrate. Whether that meant that they'd cleared it, or time simply had run out, I didn't know. It had the other guide and me out of our chairs and out of the trailer in a heartbeat.

The trailers sat about a hundred yards from the portal, and two combat espers stood watch between those spots. They served as guards in case any monsters slipped through the lines that the squads had created inside. They remained as guards even as the other guide and I approached the portal.

Something I didn't expect hit me.

Fear.

Sure, I felt fear around portals no matter what. Anyone with half a brain would. Only an idiot wouldn't know the kind of danger that that thing signaled.

This wasn't fear of the portal though, not of the dungeon or even of the monsters inside. Instead, this was all about what would come through that portal. Or rather, what might *not* come back through at all.

I'd been stationed at portals before, with other squads, and I'd never really given a fuck whether they came back or not. In fact, there were times when a part of me almost wished they wouldn't. If they never came back, I would never have to guide them. I'd never have to address that pain inside me, the anxiety, the helplessness.

This time though, the idea of any one of those four fuckwits not coming through that portal terrified me.

In fact, a very stupid part of me felt drawn toward the shimmering boundary, compelled to enter it and retrieve them as though they were my property. As though no dungeon was going to get the chance to take them from me.

Thankfully, before I made a fool of myself like that, the purple shifted, swirling, and dark figures appeared through the center of it. It took a long moment for them to fully pass, to move from shadow to substantive figure.

I was able to identify them as they appeared. First, it was the other team. The guide I'd spent time with squealed, then rushed forward like greeting a husband back from war.

It gave me a moment to stare, to wonder what it would be like to feel that way. She ran over, greeted by the team like some long-lost lover. It annoyed me, especially after the things she said, but I could hardly deny that a part of me craved that kind of closeness.

My attention returned to the portal just as three figures broke through the surface. Carter was, yet again, covered in monster blood. Beside him walked Kenyon walked, with Shear next to him, and while both looked tired, neither showed any obvious injuries.

Those nerves inside me didn't go away though, because three wasn't the full number that should have returned.

I took two large steps forward before I stopped myself, and the last person appeared in the purple shimmer of the portal. I recognized that figure even before it all came into view. Except when Ingram did appear, he made Carter look clean and put together.

He limped and held his arm against his front, tight to his stomach as though it didn't work right.

I had no chance to stop myself this time.

I rushed forward at a dead run, and even when Kenyon tried to stop me, I ducked around them. The portal collapsed in on itself just as Ingram passed through. It told me they'd cleared the dungeon, either by monster or heart, so at least they'd done their job. None of that really mattered, however, in the face of the way that Ingram walked.

I skidded to a stop just in front of him, staring up into his face. He wore a strange expression, some weird level of contentment. How could someone look that happy when hurt and covered in so much blood?

It made me wonder if I knew him at all. Or, maybe it was better to say it made me recognize I didn't know him, that I might not ever really know him or understand him.

"You're hurt." My words were stupid — even I knew that much. The problem was that my brain refused to work. Seeing him that banged up bothered me.

"I'm fine." His word slammed shut the door on any sort of conversation.

"You are not. Look at the way you're holding your arm." I gestured at him as though that had to prove the point.

He shifted to hide it, as though leaning the other direction would make me forget what I'd seen, as though I couldn't see any longer that he still had that arm pinned to his side.

"Kenyon already looked at it and healed me."

"Then why are you still like this?"

"Because it still takes a while to fully go away. What are you, my mother?"

Those words stung, more because he spoke true. I thought over to that other guide, to how annoyed I'd been by her actions, but she'd been welcomed, hadn't she? They had at least a false sense of closeness—we didn't.

I dropped my hands and curled them into tight fists when I didn't know what else to do with the energy coursing inside me. I didn't even understand *why* it bothered me so much.

"You probably need guiding," I said, the words soft, quiet, meek. I hated that the worst.

His silence spoke more than his words had. It was one hell of a rejection.

"I can tell you need guiding," I pushed.

He leaned in, and it took everything I had not to pull away. He didn't touch me, but he got so close I could feel his breath against my ear. "Listen here, *Blizzard*, what I need is something I'm pretty sure you're not offering. You'd probably do well to learn not to offer shit when you're not ready for it."

His nearness made it hard to think. I struggled to work through my own thoughts, to come up with a response, so leave it to my mouth to move before my brain could get involved. "I can feel the corruption. There's no reason to say no."

"You think? Because I can assure you that if you guide me, your little no-touching rule is going right the fuck out the window. You think I couldn't feel you the last time we did this? You can act a prude, you can act like you don't want it, but I can fucking *smell* you. I know exactly how wet you get. I can *feel* what you want from me. And with me in this mood? Trust me, I'm going to take full advantage of it." He crowded me, stepping in even closer so the heat of his body seared me. "I gotta wonder if you've ever experienced that.

You ever guided someone while they were between those pretty thighs of yours? While their tongue was lapping at your clit? I've heard that as good as it is for the esper, it's even better for the guide."

His words reached so deep that I couldn't believe it. They went past fantasy, to desires I didn't even know I had. Other espers had tried to say things like that to me, but it had never mattered. It had never sparked anything inside of me beyond disgust. So why was it that when Ingram said it, it tempted me? When he made those promises, I wanted him to prove them.

I wanted to know if he spoke the truth, if he could get me there, if I could be normal and feel that way. That desire scared me as much as it excited me. It was new, didn't feel like me, and the unknown nature terrified me.

"This isn't about that," I whispered, wishing my voice were stronger, more certain. "You need guiding — that's all that matters."

"You sure? Because I can see the way your nipples are hard, and I'm pretty fucking sure that ain't the only sign. So you giving in? You going to spread those pretty little thighs of yours? First me, then the others? Gonne let all three of us fuck any hole on you we want? Ain't you just a giver, then?"

His words shocked me, graphic and daring. Before I thought about it, my palm flew, striking him on his cheek.

Which was entirely unacceptable. He was clearly hurt, but that seemed the only reaction available to me. It was as though that woke me up, a way to break this spell between us, to remove the hold he — and the words he'd said — had on me.

He didn't react to the hit, not so much as moving, as though it hadn't happened at all. He chuckled, then said in a soft voice, "So we've both got some boundaries. Let's not cross those lines, huh?"

With that, he strolled off, past me, still limping but with his back straight. It was as though he wanted to make damn sure that he didn't appear weak. A whoosh of freezing air exploded out from the portal as it collapsed, as the purple shimmering surface disappeared and left nothing in its wake.

These smaller dungeons didn't scar the land like the larger ones, the overlap minor. It meant once it closed, little evidence remained.

However, it had left its mark on me... Weakness filled my legs, making them heavy and useless. I feared that attempting a single step would cause me to topple and fall flat on my face.

"So regular touching is a no-go, but you don't mind some roughness?" Carter's voice was as jovial as ever, as though I hadn't just slapped a man in front of him. If anything, he seemed more amused than anything.

"Shut up," I muttered.

"Why? Come on, Yun, it was nice to see a little backbone. I mean, they don't call you Blizzard for nothing. I like seeing your snarl, and Ingram could use a little frostbite now and then."

I turned toward him, rewarded by a bright smile that seemed more honest than usual. It felt as though he was telling me it really was okay, that it wasn't a big deal, that I had no reason to feel so slighted.

"Where's he going?" I asked.

Shear approached along with Kenyon, but neither of them spoke. That sure said they didn't want to answer.

But why?

It wasn't like I controlled him.

He's screwed every willing guide. The words came back to me from earlier, when the other guide had spoken about him. It explained what no one wanted to say.

If Ingram was heading off like that to be with another guide when he had one waiting for him — well, that looked pretty bad on my part. It was one hell of a slight against me, as though I'd failed — especially when I'd offered.

"Right," I said, hating the way it hurt. There was no good reason for that to hurt my feelings, right? We had no real bond between us, weren't anything to one another beyond guide and esper — and even that was new.

Maybe this was one of those things where it really was just stupid emotions. Guiding created a closeness — no matter how temporary — between two people. Even if I refused to touch in order to prevent anything happening, to make me more comfortable, that didn't change that I might feel closer to him.

I'd heard people talk about one-night stands, about a possessiveness after that. Was that what I felt?

I blew out a long breath when I couldn't come up with anything else. "Let's go," I said, forcing myself to smile, to push down those doubts or, worse, what they might mean.

I couldn't let myself fall victim to them, to madness, to stupidity and instinct. Espers didn't give a damn about guides, not beyond what we could offer them. They all ended up the same way.

There was no happily-ever-after when it came to espers. They spent their lives fighting until it either killed them, or they gave in to the ever-growing corruption inside them.

And when that happened?

Well, they became the monsters I knew they could be.

I won't ever let that happen again.

Chapter Twenty-Four

Kenyon

The families on the beach ran around, playing, laughing, oblivious to the world around them. There was something nice about that, wasn't there?

It was pleasant, nice in a way few things in my life were.

One family drew my attention back time and again. They had a large blanket set out, with heavy items placed at each corner to keep it from blowing away. A mother, a father and three children. The two boys were older, probably in grade school, and the third was a toddler girl, given the swimsuit she wore with ruffles on the butt. The mom doted on her, giving her pieces of cut-up fruit.

It was a damn cute sight, spawning a yearning in me for something I couldn't have.

One of the things about espers was that we were always sterile. Guides could still have children, but not espers, because of the corruption. It meant that no matter how much I wanted that picture in front of me, I couldn't have it. No matter how I felt about it, there wasn't a damn thing I could do.

I'd had to give up that future when I became an esper, one future dissolving and another appearing.

The door groaned, causing me to turn. There, in the open french doors, stood Yun.

She was really damn pretty. Her dark hair was braided back in two sections, making her look younger. It barely went past the nape of her neck, with two small fluffs of hair at the ends — fucking adorable. She wore black slacks and a white T-shirt, something similar to what she'd worn each day before.

Carter had mentioned that she hadn't brought' much with her, and while her clothing was always clean, it was pretty clear that she didn't have many options. She looked nice, of course, but I was used to girls with a million different outfits, who never looked similar two days in a row. It was a far cry from this girl, who wore slight variations of the same basic outfit day after day. It was all usable, practical, and she looked nice enough, but that didn't stop me from worrying.

My sisters always had a closet full of clothing, half of which they never even wore. I didn't care if Yun didn't much care for fashion, I just hated the idea that she wore that because she didn't have other options. Still, I doubted she was about to let us take her shopping.

"Hey," I said, trying to tempt her out. Sure, this might not have been my family on the beach moment, but I'd take what I could get.

She stepped out and closed the door behind her. She said nothing at first, moving her weight from foot to foot.

Was she nervous?

She was flighty enough around us—I wouldn't doubt that she'd be a bit uneasy. Still, I got the sense she wanted to say something'.

"Just say it," I said, offering her up a friendly smile. At her glare, I shrugged. "I can tell you want to say something, so you might as well just say it. No reason to drive yourself crazy thinking about it."

"And here I thought you were dumb."

"Well, I'm not that smart, but it means I'm better at reading people. Also, I can wait as long as you can."

She blew out a long breath before her shoulders slumped. "I need to go to the store. I'd just go by myself, but Carter said I'm supposed to go with someone when I leave."

Boy, did she show she didn't like the idea of giving in to that, right? She hated having to listen to us, having to ask me for anything.

"If you're busy, that's okay. I can wait."

How quickly she backpedaled. Was she that worried about being a problem?

How can she be this adorable?

"Busy? Not a bit. A trip to the store sounds great." I got up, groaning a bit as my joints protested how long I'd sat on the hard step.

We took the truck, which I preferred over the other vehicles. I wasn't a huge fan of fast cars and preferred to drive things that were big and safe — especially when it came to driving Yun around.

"Do you like watching the ocean?"

Yun's question caught me off guard. She normally didn't ask anything about us, as though she didn't want to get drawn in any deeper than she already was. The fact that she asked me anything was a good sign, right?

"Not especially," I answered. "In fact, I didn't really want to move here."

"It's such a nice place."

"Yeah, that's what Carter and Ingram thought. I think Ingram kept saying that we'd get plenty of girls if we stayed here, and Carter said the property would only go up in value." I thought back to those days, when we'd still been new and fresh and full of hope. "We spent about our first whole year of pay on this place. We lived off ramen most nights just to save up. Plus, we agreed to do some marketing work for the owner when we bought it." I shuddered at the photo sessions we'd done for his beachside restaurant, since back then we'd been worth big money. "I don't like the ocean, actually. I grew up in a big family out in Norco — all horse and cow property there. We didn't really get to the ocean much, so I never learned to swim. The water freaks me out."

She lifted an eyebrow as though she struggled to believe it. "You can't swim? Really?"

"What? You think us espers are perfect?" The word weighed heavily on me.

Perfect.

I'd heard that so often, even before I'd become an esper. This drive to prove myself, to somehow be more than everyone else. My size, my looks, it had all made people expect certain things from me.

And I never did live up to them...

"Perfect?" She snorted.

I'd wanted her to understand that espers were held to too high a standard, that people expected too much from us, but her tone made it clear she didn't expect much of anything from us.

I found it equal parts annoying and refreshing to have her think so little of espers.

"You really don't like espers, do you?"

She didn't answer right away. Was she turning the question over in her head? Coming up with an answer? She didn't seem like the type to just say the first thing that came to mind, which I respected.

"It's not that I don't like them," she said.

"You sure about that? Because the whole no touching and that snort makes me think you're not a fan."

"What are espers for?"

I furrowed my brows, unsure of an answer.

She must have taken pity on me because she went on. "Espers have a point, right? It's to help people, to save the day. They're given such amazing gifts."

I nodded, following along. "Sure, I get that."

"What are guides for?"

That answer was an obvious enough one for me, but even I knew I shouldn't say it.

Guides were the salvation of espers. They offered us a future we wouldn't have without them. The end of every esper was corruption unless a guide saved them. They were the most important thing in the world for us, the light in a very dark world.

"Guides are everything," I said, even if that didn't come anywhere close to the full truth, even if it fell short.

She shook her head. "No. Guides exist only for espers. Without them, we have no use. Do you know why I needed this squad? Because if I got removed from another squad, the Guild wouldn't assign me again. Do you have any idea what happens to a guide who the Guild won't assign?"

I didn't answer because I had no idea. I'd never heard of such a thing.

"Exactly. Guides aren't given the documentation to get a regular job. They can't go out and get a place of their own, can't get loans. We are totally dependent on the Guild and on squads. If I don't make this work, I have nowhere to go, nothing I can do. So, yeah, maybe it isn't fair for me to dislike espers so much, but whether you had a say in it, whether you like it, you represent the boot on top of me."

I frowned, my attention back on the road as we drove, her words swirling around in my head. I didn't like them, but I also had no idea what else to say, how to deny them.

It forced me to think about the world — and her place in it — in a different way that I didn't much care for.

Chapter Twenty-Five

Ingram

I didn't feel that much better, but I was used to that. That gnawing sensation inside me never went away. It was this deep pit that nothing filled — not killing, not guiding, not sex.

Well... Yun.

She'd felt different, as though after her guiding, at least a little of that emptiness had filled. It gave me a taste of relief that nothing else had come close to.

And the fact I wanted it again terrified me.

Not because of the corruption inside me, but because of *her*. It wasn't just any guide, but that frustrating enigma of a woman specifically. Only she'd made me feel that way, and even if it felt good, I wasn't sure I liked it.

I'd gotten back to the house to find Kenyon and Yun gone. Kenyon was a healer, so not my favorite choice of guard, but he'd work. I knew he'd do whatever he could to keep her safe, and if he faced off against a civilian, he was more than enough.

If an esper wanted to fuck with her?

Too bad. What do I care?

I was on my feet before I could stop myself. We kept trackers on all the phones, so I could easily find them. I didn't even have to let them know I was there, after all. I could just make sure no one fucked with them.

Not because I care.

Not one bit.

I headed for the door just as it opened, Yun walked in and nearly ran into me. She stopped short, only a breath away. And boy did her expression darken. So much for wondering whether she was mad. That was the expression of one pissed-off woman, the sort the whole a woman scorned saying was based on.

"Ingram, what are you doing?" Kenyon held two bags and had a smile on his face, as though this were entirely normal.

Of course, Kenyon had never managed to read the room well.

"I was just checking." Yes, it was a stupid answer, but it was all my brain could come up with. I wasn't as good as Carter at making shit up.

"Check what?"

"Checking…a noise."

The look on Kenyon's face said he didn't believe me, or rather anyone with half a brain wouldn't have believed me. I got the sense he accepted it because he assumed if he didn't understand, it was a him problem, not a me problem. That made dealing with Kenyon easier some of the time.

"Where were you?" I realized just how stupid that sounded, so added on, "not that I care."

Right, because saying I don't care is the exact way to actually prove I don't give a fuck.

It was stupid, and the fact that I made such an idiot out of myself annoyed me more than I wanted to admit. Maybe this was why I didn't like talking, because it never went well.

"Yun needed to get some stuff from the store." Kenyon held up the bags as though he needed to show proof.

It made sense, because Yun hadn't exactly brought many things with her. I wondered what else they'd done. If it were anyone else, I might have thought they'd stopped off for a quickie. Kenyon wasn't the type to do that, though. The most obvious answer would have been lunch.

And that definitely was not jealousy that hit me at the thought of Kenyon and Yun sitting down for a lunch with just the two of them.

Absolutely not jealousy.

Yun didn't say a word to me, and I got the sense that was on purpose. Instead, she turned around and put her hands out until Kenyon handed her the bags. She offered a soft thank you before turning around and walking off.

"Did you notice the way she walks?"

"Ingram, I swear, if you're being a pervert..." Kenyon shook his head as though he could not believe I was saying that.

"Not like that. I mean, she's walking slow."

I didn't deny the entire pervert part because, well, that was fair. Normally, if I made a comment like that, it was probably meaning something not fit to say in mixed company. However, in this case, I meant the strange, labored motion of her gait. Normally, she walked with a smoothness, with an almost gliding nature that somehow girls managed to pull off.

However, this time, each step dragged. That was in addition to the lines etched into her face, the ones that implied she wasn't feeling all that well.

"I didn't notice anything." Kenyon peered past me to take another look.

"Aren't you supposed to be a healer? Isn't that exactly what you're supposed to notice?"

"I notice if she's sick, if she's injured. I'm not going to notice if she just didn't sleep well, or if she's in a bad mood. That's more Shear's department than mine." He might deny it but concern wormed its way into his features.

"What did she want at the store?"

"I don't know."

"You don't know? I thought you went with her?"

"Sure, I took her there, and I kept an eye on her, but it wasn't like I went through her things. That would be rude."

"What if she got something she shouldn't have gotten?" Even as I asked that, I wasn't really sure what I meant by it. Something she couldn't have? She wasn't a child. Still, not knowing bothered me.

"You're being stupid."

"Well, you'd fucking know, wouldn't you?"

Kenyon made a show of rolling his eyes and throwing his arms up as though I were just having some sort of hissy fit, which was ridiculous.

Or, maybe he wasn't that ridiculous. I had to admit, my actions didn't make a lot of sense to me either. Kenyon left, headed up the stairs, probably to his own room.

"He might punch you one of these days." Shear's voice took me off guard. He wasn't a stealth specialist like I was, couldn't sneak up on people the way I could. He still managed to mask his presence most of the time.

"He's welcome to try."

"You'd deserve it." Shear had a way of saying exactly what he thought, as though none of it had anything to do with him. He liked to comment on things like they were all outside his realm, as though they had nothing to do with him. He was just an observer, and I found that annoying as fuck.

Sometimes I wondered what it would take to get under his skin. I wanted to see what it would take to get him riled. To see him lose control. In all the years I'd known him, he never seemed to give a damn about anything. Some petty, childish little part of me wanted to see him get absolutely mad about anything.

I didn't care if it was anger, happiness or anything else. Hell, I would take him on some aphrodisiac-fueled fuck fest if it meant he seemed like an actual person for five goddamn minutes.

After this many years though, I wasn't holding out hope for at. Maybe the fucker just didn't have it in him.

"She doesn't feel good, though," Shear said.

"You're sure?"

He looked at me as though asking, 'really?' It was a fair question. I had no reason to doubt anything Shear said. I couldn't recall a single time when he'd proven himself wrong. If he said she wasn't feeling well, she wasn't feeling well.

I frowned for a moment, something else nagging at my senses. It was something familiar, something... something I couldn't quite put my finger on.

When I figured out what it was, the reason it had eluded me became clear. I knew that smell, but never expected it here, not like this, not from her.

It sent me sailing up the stairs, Shear on my heels even if he hadn't come to the same conclusion.

Chapter Twenty-Six

Yun

My stomach cramped, and I groaned at how unfair life really was. Didn't I have enough problems without *this?*

Heavy footsteps outside signaled the approach of at least two of the men, the rapid rhythm suggesting running. I expected a knock, but instead, the door handle cracked and the door opened.

Which revealed Ingram, looking nothing like he had a moment before. At the doorway, he'd been sure and snarky. Now? He looked downright panicked. He stared at the handle—still in his hand but no longer connected to the door—then pinned his hand to the small of his back like that would erase that I'd seen it.

This sure was a far cry from his normal attitude.

As though he'd just realized it as well, he exchanged his look of worry for one of general annoyance—one far more similar to what he normally wore. "You okay?"

He stared hard at me, as if trying to figure something out.

"Yeah, fine." I held my hands out to prove it.

"You sure?" He narrowed his eyes.

"What's going on?" Kenyon's voice from over Ingram's shoulder had Ingram turning.

"I *said* she's walking slow. Maybe you're even more useless than I thought because you don't seem to notice a damn thing, even when it's right in front of you."

"She doesn't feel good." Shear's voice floated through the doorway even though I couldn't see him, telling me he was probably just down the hallway past the other two.

"Just come in," I said and stepped back, not wanting them to end up shoving each other there in the hallway.

They spilled into the room like clowns from a tiny car. The room was far from small, but closed in when filled with these men.

All three stared at me, suspicion etched in those looks.

I patted my face, then down my front as though I might have missed where I had an ax sticking out of me that I had missed. What the hell was their problem?

"You're injured, right?" Ingram asked. "You take a fall or something? You're supposed to tell us if you're hurt."

"I'm not hurt."

"You smell like blood," Ingram snapped, as though his last nerve had just broken apart.

His words caused me to go still, the accusation about the last thing I expected to hear from him — especially given the seriousness of his expression.

"She's bleeding?" Kenyon asked, eyes blowing wide, turning his gaze back on me. "You're bleeding?

What happened? Is that why you needed to go to the store? You know I can take care of injuries." The words rushed from him rapid fire.

They spoke over each other so fast that even if I'd wanted to answer, they didn't give me a chance.

"She's been here the whole time — she couldn't have had anything serious happen."

"We were at the store and there wasn't anything wrong. She wasn't out of my sight for more than a minute or two."

"How could you *not* notice something like this? I mean, she's *bleeding.*"

A whistle echoed through the room. I covered my ears to protect them from the sharp sound, but it served to silence the other three.

Carter walked in, his hands in the pockets of his slacks. "You make it impossible for a man to masturbate in peace, you know that?"

Judging from how put together he was, I highly doubted he was speaking seriously when he said that.

Despite that suspicion, my brain sure enjoyed the idea of what he'd mentioned. I pictured him sitting somewhere, his head thrown back, his hand wrapped around his cock.

Not a bad sight. It intrigued me, made me wonder what it would feel like to watch him.

A snort echoed, and my gaze moved over to Shear, whose eerie eyes bore into me with a knowing look. Right, the asshole probably could tell what I was thinking even if he wasn't dipping directly into my brain in that moment.

"She's *bleeding,*" Ingram said like a child telling on their sibling, jamming a finger my direction.

"She needed to go to the store, and she was walking slow," Kenyon added.

Carter stared at them, lines appearing between his brows. After a moment, he put his hands on his hips and let his head drop back, sighing loudly. "Seriously? That's what caused this whole thing?"

"Bleeding is a big deal," Ingram argued.

Carter shook his head, then pointed toward the hallway. "Out."

The others argued — quietly — but moved that way. Carter paused at the door.

"Sorry about that," he said, the muttering of the others a quiet murmur behind him. "You rest. I'll take care of them."

He didn't ask anything else, closing the door behind him, their actions as confusing as anything else.

Just as I prepared to write that whole interaction off as them being as chaotic as usual — I heard Ingram's voice from just down the hallway.

"A fucking *period*?"

Chapter Twenty-Seven

Yun

It was strange how quickly I'd gotten used to dealing with the men. It wasn't nearly as bad as I would have expected. For the most part, they let me do what I wanted. They didn't interfere in my day-to-day life, beyond the fact that they wanted to make sure I always had a guard. It meant no impromptu trips to the store, but it wasn't like I did that often, anyway.

Still, it was strange to always have people looking out for me.

I had no idea what Carter had said to them — maybe he'd sat them down for a full lesson or something — but for five days after, they'd worried over me and taken especially good care. I'd found heating pads and chocolates in my room, bubble bath in the bathroom, and they'd been quick to suggest things I might want.

In fact, the very next day, I'd found a plethora of pads, tampons, and even a menstrual cup under the bathroom sink. Part of me chuckled at the idea of any of these four going to the store to get such things, of them standing there in confusion while they tried to work out what a girl might want or need, but I couldn't deny that it was nice.

I'd worked with countless squads before, and not a single one had seemed to give a damn about my needs. Even when there were women espers, they didn't care.

Thankfully, my periods weren't that drawn out, so after a few days of feeling crampy and tired, I was back to normal by the time we had another mission.

This one was just training—more like a lesson than anything else.

"What is this, daycare?" Ingram said, the words loud enough that anyone passing could hear him.

I had a feeling he'd never gotten a handle on the whole whispering thing—or maybe he did it on purpose.

It was funny for him to refer to the other espers as children, given they were all in their twenties—hardly kids. "They're adults," I pointed out.

"Barely. I mean, they're here because they've never seen a stable dungeon before. Might as well be kids."

"Why are you here, then?"

He pressed his lips together and looked the other way.

Seems he doesn't want to answer that.

"Yun!" Kaiden's cheerful voice made me smile before I even spotted him.

I turned, but found Carter's wide back blocking my view.

"Whoa, buddy."

I pushed Carter's back. "What are you doing?"

"Do you know him?" Carter asked, still not moving from between us.

"Of course I do."

Carter made an unhappy noise but stepped aside. "I don't like when people come rushing at our guide."

"Yeah, well, before she was *your guide,* she was *my* friend." Kaiden didn't show a speck of worry before he wrapped his arms around me and pulled me into a tight hug. In fact, I suspected he took his sweet time just to piss Carter off.

That was pretty on brand for Kaiden.

Finally, he pulled back, smiling as though he had no idea that four espers shot looks at him that could castrate a bull. "Fancy seeing you here."

"Yeah, well, I didn't think *you'd* be here. Isn't this a bit under your radar usually? You're way too big a deal for something like this."

He shrugged. "Training newbies is important. There aren't that many guides who've worked this dungeon, so when they asked, I figured I'd say yes. Besides, I might have seen a certain squad's name on the list and wanted to catch up."

Carter frowned, then butted in, "You're Kaiden Swarth? The guide?"

Kaiden didn't bother to give Carter one of his winning smiles, the sort that could get an esper to give up damn near everything for him. Instead, his look was just about as friendly as Carter's. "That's right, and this girl here is my precious friend. You've been taking care of her?"

Wow, talk about a threat.

If anyone thought guides were automatically sweet or weak, they'd never met Kaiden. That man was just as vicious as an esper, something that had always amazed me. That was probably one reason I'd adored him right from the start.

"Of course we have," Kenyon answered. "What do you take us for?"

"I take you for a squad that has to attend this because you so fucked up the last time you went into the Pitt."

That caught my attention. *The last time?*

I hadn't known they'd entered The Pitt before. The timeline fit, but the Guild liked to bury any story that didn't paint them in a good light, which meant unless you lived through it, you weren't likely to find much evidence of any problems. It was all word of mouth after that.

I expected Carter to snark back—he usually did—but he didn't say a word.

When I turned toward him, I found a haunting expression on his face. It was a turbulent mixture of anger and pain, the sure sign that whatever went on in his head wasn't good.

It made me wonder what exactly everyone else seemed to know, what I didn't know.

And a part of me didn't much want to find out.

Chapter Twenty-Eight

Shear

Having Yun out of my sight made me uneasy. I wasn't sure why — I rarely cared much about anyone else.

It was like having a string pulled across my bare skin, slowly and unending and impossible to ignore as it agitated the hairs, the sensation soft and almost ticklish. No matter what happened, it drew my focus back toward them, wanting to walk into the room, to go speak to them.

"She's fine," Carter said.

"You sure? How do we know she's fine?" Ingram asked.

"She's with the other guides in the private guide room. That's the safest place for them," Carter pressed. "Nothing is getting in there."

"I don't like it," I said before I could stop myself.

Carter lifted an eyebrow. "It's bad enough for *you* to care? Well, fuck, maybe we should be worried."

I wanted to ignore his statement, but I'd started this by stupidly opening my mouth. "People are easily swayed, especially when alone. I dislike her being with the others."

"Who knows what they're telling her?" Kenyon muttered.

"You can't just lock her up," Carter pointed out.

"Of course we can. She's only a guide. She can't get past locks," I said.

Carter sighed, as though I'd missed the point.

Perhaps I had, but that didn't make me wrong. We *could* lock her up. We could restrict her movements so she wouldn't go out of our sight, so she was never at risk.

Guides were protected by the Guild, but that didn't mean they'd care if we were overly careful with her. If anything, they'd consider watching her more closely, ensuring her safety, as a positive and reasonable measure.

"You want her to run? Because that's how you get her to run away." Carter shook his head. "You might be great at recognizing others' thoughts and feelings, but you sure don't understand people that well."

I crossed my arms, hating that he wasn't wrong. It was true that I'd never quite figured out how minds worked. It felt like nothing more than a constant form of observation. I knew what people thought and felt in the moment, but working out why they felt that way? What they might think next?

Perhaps it was because I was a mentalist, because I'd turned into an esper younger than most.

That was what my records said, at least. The doctors I'd seen from that early age had chalked up my faulty social skills to my lack of use. I'd never had to develop them since my powers fed me that information.

Whatever the reason, it usually had me keeping my mouth shut instead of risking others realizing how little I actually understood.

We headed into the large space where the class would take place. It had a stage up front and a large projector screen, no doubt hooked to a computer with all the scary pictures of The Pitt.

Being here *was* a massive waste of time for us. We'd not only dealt with stable dungeons in the past, but had personally come to *this one* and survived it. I doubted there were many working espers who could say the same.

Still, we'd gotten told to attend because they thought we needed the *refresher*. It was a not-so-subtle way of reminding us that our last time hadn't gone well.

Or rather, that the Guild blamed us for the outcome.

Eyes turned our ways, the reaction more hostile than usual. Generally, we got pity or derision, but right now?

Hatred.

Anger.

Rage.

Why? Probably because the idea of going into a dungeon with a squad they saw as untrustworthy could put the entire mission in danger. It was like building a bridge—every last section had to stand, because if any fell, the whole thing would collapse.

They didn't want us to be that weak link that took them all down.

"You're this way," a low-rank esper said, one of the people working the event to keep it running smoothly. They couldn't stand in a fight for a job like this one, so instead, they took on the administrative tasks. We followed the woman to a set of chairs near the front and to the left. It was like getting sat up near the teacher's desk at school. She left us there, and most of the spots were still open.

I can't believe we're back here again.

We didn't have a choice, didn't have a way to get out of it, but that didn't change just how fucking much I hated it. This dungeon had almost killed us before, had ended up destroying our lives, and they expected us to face it again?

Hadn't we paid our price? Hadn't we done what we needed to do?

It was someone else's turn to take over now, to throw themselves into this mess.

Despite me thinking that, however, I sure as hell didn't want to suffer the fate of an esper who got thrown out of the Guild.

No thanks.

It meant we had to sit there and do as we were told, that we had to accept this bullshit assignment. My gaze moved over to the seat beside me, the one with Yun's name printed on the card.

This time, we have something worth protecting...

Chapter Twenty-Nine

Yun

Kaiden plopped down on the large couch and patted the seat beside him. He had that same smile, as if this were the easiest thing in the world. Then again, everything seemed to come easily to him. It was one of the things I loved about him, but it also frustrated me.

I took the seat. Kaiden was one of the few men who didn't freak me out. Part of that was that he wasn't an esper, but another was just him as a person. It wasn't that I didn't know that he was capable of violence — anyone was. It was that some part of me never believed he would use it against me.

"You've looked better."

"That's not something you're supposed to say to a woman."

"Well, it's true. I mean, you never look all that rested or happy, but you look even more tired than usual." He caught my chin and lifted my face, tilting it side to side to examine it from every angle. "Maybe this squad isn't a good fit."

I knocked away his hand. "It's not like I have a lot of choices. This is my last chance before the Guild is through with me."

"They always say things like that. They're not about to throw away a guide."

"They will if the guide is useless, or worse, dangerous. Of course, the idea that they might not let go of a guide even then, that's scarier." I thought about all the uses a guide might have beyond the expected. Little research had been done on guides, because the Guild considered them far too valuable to experiment on. If I had no choices, no use, no friends or family or anyone to miss me, the Guild could do anything they wanted to me without recourse.

A weight settled on my hand, pulling me back from those terrible thoughts. Kaiden stared at me with more caring and understanding than I would have expected. He played the part of a playboy, moving from esper to esper, from squad to squad, without ever laying down roots. He pretended that nothing mattered to him at all—well, nothing but me. It was times like these, when I glimpsed beneath that mask, that I recognized the depths of care he actually held.

"You silly little girl, do you really think I'd let anything happen to you?" And just like that, he did what he always did. He reassured me, making me feel less alone in all of this.

My eyes burned, but I refused to give in. I wasn't about to cry like the little girl he called me, not about to go back out to my men with swollen eyes that I would have to explain. In fact, I had a feeling they might go have a word with Kaiden after that, as though they needed to find out exactly what had made me cry.

"Now that we're past that, I want details." He sat back as though this was the most normal conversation in the world to have. "Come on, I want all the specifics. Guides don't live in a house with a squad of S-Rank espers without there being some filthy, wonderful details."

I made a point of rolling my eyes, which helped clear away the remaining tears. "You know me, Kaidan, there are no dirty details to share."

"Are you serious?" Pure shock ricocheted over his features. "You've been there for over six weeks, and you're telling me *nothing* has happened? I find that pretty much impossible to believe."

"Yeah, well, believe it or not, that's the truth. Just because we're living together doesn't mean I'm gonna let them do whatever they want."

"What about whatever *you* want?" Whatever expression was on my face had Kaiden laughing. "Is it *that* impossible for you to think that you might be interested? Come on, Yun, you're not dead."

Not dead, no, but I wondered if a part of me hadn't died. My mind traveled backward in a way it hadn't since just after it had happened.

As the years had passed, I didn't get drawn into memories as quickly, as time and space distanced me from that horror. That it would so quickly wrap around me again made me wonder the change.

Stress?

The nightmares?

The upcoming time at The Pitt?

The men?

"Yun." The sharp name drew me back before I fell headlong into the memories, dragging me back to safety.

I blinked slowly, staring at Kaiden, his familiar light blue eyes grounding me. I shuddered as the energy slipped from me, the fear, the anxiety. I swallowed, the action so thick it hurt, but it helped clear my head.

He tilted his head. "You're still doing that badly?"

"No, not usually."

"You haven't been like this for a long time. You were doing better."

I pulled my leg up, resting my heel on the edge of the couch and wrapping my arms around that knee. "I've been having nightmares again."

He pressed his lips together. "Those had gone away, hadn't they?"

"They're different, now. Before it was a memory of what happened. Now? Now it's like *he's* talking to me, taunting me."

"How often?"

"Almost every night. Sometimes it's not as bad, sometimes it's worse, but almost every night I see him. It's like I'm back there, in that dark forest, and he's laughing at me, telling me we're connected, that we're inevitable." I held myself tighter, my voice thin and strained as I spoke.

"Do you know why that's happening? I mean, there are plenty of reasons I can think of, but do you think there's a specific reason? Is it the squad?"

"I don't think so. It started before I met them, before I even knew that I was going to have to work The Pitt."

"But you knew it was opening again. Maybe it's as simple as that. You knew it was going to open — that's almost an anniversary. Perhaps your brain is acting out because of that."

I mulled that over, and it was possible, but something about it felt strange. "What if he's right?"

"What?"

I pushed myself to keep talking even though the words hurt. "What if we *are* bound? Interaction between guide and esper can create a bond—what if I did that?"

"That's not possible."

"How can you be sure? How can you know that? No one knows what happens between a guide and a corrupted because it's never happened. Maybe he really is talking to me, maybe I can't escape him, maybe I never really got away at all." The words poured from me, allowing the panic to grow until it consumed me.

The things I'd feared but never risked saying swelled, aided by the fact that I spoke to Kaiden. I admitted to him things I'd never dare say to anyone else.

He pulled me against his chest, the hug tight, his voice whispered into my ear but surprisingly strong. "It's not real, Yun."

Even if he said that, I didn't believe it. I *couldn't*.

He wanted to reassure me, and as much as I trusted Kaiden, that didn't mean he knew what he was talking about. I'd learned that life wasn't as simple as truth and lie.

Maybe my experience had broken me. Maybe it had damaged me so badly that there was no chance of coming back from it, like a part of me had been burned so severely that it would never heal.

The spiral took over, plunging me into the despair that had threatened me, growing over the past weeks and months until I had no idea how to escape it.

At least, until a familiar sensation in my head eased me.

"If you don't breathe, you'll pass out. If you pass out, Kenyon will have a hissy fit." Shear's voice soothed me, confident, without the tiniest bit of panic. Even Kaiden seemed overwhelmed by my reaction, but Shear didn't.

He spoke with the same solid voice as always, and that alone reassured me.

"I told you to stay out of my head."

"Then don't freak out, and I won't need to. Trust me, I don't want to be in your mess of a brain any more than you want me here."

I could almost hear him sneer as he said that, like my brain was a teardown in a bad neighborhood.

Which wasn't the least accurate way to describe my brain — especially right now.

"What happened that got you to this state?" His question came out with an edge of curiosity. If it had been pity, I probably would have reacted differently. I *hated* pity.

Curiosity I could deal with.

"Fuck off," I responded, half-heartedly.

"Gladly. The meeting will start soon. If you don't hurry up, someone will come and collect you."

I responded to him with a mental middle finger, surprised when I pulled away from Kaiden, when I opened my eyes and found that I actually felt better. The panic that had threatened to yank me into a pool I wasn't sure I could ever surface from again had dissipated, had dried up until my toes actually touched the ground.

"You okay?" Kaidan stared at me, confusion coloring his expression.

Of course, Kaidan wasn't privy to my little conversation.

I nodded. "Yeah, I'm okay, now." At his furrowed brows, I shrugged. "Shear."

He cocked an eyebrow. "You let a mentalist into your head?"

"It's not like I invited him." I pulled away and stood, rubbing the heels of my palms against my eyes to help get rid of any lingering signs of my little breakdown. Usually, after something like that, I was so worn out that it would take hours to feel like myself again. Somehow, I felt rather refreshed...

I doubted it was because a meltdown helped me, and it made me suspect it had more to do with whatever Shear had done.

"Yet you accepted it. You think I don't remember when a mentalist tried to help you with a headache one time?" He pressed his lips together, staring at me.

"What?"

"Nothing really. Just interesting that you'd let this happen. You better get back—we've both got a job to do."

Something about the way Kaiden said it kept me quiet, a speculation there in his voice that I didn't care for. It felt like he was saying something that I didn't want to hear. So instead, I headed out of the guide room and into the main space.

Despite all the people moving around it, the chaos, my eyes settled directly on the espers I looked for. There, near the front, sat Kenyon, Carter, Ingram and Shear, drawing me to a stop as I stared at them.

Did I trust them? It was hard to believe it, hard to think it possible, but that look Kaiden had given me, the point he'd been trying to make, it all echoed around in my head.

I didn't have an answer, hadn't come up with an understanding, but at the very least, it helped distract me. Even The Pitt didn't feel quite so overwhelming.

Maybe because I'm not alone...

And, boy, didn't that feel like the most dangerous thought I'd had?

Chapter Thirty

Carter

Having to sit here and listen to someone tell me about The Pitt annoyed me more than I wanted to admit. It didn't dim my false smile, of course. No, nothing could shake that. It was easy to sit back, my hands folded over my stomach, my legs kicked forward beneath the table and pretend that none of this mattered to me.

The person up front was Inlan Price, the mouthpiece of the Guild, at least for the espers. He liked the spotlight, loved being up there telling everyone what to do even though the asshole didn't know anything from the last time The Pitt had opened — he'd been way too far back to see shit.

He'd enjoyed his spot at the back, telling others what to do, sending better espers off to their deaths so he could take the glory on television the next day.

My only benefit was that it was also his job to stand there and apologize for *my* behavior.

"The Pitt is one of the most dangerous stable dungeons currently active," Inlan explained, the screen behind him showing images from The Pitt.

Funny how it appeared like most other dungeons, yet I'd have recognized it anytime. That place had tattooed itself onto my mind, the place where everything had changed.

I'd walked into that dungeon a fucking hero, the cover model of half the damn magazines out there, and by the time I exited?

I peered around, noting the way no one sat too close to us, the looks we got, the snide little comments, and that showed what had happened when we'd come out.

We'd lost everything.

And here I am, ready to go in again.

"One of the most dangerous things about this dungeon is the corruption gain. It causes corruption levels to rise at five times that of other similarly ranked dungeons. This means that the presence of guides is going to be instrumental to this mission. We will have both squad specific guides located in well-protected areas near the portal, along with many floating guides to fill in the blanks. The most important thing is that we keep sessions short to ensure espers remain at optimal levels."

"It can't be that bad, can it?" someone asked from the peanut gallery. I didn't recognize the voice, but I didn't bother myself with learning anything about new espers. There were so many of them coming in each year, and it would be a full-time job trying to keep track of them.

I wasn't the HR department for the Guild—no reason for me to worry about that.

Inlan at least had the decency to put the esper in place with a sharp look that shut him up. "Do you know how many espers we lost to corruption last time The Pitt opened?"

The esper huffed.

"I'm serious. Answer."

"Two?" the esper guessed, but his tone suggested he saw it as the trap it was.

"Fifteen."

The esper at least appeared properly scolded. "A stable dungeon will have casualties, of course—"

Inland cut him off as though he weren't speaking at all. "Fifteen to *corruption*. Another thirty died or were declared missing in action when the portal closed, but fifteen turned."

The gravity of that rushed through the crowd, silencing everyone. It was normal to lose espers, but to have them turn during a mission? To have so many killed by corruption rather than actual damage?

The truth was that most espers would happily take a bloody death rather than losing themselves, instead of becoming shadows of the people they used to be.

Inlan took the silence as understanding, because he released the mouthy esper by looking away. "Since we are on that topic, I would like to introduce Kaiden Phillips, one of our top guides. He will share his insights, so pay attention."

Kaiden stepped onto the stage from a table to the left, looking different from earlier. When he'd run up to Yun, when he'd wrapped his arms around her as though he had every right, he'd seemed younger, carefree. Now, however, he seemed like the high-ranking guide I knew him to be.

Kaiden was the sort of guide that *everyone* knew. He was likely the most powerful guide, and despite some of his personal life getting in the way for him, no one would doubt his knowledge or place in our world.

I'd never worked with him, not even when we sat up at the top as well. It hadn't been any real choice — back then we'd always had our own guide and Kaiden had always refused to settle down with his own squad.

And there was the whole rumor that he was a top.

Not a lot of espers were willing to let a guide top them — and I wasn't interested in that — but it wasn't like he didn't still have a place.

Besides, if anyone knew better than to believe every rumor, I did.

"I've interacted with The Pitt twice," Kaiden said, his hands folded behind him, resting at the small of his back. The position pushed his chest out and made him look larger. Hell, he could almost pass for an esper. He proved that not all guides were women or waify, feminine men.

Maybe I'd let him top me…

A sharp look from my side said Shear had probably caught a strand of that thought. I didn't bother to deny it — Shear knew me too well for me to try. Instead, I gestured toward the stage as though to scold him for paying attention to my perverted musings instead of the point of our being here.

Math — not my strong suit — kicked me in the head as I tried to work out how Kaiden could have been around for The Pitt twice. It only opened every ten years, and Kaiden couldn't have been older than thirty? Maybe he just looked good for his age?

"My first exposure to The Pitt was when I was twelve — my first stable dungeon after appearing as a guide. I was still in training at the time, and this was when The Pitt appeared outside of Phoenix. We had twenty guides working that day, plus others in training like myself, and we could not get ahead of the corruption levels. We lost only two espers that day to monsters, but twenty fell to corruption." He paused at the end of that statement, as though to ensure it sank in.

He didn't really need to — not with a group of espers.

Guides prevented corruption, sure, they helped give us more time, but *no one* understood the danger of corruption like the one staring down the muzzle of that gun. I knew exactly what it could mean, what it *would* mean, eventually, if I didn't get myself killed by a monster first, if I didn't take my own fate into my hands and deal with the problem myself first.

It was just a long fucking path with a single possible outcome. I either died or I ended up as much a monster as those I'd spent my life killing.

There weren't other options, not for espers, not since we'd started appearing around eighty years ago.

Still, sometimes guides liked to act like they were the experts of it, like it was their job to make sure espers understood the danger.

Kaiden struck me as that sort of asshole.

Or maybe I just really disliked him because of how close he was to Yun. Some part of me wanted to put a claim on her, to make sure he understood that he was second to us. I didn't care that he'd known her longer, that she sure didn't smile like *that* when she saw us. We were espers and guide.

She'd guided us, lived with us, was under *our* protection. That meant we had a connection with her that Kaiden never would.

That thought helped me to settle deeper into the chair, scooting down slightly so I looked like a delinquent at the back of a classroom.

"You have already heard what happened the last time The Pitt opened right in the middle of San Diego, near the beach. We lost over a thousand civilians by the time the portal closed, and more in the months and years since with breakthrough monsters. The San Diego appearance was an absolute disaster, aided by a lack of Guild planning, a failure of squads to work together, and..." Kaiden's gaze moved over to us, a sharpness there that said he knew what had happened—or at least the official story.

I smiled as though I couldn't feel the daggers there.

"Other issues," he finished. "We can't have that happen again. That is why we are putting so much into these practices first. I will handle training with guides ahead of time while the espers receive their own training over the next month until The Pitt appears. We will be prepared to travel to where The Pitt opens as soon as it starts to appear." He gestured to Inlan, signaling he had nothing else to say.

Inlan took center stage again. "Part of what this meeting is for is to alert you all about what is coming up. Our joint missions so far have taught us something important—squads don't work well together. If we want to create a cohesive group to ensure we are ready for The Pitt, we have to take more drastic measures. For that reason, we have decided to move forward our timeline. You all have one week to finish your preparations, to settle your plans, because every squad involved in The Pitt offensive *will* arrive at our training location in Nevada in one week to give us time to actually prepare."

I lifted my eyebrow at that—it was the last thing I'd expected to hear. Working together was one thing—a stupid idea, but whatever—but housing and training us together? Full-grown adult espers used to having our own way?

I chuckled to myself at what a fucking disaster this was going to be.

Chapter Thirty-One

Yun

Well, not having that much stuff made it easier to pack everything. Kenyon had brought me a number of suitcases, all appearing brand new and worth way more than anything I had to put inside them. Instead, I'd just ensured everything I had was clean and placed it back into the bag I'd brought with me. It was easy since I hadn't really put any of it away.

"You sad to be leaving?" Kenyon asked from the doorway of my room.

"Maybe sad to be losing out on the nice bathtub, but otherwise?" I shrugged. "One place is pretty much like the next."

"You didn't get accustomed *at all* to being here?" His voice sounded almost hurt by my disinterest.

I turned and sat on the edge of the bed, willing to meet his gaze to have this talk. "You don't get it. Espers settle down, but guides? We get moved around more. Easy come, easy go."

"Not exactly. I mean, this is just a temporary relocation while we train. After that, we're coming right back here."

After that.

Such a simple phrase that meant so much more. That was training, that was The Pitt, *that* was my biggest nightmare. He was assuming a lot, that we'd survive, that they'd still want me at the end.

That I wasn't headed toward something that would end up killing me.

The truth was, none of us knew that. None of us could say what would happen, and I didn't know if it was experience or paranoia, but I couldn't imagine returning.

The truth was that no matter how much I wanted this, my history had taught me never to get too comfortable in any one place.

"Why do you look like you don't believe me?"

I hated how Kenyon looked almost insulted by my suspicion. It went to show how different we really were, how different our lives had been. He couldn't imagine not making it back.

Truth be told, where I would go afterward was the least of my worries. Could something kill me? Sure. I could get hit by a car crossing the road tomorrow.

That wasn't the biggest of my fears.

"I just don't like getting ahead of myself."

"How is it getting ahead of yourself? Just see it as a vacation. You pack up the things you need, you go, you come back. It's not like you joined us just for this mission. We didn't even know about this mission when you joined."

"That might be true, but I just have this feeling. Call it intuition, maybe. I've never stayed anywhere that long." The part that I didn't utter out loud was that no one had ever wanted me around that long.

No, that wasn't entirely fair. There were times when espers wanted me to stay, when I fought it the entire time. There were times when I ran from the very start, when no matter how much they wanted me to let them in, I couldn't.

How many times that Kadian told me to give in?

He'd sworn by espers, told me I needed to accept my place, that I was only hurting myself by fighting, but good advice was rarely easily taken. It didn't matter if he said people were safe, my body and mind never truly believed it.

I knew *exactly* what any of them could turn into at any time.

"Have you ever stayed at a place like this before?" I asked to change the subject.

Kenyon sat on my bed, kicking his feet out in front of him like he didn't have a care in the world. "A few times. Never for anything this big, and not for a long time. Espers usually train in groups like this right after they turn. There are a few places across the globe that deal with newly changed espers."

"Like Ruby?" I asked, the name every civilian was familiar with.

He nodded. "Sure, like Ruby. They're all named after gems, but Ruby is the one most people know. It's the celebrity location that gets all the news."

"Where did you train?"

"Well, Ruby is for Rank A. The Guild likes A-Ranks because they look pretty on camera and seem flashy without scaring the normies. Rank-S espers usually go to Diamond. That's where I went."

"The others, too?"

"Most of us, yeah. Not Shear, though."

"Why not Shear?"

"He went to Obsidian." I hadn't heard of that one, and it must have shown on my face because Kenyon kept speaking. "Obsidian is a small training facility in Washington. Special cases go there."

"Why is Shear special?" As soon as I asked, I almost laughed at my own question. Obviously, Shear wasn't normal—anyone who spoke to him would know that much. "I mean, I get that he's different, but I don't really understand why."

Kenyon rambled, and I got the sense that he probably didn't know how to stop himself. Kenyon seemed like the type to just keep his mouth moving no matter what. It was probably why such stupid things flew out of it so often.

"Most espers change after puberty. A few change during puberty, and they can change all the way until they're elderly, but the average age is around nineteen or twenty. He, on the other hand, never changed. Or, if he did, there's no signs of it."

"What are you talking about? Every esper has to change into one. And it's not like it's that hidden when it happens." I thought about the fevers, the aches, all the signs that usually landed an esper in the hospital when it happened. And all of that didn't include the new skills that often showed immediately.

It was pretty easy to tell an esper had awakened when they suddenly started raining down fire every time they got mad.

"Exactly. As far as I know, Shear has always been an esper. It wasn't until he started talking that his parents realized something was weird. He knew things that he shouldn't, and once he had language, he started communicating mentally with people. The guess now is that he was born an esper. It could have happened sometime when he was still an infant, but that's just about as weird. Carter says that's why he's so fucked up. Because he didn't grow up normally, because he never learned the things most kids learned. He was five when he went to Obsidian."

"What's Obsidian like?" I tried the picture a child, almost a baby, trying to survive with other espers. It seemed cruel to yank him away from his family, from everything he knew, from every sense of support and safety he had.

Was that pity I felt?

Maybe it helped me to understand the strange man a little better. No one who grew up like that could grow up normally.

"No idea. Obsidian is the sort of place people only go when they have to, and they don't talk about it afterward. Shear isn't a big sharing sort of person, in case you didn't notice. He's been pretty hush-hush about his time there." He paused for a moment, a rare look of concern on his normally happy face. "He gets called back there usually once a year or so, and whenever that happens, he gets even more quiet. Afterward, he's like a different person for a week or so. Nothing is physically wrong with him—I'd be able to tell—but he isn't himself. All I can say for sure is that I'm glad I've never gone to Obsidian."

I frowned as I considered that, as I thought about the places these men *did* go. It was crazy to me to think that there was anything that would frighten them. They laughed their way through dungeons, through almost certain death, but a training facility could get *that* look on their faces?

Kenyon got up with a quick jump, as though he'd just realized he'd probably said *way* too much. "Well, we're supposed to catch the plane in about two hours, so finish up. They feed us on the plane usually, but it's not like, good food, so maybe we'll drive through somewhere first."

With that, he breezed out of my room, leaving me there to look around and wonder if I'd ever make it back here.

And accept the fact that I really hoped I did...

What a strange feeling.

Chapter Thirty-Two

Ingram

Well, this could be worse.

Fuck knew I'd spent enough missions sleeping on the ground with fucking rocks in my back that anything with a bed was one hell of a luxury at this point.

The plane ride had been easy enough — they had their own military crafts that they shoved us into for the trip. We met up at a small, private airport and traveled with only four squads — none of which I knew or gave a fuck about.

Kenyon had thrown up in the bathroom — that boy never did like flying — and Yun had slept through the whole thing.

It wasn't that long a flight, thankfully, before we were escorted to one of the small trailers they used to house the squads. It made sense to set the place up like an RV park, with each trailer functioning as a little house. It wasn't comfortable, but it had the essentials we needed.

Beds. Showers. A small kitchenette.

Good enough.

Carter was with Kenyon and Shear getting booked in. I'd gotten pulled aside first thing for my little meet and greet — thanks to my reputation and the way I looked, most likely — which left Yun and me wasting time in the trailer.

The sun had gone down a few hours ago, and she looked as though she were dragging ass already.

"You can sleep." I gestured at the large room at the back — the only regular room in the place — where we'd all agreed she could sleep. Women needed doors and shit, so the rest of us could bunk on the other beds around the place.

Her expression said she didn't trust me that far. "That's hardly a door," she pointed out, the pocket door tucked away little more than a piece of paper.

"And the door at home wouldn't stop me either. If you want to worry — worry — but at least do it about shit that matters. Your eyes are drooping closed every few minutes. It'll take the others at least another two hours to get through all their screening. No reason to stay up all night for nothing — tomorrow's coming early, whether you're ready for it or not."

She pressed her lips together, that little spark of anger, something that I liked *way* more than I had any right to.

Fuck, hadn't that gotten me into trouble enough times before? I didn't care for weak women, for ones who sat down and shut up. They were boring. It was why I'd ended up with crazy women who had no problem putting me six feet under when I disappointed them—and I always disappointed them, eventually.

They wanted something I didn't, didn't understand the arrangement I was looking for. Didn't matter how clear I was with them, they always thought they were special.

"If you're tired but can't fall asleep, I'm pretty sure I could help you." The words left my lips before I thought about them, before I realized how fucking stupid they were.

She snorted. "Thanks, but no thanks."

"You sure? You've been with us a while and I'm pretty sure you haven't gotten any at least since then. You've gotta be pent up by now."

"What would you know about that?" Her voice came out sharp and angry.

Sure, I'd seen plenty of guides get pissed over espers stepping out, acting like scorned lovers, but the anger from Yun seemed larger than it should have been. What exactly was she so angry about?

I thought back to the portal, to when I'd turned her down.

Oh, that…

Yeah, women tended not to like getting ditched like that, huh?

"You want to shame me? Go for it. Wouldn't be the first time."

She blew out a long breath. "I'm not shaming you—I'm trying to figure you out. Why would you do that to yourself?"

"To myself? What, like I'm some precious thing that's gonna get dirtied? Stop with the fucking princess shit and fairytales—it's exhausting. If I want to fuck my way through the population of San Diego, who the fuck are you to tell me I shouldn't?"

She jerked her gaze away, her cheeks flushed pink.

It made me feel as though I were on the attack, and I wanted to keep it going. I wanted to corner her, to force her to submit. "Maybe if you tried that once in a while, you wouldn't be such an insufferable bitch all the time."

The word that hung between us was the one I didn't say, the one that lingered on my tongue but remained silent. Even I didn't want to push things that far, after all.

Frigid.

That's what my brain screamed, what she thought, no doubt. It's what the espers called her. Blizzard was the name and why? Because she was cold, frigid, but also devastating.

I expected her to yell back, to throw out man whore or some other insult, to stand toe-to-toe with me as she usually did. Instead, she drew her hands into fists and got up, off the seat, then headed back to the room. The slam of the door was impressive, given how thin it was.

Yeah, that was the Blizzard, huh?

I sat there, in the main space of the trailer, guilt gnawing at me. I didn't normally feel that guilty, but something about running her off caused the unfamiliar feeling to prick at me.

She'd already gotten dragged here because she was our guide, forced to deal with a bunch of espers in a tiny trailer, and now I'd fucked with her enough to run her into a tiny room.

I sighed, ready to make it up to her later.

At least I was until a gasping noise floated through the door.

Is she crying? Talk about a lance through the heart sort of pain... Pissing her off? That was fine. I was pretty comfortable in that position. But to think that I'd actually made her *cry?* That was too much.

Even I wasn't enough of an asshole to be okay with that sort of bullshit.

I got up and went to the door, ready to apologize — first time for everything. I pulled the door to the side, mid-conversation already. "Look, I'm sorry, I didn't mean to make you — "

The words dried right up in my throat, falling silent as I stared at what was very much *not* the sight I'd expected.

I'd thought I'd find her crying, curled up on the bed, wiping her tears away as she used a pillow to muffle the sound.

That sure as shit wasn't the sight laid out in front of me.

Instead, there was not-so-sweet little Yun lying on her back, her pretty thighs spread wide, her frustratingly tight leggings gone, her hand in the heavenly space between. She stroked her clit with two fingers, her other cupping her breast through her shirt, her thumb brushing over the nipple.

Fuck, I had never seen anything that sexy in my entire life. I'd seen women do things that would shock a whore, but *none* had made me feel like this, none had made me want anyone this badly.

Her hands stilled — it seemed my voice was enough to kick her free of whatever she thought about. I tore my gaze from her cunt, moving up her body to her wide eyes.

Normally, people would cover themselves, but she just lay there, frozen in place.

And just like that, I was pretty sure I'd just fallen for her.

Chapter Thirty-Three

Yun

I wanted to crawl into a hole so small that I could never escape it.

I'd been scared before, hated where I'd ended up, but I'd never experienced humiliation like this.

It was good to know that no matter how crazy my life got, there were still times I got to experience something totally new.

Ingram stood there, in the doorway, staring at me like I was the most delicious meal he'd ever laid eyes on. I didn't come close to believing that, though, since I knew he had more than his share of women in his background. I wasn't nearly confident or foolish enough to think I was the prettiest girl around, so I didn't get the reason for him staring like that'.

The strangest part of it was the tension there, between us.

I recalled when another esper had walked in on me in the shower. It had been an honest mistake — at least, his shock had made it seem that way — but when he'd spotted me, he'd gotten a door slammed in his face. I hadn't needed to think twice about it, making my feelings and rejection beyond clear.

This was different.

This sparking electricity ran between us, something that pinned me in place, that made me wonder…*what if?*

I couldn't answer that. Fuck, I didn't even know what I was asking exactly. What if I didn't turn him away? What if I gave in, just a little, and experienced something for the first time?

I'd never wanted that before, had never even been tempted by the idea. It had turned my stomach, made me flinch away and react by baring my teeth.

This time, though? I wondered what it felt like, how it would end if I gave in.

"Curious?" His voice came out rough and low, making him sound like the predator he was.

I dragged my tongue across my lips then nodded, unable to lie, to deny it. What would be the point? There was no way he couldn't read it on my face.

There were times to lie and times to just admit the truth — half-naked and legs spread seemed like as good a time as any to admit it.

Especially to Ingram.

I might have felt differently if Kenyon stood there, or Carter, but Ingram? The man was a walking dildo from what I'd seen, so I had no reason to feel self-conscious about anything.

His lips curled up on one side into a smirk that made my heart speed faster. He took a step forward, the action causing me to scoot further away up on the bed.

He tilted his head, his smile dimming for a moment before he slid shut the useless door again—this time with him on the inside. "You're still gonna play that whole no-touching game?"

I gulped, but nodded. Sure, this was embarrassing enough, but I didn't think I could handle the idea of him actually putting his hands on me. That was too much space for me to cross, no matter how it might tempt me.

And I didn't want to lose control and end up hurting him.

He came closer, seating himself at the end of the bed, his gaze intense and locked on me. It made him a monster, and me? The prey that he chased. Was this what they saw before they died?

No, that wasn't it. He was a stealth specialist—they saw nothing before they died.

"Go on, then. You don't let anyone else touch you, so I want to see you doing it yourself. I want to see your fingers between your legs, rubbing that pretty little clit of yours again."

"And you'll just sit there?" Boy, did I sound untrusting.

Not that anyone would blame me. Who would trust him? Especially with that smirk?

He laughed as though my question were stupid. "*Just* sit here? Not a fucking chance, not when I've got a show like this in front of me. Don't worry, though, no matter what a pervert I am, I'm not about to touch someone who doesn't want it." He undid his pants with a quick jerk of his fingers, then pulled down the zipper. They were loose pants, which meant the fabric moved down enough for him to draw his cock from them—my first time seeing him like that.

And I could understand how he got so many willing partners. He was thick and long, with a line of piercings that ran up the bottom of his shaft.

What the hell?

"I hear it feels fucking fantastic," he all but growled, his hand already moving along his shaft. "At least, I've never gotten any complaints when I've fucked someone with these." He dragged his fingers over each piercing, the action drawing my attention like a lure.

I shivered, which made me realize I'd started to move my fingers against my clit again without even noticing. It was like the sight of him turned me on so much that I couldn't help it, sucked into the moment by the promise in his voice and the sudden dryness in my mouth.

Maybe I should have put an end to this, should have drawn clearer lines between us, held those lines as I had typically always done before. Except, that proved impossible.

I guided him at the same time, the action instinctual and driving up my need more. As the corruption poured into me, I didn't bother to ignore it as I usually did, didn't try to shove the sensations and cravings into a tiny box buried inside me so deeply that I couldn't access it.

Why not experience it just this once? Just let myself fall into that abyss, no matter how terrifying, how difficult?

I didn't bother to even hide my interest—what was the point in doing that when he could see exactly how much I wanted this—and watched him. Somehow, the movement of his hand over his cock was one of the hottest things I'd ever seen.

Why?

The sight of anyone — clothed or unclothed — hadn't ever done a thing for me.

There had been a time, back before everything had changed, when I'd thought — maybe? It hadn't been interest so much as curiosity, a desire to know something that I hadn't experienced.

As a preteen, and into my early teen years, I'd seen what most kids did — brief glimpses of movies where they showed people naked.

That had been rather innocent, though — nothing like this.

And those men hadn't looked anything like Ingram, either.

His shirt rode up, exposing his stomach, the muscles standing out sharply, showing just how little fat he had. Tattoos rested over that skin, making me wonder if there was a bit of him unadorned by tattoos or piercings. Some were colorful, others monochrome, some with bright lines and others faded, suggesting they'd been added years ago.

It made me want to have him stripped entirely, to trace the line of each tattoo, to see him in all his glory. I wanted the time to taste him, to savor every inch of him, to do as I pleased for once.

I lacked the bravery for that, so instead I allowed my gaze to take him in, at least what little I could see.

"That look you have…"

His voice came out thick and heady, something I wanted to feel whispered against my ear. I craved the feeling of someone wanting me, of losing myself.

I imagined it as I teased my clit, chasing the sensations that drew me closer to my release.

In my mind, I wasn't broken, wasn't a shell of the person I could have been. Instead, I welcomed Ingram, both of us hungry for the same thing, willing to find that pleasure in each other, capable of giving ourselves over to it.

He'd be rough—I was sure of it. Nothing about him screamed gentle, after all. He had the experience to turn my own body against me, and I wanted him to expend every bit of that knowledge on me.

"You know, I could fuck you. Guarantee you'd enjoy it, that I wouldn't stop until you had your fill. Could waste away the boring fucking hours here doing something a lot more fun."

I shook my head but kept my hand moving, stroking over my sensitive clit, wishing for a moment that I'd packed all 'the toys Ingram had' left for me. A vibrator right about now would have easily gotten the job done, pushing me over that edge without nearly as much work.

"You sure are taking your time," Ingram said. "You fuck yourself like a girl not used to doing it."

I turned my gaze from his, unable to stop the shame there. *Not even good at this, huh?*

"Look at me." The words were rumbled out, a demand that had me looking right at him. "You really don't have much experience, huh? Ain't making fun of you, just pointing it out. Fuck, it's a turn-on. I'm not usually into virgins or prudes, but something about you makes me think I might have had that all turned around. Come on, sweetheart, do whatever feels good. I want to watch you get yourself off, see how you figure out what feels best, what you like, what you don't. Make it easier when you finally let me between those thighs of yours."

Normally, words like that would cause me to freak out, would repel me, make me want to run. The way he spoke made my cunt twitch in desperation, wanting something that had been denied to me my whole life.

He stared, and I wondered if he could tell the effect his voice had on me. Did he know it excited me? Did he realize how close to begging him I felt?

The fire in his eyes told me he probably knew *exactly* how little it would take to agree. I'd fold so quickly, with the tiniest push.

"You'd say yes if I asked again, wouldn't you?" He laughed, the tone broken by a deep, masculine groan. "I'm not about to do that, though. I want you *begging* for me when I do fuck you—when, not if. You aren't ready to submit like that yet, and that's fine with me. I don't have a problem waiting until you're just that hard up, until you don't have a speck of doubt. Until then, why don't you be my good girl and come?"

Those words lit a fire inside of me, made it impossible to resist anything. Why? The idea of being called a good girl was insulting.

At least when I was wearing pants. It seemed pantsless was an entirely different thing, and I reacted in the opposite way. A surge of pleasure rushed through me—a mixture of his words along with the guiding I did automatically, the flow of energy from him to me—and it pulled me like the current in a river, something I couldn't resist or fight against. It poured over me, crashing into me with such power that I could only arch my back and experience it.

My eyes shut, as though my brain couldn't filter through all the stimuli that assaulted me. I parted my lips but couldn't draw breath as I came hard, as the muscles in my back and my thighs all tightened to an almost painful point.

I remained on that edge for so long that my chest ached. It eased, my body going lax, my muscles too weak to even consider moving. I opened my eyes again to find Ingram there, his eyes brighter than usual, a sure sign of his emotions, his desires. His chest rose and fell in rapid pants, the seed that covered his hand showed that he'd come, but he was far from satisfied.

It left me confused, unsure how to address this, how to figure out where to go from here. I felt as though I'd crossed a line I'd never thought I would, one I'd guarded with everything I was for so long.

"Close your eyes and get some rest," Ingram said. "Best way to work through shit in my experience."

"And you sure know how to deal with this sort of thing, don't you?"

He smirked as he rose, not bothering to do up his pants, to hide anything. He just kept the hand sticky with his cum away from him. "Yeah, I do, so listen to me and stop overthinking. Sweet dreams, Blizzard." He offered a wink, then walked out, leaving me there all on my own.

How the hell was I going to face any of them tomorrow?

Post-nut clarity is a bitch.

Chapter Thirty-Four

Carter

"You want to hit me? Do it and get it over with."
Ingram crossed his arms as he stared at me, not looking
worried at all about what I might do.

Which made me want to hit him all the more. I could
smell Yun on the asshole, despite the shower I knew
Ingram had taken. How could he smell that much like
her? I doubted she'd let him touch her, yet her scent
clung to him like cologne.

And it pissed me off.

It set off all the territorial instincts inside me, made
me want to go in and cover her in my scent.

Not that she'd let me...

"Hit you? Why would I do that?" I smiled widely,
my trademark carefree attitude hiding my real feelings
as it always did.

He made a derisive noise. "The fact that you can
smile like that makes you one terrifying asshole, you

know that? You can smile right before you take someone's throat out—I've seen you do it. The wider that smile gets, the more I start questioning what's going on in that freak show of a brain of yours."

"No idea what you're talking about," I lied, then held out half of the croissant that I'd been eating to him. "So we've got rank testing today, right?"

Ingram took the piece and popped it into his mouth, chewing quickly before swallowing it down. "That's what I've heard. Fuck, how long's it been since we had to be graded?"

"Not since I left Diamond. Feels nice to show off sometimes."

"Speak for yourself. I don't like getting watched like a fucking science experiment or a circus show. I've been an S-Rank and stealth for fifteen years. No fucking point in this bullshit again."

I understood his feelings—and honestly, I shared them—but bitching about it wouldn't change anything. At the end of the day, if they wanted us ranked again, if they wanted to ensure everyone was what they said, they were going to do that. Better to hide my reaction to it, to bury that down deep and not let anyone see anything real.

It was the only way to make it in the world, to keep that all close to the chest, to play the game.

And I was fantastic at that.

So I kept that smile in place and shrugged. "You'll be fine. It's not even a big deal for you to rank compared to the rest of us. One day of stretching your esper legs and it's done. We'll have a delicious dinner, we'll talk to other squads, it'll be a great day."

Ingram rolled his eyes before stealing another piece of my breakfast. He opened his mouth as though to speak when his gaze moved past me and toward the doorway that led into the large meeting room where we stood.

The vibrations that rushed through the room, the way he stood a bit taller, it all told me who had walked in without me having to turn.

Yun.

Even if I didn't need to, I couldn't stop myself from looking, my gaze finding hers with an ease that was almost terrifying. She walked in, her shirt undone slightly more than usual — or was I just more aware of it? — those black slacks hugging her thighs in a way that was far too tempting. Her hair was pulled back, French braided to the nape of her neck and secured there with a small bit of hair from the bottom. It made her look competent and capable, like any other badass here.

Mine.

The word bubbled up through my mind, percolating until it sloshed around, filling every last crevice.

I shook it away, smiling when her gaze found me, when she headed my way.

"You didn't grab any food?" I asked. "There's a table just outside that door with pastries and fruit."

"I'm not hungry." She crossed her arms and boy, did she make a valiant attempt to *not* look at Ingram. Whatever happened between them, at least I didn't have to worry that she'd fallen hopelessly in love with him or something. The tension there said she wasn't even close to addressing whatever they'd done. "Where's Kenyon and Shear?"

"Kenyon is checking in the with medical. They do healer testing there."

"And Shear?"

I shrugged. "He's probably trying to avoid coming. He doesn't like doing these sorts of tests, but I'm sure he'll show up before long. Where are you scheduled today?"

"Guides are testing in the western wing."

"All of them?" I lifted an eyebrow, surprised by that. "Normally, guides are tested in a few groups."

"Yeah, it seemed weird to me, too."

I considered it, then let out a soft laugh. "They're trying to create a sense of community between guides and espers. It's military tactics 101. Get people shoved together in close quarters, force them to rely on each other, and you'll end up with a bond between them. Squads don't tend to do well together, so they're trying to force it."

"They're also probably trying to make guides feel responsible for one another so they'll care for other squads," Ingram pointed out.

Yun's expression darkened.

"Don't worry—won't happen." The reassurance left me unconsidered. It wasn't just an attempt to make her relax or win her favor, but rather an absolute fact in my mind.

I wasn't about to share her with other squads.

Fuck that.

I had no intention of handing over *my* guide to anyone. There were enough other guides for that, and I didn't mind taking apart any esper stupid enough to even think they could touch what was mine.

Especially given the fear on Yun's face. Her expression said she didn't want that to happen anymore than I did, and that solidified my response. I wasn't about to let something happen that she didn't want.

Not a fucking chance.

Still, despite the way my brain freaked out, I kept my expression neutral and my voice casual. No reason to let her in on how exactly I felt about it all.

"If they say we have to…" Yun pressed.

"Don't worry about that. Consider this a benefit of working with a squad — you don't have to think about stuff like that. You've got us to handle the Guild for you." I doubted my smile reassured her much — she'd glimpsed the mess beneath it a time or two — but I still offered it in an attempt to make her understand that it was our job to keep her safe.

It was the push and pull of guides and espers. She kept us from losing ourselves, from becoming a corrupted, and in exchange? We took care of her. It wasn't enough, wouldn't ever be enough for what she did for us, but it was our privilege and responsibility to keep her safe.

That meant from monsters, from other espers, and even from the Guild if we had to.

She narrowed her eyes until only a slit of darkness remained. *Seems she doesn't believe me.*

It was hard to blame her, given how many times she'd gotten herself thrown out on her ass from other squads. It wasn't like she had any reason to believe us, to put any trust in us.

"This place smells of desperation." Shear's odd comment broke the tension, a strange talent of his to throw any conversation into disarray without even meaning to. He had no food, but I didn't offer him any, either.

He could feed himself if he needed to.

"It smells like cheap body spray," Yun countered.

"That, too, but I mean the acidic smell of desperate ambition. All these espers and guides are hoping they can prove themselves and move up in the world. They don't see this as a mission to save people, but as one to benefit them." He crossed his arms as he cast a disgruntled look over the crowd.

Leave it to Shear to identify the nonsense of others, to not just willingly accept it. He lacked the social skills or planning mindset to keep the facts to himself, too. He simply blurted it out as it came to him, no matter how useful those details might have proven if he'd just played the game.

"Isn't that normal?" Yun asked. "People always want to better their position."

"It's a losing game," Ingram muttered. "No one stays in the top spot for long, and the fall down from it fucking hurts." He shook his head, the shadows in his eyes ones that I knew all too well.

Yun stared at him — the first time she'd really looked at him this morning, like his words were enough to help her forget about whatever had happened between them.

Then again, she didn't understand. She couldn't. The limelight sounded great to those who didn't stand in it, but they had no idea what it did to a person, what someone had to sacrifice to keep it, or just how hard it hit when it went away.

Good. I didn't want her to know, because understanding would mean pain for her, and I found myself reluctant to hope for that.

"It isn't like that's a surprise," I said to ease the conversation. "Every grouping like this has espers hoping for a leg up somewhere. It's to be expected. Just keep your head on straight and do what you need to do, and it'll be the same as ever."

A ding from above us had me glancing up toward a PA system just before a distorted voice echoed over the crowd. "Rank testing will start in ten minutes. Please make your way to your section. Thank you."

"Show time." I clapped my hands loudly as though excited to get this over with, then smirked at Yun. "Try not to miss us too much."

I left her sputtering out a broken reply when I winked and turned, heading toward the door, leaving her there with a million responses — none of them nice, I was sure.

Maybe I'd never outgrown being a young boy desperate to pull the pigtails of the girl I liked. If she was annoyed with me, at least she was thinking about me.

That had to be enough.

Chapter Thirty-Five

Yun

I would have figured that being surrounded by guides would make me more comfortable, but it never quite worked out that way. Instead, I felt almost more unnerved, as though they could see right through me, like they knew everything that was wrong with me.

I felt like a broken version, and every last one of them knew it.

Which wasn't too far off from the truth, given the looks I got.

It wasn't like it shocked me. I'd been used to guides staring at me like that, which was one reason I preferred not dealing with them when possible.

Kaiden wasn't anywhere that I could see — and it wasn't fair to expect him to protect me.

Instead, I pulled my shoulders back and walked into the busy room as though I had no idea that anyone thought anything about me. It wasn't fake it 'til you make it so much as 'fuck 'em.'

I spotted a few people I recognized, but none I was close to. I passed by those meandering around the large room and headed for the check-in table. Civilians worked that location — two older men who sat with open laptops in front of them.

"I'm checking in," I said. "Yun Moore."

The man on the left typed, his gaze on the screen rather than me. Then again, civilians tended to do that.

They either had hero worship — putting us on some pedestal anyone would fall from — or they acted like we were tools to sacrifice for their wellbeing.

It seemed from the lack of any basic niceties that they viewed guides the second way, as something for their benefit, but not really human at all.

"Rank S. Assigned to Squad S412." He rambled, his voice bored. "You'll be ranked again today."

"How are they testing?"

"Blood draws to check for corruption antigens, then sample guidings."

Blood draws, great.

The sample guiding was less of a problem, but the blood draws?

Something about needles just set my teeth on edge, making me want to flinch away. Worse than the needle was the tourniquet. The way they hugged tight around my arm, the sensation of helplessness — I hated it all.

Still, I smiled as though it didn't bother me. "So where do I go?"

"You'll get called when it's your turn. Listen for your name." He handed me a stack of papers. "Give these to the nurse who's doing the draw." With that, he returned to his laptop as though I wasn't even worth a goodbye or good luck.

I held back the words I wanted to say and stepped away from the table. No reason to cause more of a problem here. Fuck knew I'd gotten myself into trouble enough times, and I didn't need any more reasons for them to dislike me.

The room filled up more and more, and I had to admit, guides were an interesting group. Where espers had this power behind them, something almost tangible, guides held an ethereal quality.

They glided more than walked, with this lightness that seemed to absorb any darkness around them.

It made me wonder if I could ever be that sort of person. Could I ever feel that way?

Across the room I spotted the guide who embodied that description more than any other—Mercy.

She smiled widely. Her blonde hair hung down in loose curls around her, and she wore a sundress that hung to just above her knees. She laughed as though she had no worries in the entire world, as though nothing could touch her.

Again, a thought that would do nothing good slipped through my mind.

What if I could be like that?

Would my life be easier? No doubt about that, really. Squads would accept me happily, would fight over me. They'd cherish me, claiming me as their own, giving a damn.

Except, no matter how tempting the thought might have been for a moment, I knew it wasn't possible.

From what I knew, Mercy had been flagged as a guide young, after living an idyllic life. Rich parents, a wonderful home, never had anything bad happen.

She'd gotten trained after ranking in as an S, then had her pick of assignments. Even though any squad would take her in a second, she'd decided to float, going where needed, only working with squads short term.

She was the epitome of what a guide should be—poised, sweet, sexy in a way that made me question my own sexuality. Basically, she was everything I wasn't, and worse, she was even nice to me. It made it that much harder to hate her.

"Yun Moore."

I snapped my head around toward the back of the room, where a nurse in blue scrubs stood next to one of the steel-and-cloth dividers. She checked the tablet in her hand and called my name again.

I headed over and gave her the paperwork, then sat where she indicated. The tightened grasp of the thin rubber used around my arm had me closing my eyes and breathing slowly.

At least she found a vein easily, proving that while she might not be nice, she was competent.

I'd take competent over nice any day, especially when it came to medical know-how.

She pressed a piece of gauze against the pinprick wound, then wrapped a pink bandage around it, just above my elbow, the material sticking to itself. "Go sit in the next area for a few minutes to make sure you're not dizzy, and they'll tell you what to do afterward." She pointed the opposite direction from where I'd walked in.

Which meant that the back of the large room was sectioned off into at least two or three areas, intended for guides to move through them one at a time.

Right after I passed from the area for blood draws, the nurse called another name, moving us through like cattle. I sat in the chair she'd indicated, giving me a look at the next room.

It had four sections, telling me they expected this area to bottleneck. It made sense, as doing sample guidings was time-consuming.

Guiding espers was a back-and-forth sort of deal, which meant we pulled different amounts based on the esper. The closer the two were in terms of rank, the more intimate they were, the higher the compatibility, the easier it was, but it all changed based on the esper.

With a sample like this, corruption was contained inside a low-level heart, and the guide removed the corruption from the heart. Using a known factor would help them evaluate a guide's skills on their own—they'd be able to see how well the guide did compared to others without the bond or esper playing a part.

It wasn't that pleasant, of course, because removing corruption from a sample was more work, required more effort from the guide.

The heart was small and cube-shaped, appearing more like a piece of dull obsidian.

A guide stumbled away from the cube, a civilian catching him before he hit the ground.

Yeah, not a wonderfully good time.

The civilian escorted the guide away before another nurse in scrubs met my gaze, then gestured for me to approach.

I used the armrests of the chair to push myself to my feet, then followed her order. Someone else traded out the cube with a fresh one, this one humming with corruption. They used gloves, then set it right into the space carved out of the metal structure.

Civilians didn't react well to corruption, so they tended to avoid it when possible.

"Your records show you're an S-Rank, right?"

"Yes, S-Rank."

She nodded, tapping her fingers on the screen of the tablet. "Any recent changes to abilities? Any problems with guiding?"

"No."

She ran through the questions with an ease that said she did it often, that she was used to this work. Some nurses and doctors specialized in guides or espers, and that seemed to be the case with this one.

"We're going to use an S-Rank sample for you. Now, if you aren't S-Rank, there's a risk to doing that. The corruption could overwhelm you, so make sure you're honest."

I almost laughed at her warning, as though I hadn't been through this enough to fully understand the risk.

A lower-level guide couldn't handle as much corruption, meaning they could accidentally take in more than they could filter. It wouldn't usually do long-term harm, but it would knock them out and it wasn't all that pleasant a recovery.

However, despite all my flaws, all my problems, there was no doubt as to my rank or abilities.

It was one of the few things I could manage.

And at least this time it was just a sample, which meant I didn't have to worry about the whole 'no-touching' thing.

"Go on. An average time would be five minutes to clear the corruption."

I nodded and walked up to the heart, the sickening sense of corruption thickening as I neared it. I could smell it, feel it in the air. It was worse than an esper, since this corruption felt stagnant, as though it had festered and rotted.

However, it was just a cube, and that reassured me. It was nothing more than a rock capable of holding corruption inside of it.

I shook my hand once, then set it on the side of the cube. A beep signaled the start as the nurse pressed a button on her watch.

A timer, no doubt.

I pulled the corruption from the cube quickly, allowing it to rush into me. It was easier in some ways than guiding an esper — less complicated, at least — but I had to do all the work myself. I drew that power into me, feeling my body already filtering it, changing it, absorbing it and rendering it harmless.

Five minutes?

A joke.

The corruption slipped into me, comfortable in a way that unnerved me, easy in a way it shouldn't have been. It almost felt like the corruption was rushing from the cube to me eagerly, as though it knew exactly where it wanted to be. It terrified me how easy it really was, how little effort it took.

The words in my head came back to me, the fact I was ruined, that I was bonded with *him.* It made me remember what he'd said, made me question that.

Was it because I really was broken? Had what happened altered me so much that I wasn't normal anymore?

Those doubts wrapped around me tighter and tighter until they strangled me, but even that didn't stop the flow of the corruption. It felt as though only a few moments passed before the corruption slowed and stopped, all of it emptied from the cube and into me. It no longer hummed with that energy signature, telling me I'd drained it.

A low whistle had me spinning, fear beating at me after all the thoughts that had tumbled around in my skull. Instead of my past, instead of the terrors that lurked in my mind, I found only the nurse staring at me, her gaze moving between her watch and me.

"Forty-two seconds," she said, frowning as though she couldn't believe it.

Then again, given that the average for my rank was five minutes, I'd beat it by four minutes and some change. I hadn't intended to show it up that far, but that didn't change anything.

The look she gave me said she wasn't impressed, but rather suspicious.

Yeah, great job making friends…

Chapter Thirty-Six

Shear

I closed my eyes against the pain in my head, the sharp, stabbing sensation that reached deeper than physical pain. It felt like an attack on my psyche itself, something I wanted to yank away from but knew better than to attempt.

Resistance always proved fruitless. It never got me where I wanted to go and just increased the amount I suffered.

So I didn't try to stop that clawing sensation in my head, the one spawned from a debuffer putting up a shield to stop mentalists from fiddling around in anyone's head. It wasn't just a matter of not using my powers, however, it also affected my brain. It sizzled through my gray matter, causing that agony.

I *hated* when they pitted us against each other.

Fighting monsters or dealing with civilians was one thing. I could do that anytime without a problem.

Fighting against other espers always took me backward, reminded me of the years I spent training. All I had wanted back then was *someone* to trust, to rely on, but Obsidian had made it clear that wasn't a luxury afforded to espers.

It meant when this training camp pitted us against each other, it turned my stomach. They wanted us to learn to work together, but decided to make us enemies instead?

I could almost hear Carter in my ear telling me they weren't doing that, that friendly competition would help people bond.

I knew the truth, though, because I could *hear* it all in the heads of the civilians who watched over us.

They wanted to see how far they could push us, wanted to see what we could do and had a morbid fascination.

Civilians always did, in my experience.

It took me back to Obsidian, back to when I'd been nothing but a science experiment for them, too young to control my reactions, to know how to handle it.

I wasn't a child anymore, though.

"Debuffer?" Ingram asked from beside me, all of us in a large gymnasium, the lights turned so low and a lack of windows making it nearly impossible to see anything.

I nodded. "Rank-S putting out an anti-mentalist blanket."

Ingram glanced away, his eyes catching the stray light to make them almost glow. "Near the back. Got him." He didn't have to tell me what he planned to do—I never had to fear that Ingram wouldn't handle problems.

He was difficult and broken, but loyal.

He disappeared, the darkness closing in on me, the blindness almost terrifying. It stole my most trusted and relied upon sense from me, plunged me into a void where I couldn't understand the world around me. The lack of light mattered so much less to me than losing my abilities.

Few debuffers had the strength to put me in such a state. The fact that they'd found one unnerved me.

However, this was *our* rank test, not the other squad's, so that meant the Guild would pick the perfect people able to counter us.

I had no idea where Kenyon or Carter were within the space, unable to sense them, unable to see them. My vision was the same as a civilian's, my other senses and skills no better than any human.

It meant I had no idea what exactly they were doing, but history had taught me they had things well in hand. If only I could get rid of this horrid pain...

If I could unbind myself, I'd end this immediately. I didn't care for showing off, but neither would I just let things continue if I could end them. I wasn't like Carter, willing to lessen myself to play a game.

A scream echoed through the space, and the pain in my head lessened, though it didn't disappear.

Not gone?

I let out a soft laugh at the realization of how they'd managed this, of their fear when it came to me. They'd gotten not one but *two* debuffers to screw with my head. It explained why they'd had such an upper hand and it did something I rarely experienced—it angered me.

Normally, emotions were just information, something I saw in others. I didn't have to suffer through them myself. It surprised me when it sprang up now at the idea that they would try such a dirty trick against me.

The roar of a monster echoed in the room, but I ignored it. Now with only one esper screwing with my mind, I could identify the others around the space with ease, their minds like spotlights in the darkness, standing out for me to attack.

Three monsters, all Rank S, one already dead. Ingram shifted closer to one of the monsters — moving in the shadows, only identifiable to me because of our bond, because of our years of working together. Carter went after two others, the darkness not a problem for him. Kenyon stood to the back, his eyes closed, telling me he sensed the health of us rather than focusing on the enemies or trying to see.

He trusted that the rest of us would ensure he didn't get targeted.

Other than the monsters, one debuffer stood near a doorway across the gym and another was already down — thanks to Ingram. A third esper stood, and I got the sense they were there to keep things dark, to control the temperature, to cause the wind to whip through the space and throw us off balance.

In other words, the civilians in charge wanted to figure out how we handled monsters, so they needed to throw anything they could at us. They wanted to give us the unpredictable, to see how we would react in a situation that got out of hand.

And if something in here ended us?

Well, we were only worth as much as we were useful. A weak esper was no different from a dead one to them.

It made me think about each of us, about the things we'd sacrificed, the things they'd put us through.

Worse, I thought about Yun, about what they might have done to her.

And something that had never happened before occurred—I lost my temper. I'd gotten angry before, something fleeting and frustrating but controllable. This took it to another level, it exploded through me, filling me.

Rage like I'd not known myself capable of exploded through me, causing me to put my hands out, to let it flow from me. I didn't think about it, didn't direct it, and it was met with absolute silence.

No screams, no roars, no sense of panic.

The darkness sank away when the large florescent lights flickered on.

We'd entered in the dark, so I hadn't gotten a look at the layout before. Civilians stood on the second level, on a metal pathway that kept them up above the fray and followed along the walls. They wore night-vision goggles, allowing them to watch the test even without the lights.

They didn't move, though, not to turn off the goggles, not to react, nothing. Similarly, through the space on the bottom level, the three monsters and the two espers not part of my squad remained frighteningly still, as though dead.

Only my squad remained unaffected by my hold, the grasp I had on each mind in the building, the fingers of my power so deep into their psyche they couldn't even consider resisting. I *felt* their fear, their panic, but they couldn't budge, couldn't worm their way out of my hold.

And I could end them all *so* easily. It would take so little for me to make sure that no one in this building was a threat again, to crush them. All of them, or just the monsters, or just the espers—it didn't matter.

"Release them." The voice came from the sound system, and my powers reached out, searching for the person, wanting to control them, to drag them down just like the others.

Except...they were too far away. Watching through the cameras?

Must be.

"That's enough," Carter said, his voice careful as he looked toward me.

"We were meant to kill the monsters. I'm doing that."

"You're holding humans, not just monsters," the voice on the loudspeaker said.

I shifted my gaze around until I located the camera in the corner. When I spoke again, I did so to the person on the other side. "Is there a difference? Human. Creature. Esper. They're all monsters." My powers reached out even farther, stretching, searching, until they latched onto the man on the other side of that camera, the mind who spoke through the PA system.

He was terrified—his brain lit up in all the primal places, the deep spots, the ones that initiated fight or flight in people. He was so far away, nearly a mile, at the other end of the complex, but that wasn't far enough, not to save him from me.

"Enough."

The voice in my head wasn't my own—it was Yun's. It drifted past that temper in a way even Carter hadn't managed, dragging me back from that edge. She couldn't connect with me, so had I found her mind? Had I reached for her without meaning to? Sought her in my moment of madness?

The reason didn't change the facts, and her mind was enough to ease me, to allow me to take a deep breath, to wrestle my control back.

I crushed the minds of the three monsters, their bodies hitting the floor in motionless heaps. I also released the two espers along with the civilians, offering one last mental push to the one who had spoken through the cameras.

Carter put his hands on his hips and smiled as though nothing strange had just happened. "Well, looks like we won."

I shook my head, rewarded with the knowledge that the man behind the camera, the one in charge of this entire little stunt, was wiping blood from his nose.

Serves him right.

Chapter Thirty-Seven

Yun

Exhaustion hung on me, causing my feet to drag as I entered the trailer, glad to finally have finished.

After my great time, I'd found myself in a number of meetings with a few of the medical staff. They wanted to understand how I'd done it, but I didn't have an answer for that. Honestly, dealing with them was far worse than the actual tests. The questions had come, one after another, as though they would figure out how I'd done it using some questionnaire.

The answer they wanted wasn't one I could give them anyway — and even if I could, I doubted they'd want to know it.

Or worse...if they knew, if they understood how it had happened, would they try to replicate it?

My mind seized that thought, the horror of it. Would they do that? Put others through what I went through just because it might strengthen their powers?

The fear filled me so completely that I didn't pick my feet up enough as I went up the final step into the trailer, my toes catching on the ledge and pitching me forward. It happened so fast I couldn't even brace for it, would have ended up flat on my face if not for a strong arm catching me.

It knocked the breath from me, since it wrapped around my stomach to stop my fall, but at least I didn't smash my face against the floor.

"That excited to see us?" Carter's playful voice was the only reason I didn't react badly at his touch — well, that and the fact that he helped me regain my balance, then backed off. "You're like a little kid, rushing so fast you trip over your feet."

"I tripped over the step." I gestured toward the stairs as though proving it, my cheeks warm. I might have argued more if it wasn't for a delectable scent filling the trailer. It drew me to a stop.

It was thick, heady, rich. I could identify onions and the sear of chicken? I turned my head toward the small kitchen space along one wall of the trailer. It only had one induction burner, but steam escaped the top of a rice cooker plugged in beside it. Kenyon stood before the large pan on the burner, a wooden spoon in his hand that he used to stir whatever was there.

My stomach grumbled loud enough that even humans would hear it, which meant there was no way a trailer full of espers wouldn't.

Which made me recognize I hadn't eaten since this morning, not since before the guiding test. The corruption had stolen my appetite, and the business of the day had made it so I hadn't even realized I was hungry.

Kenyon turned, glancing over his shoulder toward me with a smile. "Good timing—we're going to eat outside. Why don't you go take a seat?"

The exhaustion that had pulled at me eased at the idea of a nice home-cooked meal. Sure, this wasn't our home—I didn't really have one—but it was comfortable and as safe as I could hope for. I turned and went back down the stairs, realizing for the first time that a picnic table sat out there, a string of lights hanging above it from the awning of the trailer. It looked downright cozy.

Ingram already sat on one side with Shear next him, neither speaking. I hadn't noticed them because the table sat near the back of the trailer, and I'd come in from the other side. I took a seat across from them both.

They lifted their gaze but didn't question me, with Shear staring silently and Ingram returning to his phone as though he had better things to deal with.

Fine by me. I didn't know how to deal with him after what had happened, so I'd prefer he act as though I didn't exist. It made my life easier.

A few moments later, Carter appeared with plates balanced on his arms, Kenyon just behind him with glasses of water. They put them out before each of us and took their spots—one on each side of me.

The plates were paper, piled high with rice and a yellow curry mixed with large chunks of chicken, carrots, onions and potatoes.

One deep inhalation drew that delicious scent into my lungs, allowing me to savor it before I picked up a fork and took the first bite. It had spice to it, leaving a lingering burn on my tongue, but the flavor was deep and wonderfully balanced. The rice eased the burn, mixing perfectly.

I lifted my gaze to find all four of them staring at me.

My cheeks burned worse than the curry when I realized I'd actually moaned as I'd eaten. It was good, but that was just absurd.

Carter chuckled, a low, amused sound before he spoke as though to break the strange atmosphere. "I heard you were *quite* the topic."

I blew out a long breath. Wasn't I always the topic of conversation? It wasn't anything new, but rather an annoying fact that never quite went away. "Oh, really?" I asked as though I didn't know. Better to act as though it didn't bother me than let them see me sweat.

"Heard she scored highest of the S-Ranks," Ingram added.

"Great job," Kenyon said from around a mouthful of food.

I frowned, the words all strange. Praise wasn't something I was accustomed to, not anymore. That was the sort of thing loving parents did, so I hadn't experienced it since before I'd lost my own. It felt like when people reached out to stray dogs—no matter how wholesome the intention, the stray didn't trust it enough to enjoy it.

I reacted similarly, with distrust, waiting for the other shoe to drop, for them to twist it somehow.

However, that didn't happen. Instead, they went on with their conversation, letting the compliments rest on me, forcing me to sit with them.

"How mad were they?" Carter asked, looking over at Shear.

"Does it matter?"

That took me back to earlier, when I'd felt a rush of power that I'd immediately identified as Shear. It had been so strange that I had wondered at first if I'd felt it at all. He was usually so well controlled, to feel him in that way had surprised me.

Almost as much as it has surprised me that he'd reach for *me*. Of all things he could have done, why would he reach for me? And why was it that my response — as straightforward as it had been — had somehow allowed him to gain his own control again.

"Can you blame them?" Ingram asked, pointing his fork at Shear. "He made a big ol' spectacle of himself. What was that all about? You're usually way too smart to pull that sort of shit. Way to rile them up."

"Oh, like *you're* one to talk," Carter said. "You cause problems all the time. Remember when you slept with the wife of that senator?"

"No, I don't."

"And his brother?"

Ingram smirked as though it had just come back to him. "Oh, yeah, that was fun." Not a bit of shame resting in those words — if anything, he looked rather proud.

It didn't shock me, either. It would have been more surprising if Ingram had pretended not to be a man whore, after all.

"It's not like they don't know what I can do," Shear said.

"Yeah, but they like to forget. Reminding them puts us on their radar," Carter said.

"Good. It would do them well to remember."

The way Shear said that drew my focus, a solidness to those words which seemed so unlike him.

It sure sounded like it mattered to him even if I couldn't understand why.

Chapter Thirty-Eight

Kenyon

The night pressed in on me, the sounds so different from our home on the beach. It had me struggling to fall asleep, struggling to relax enough to drift off.

I'd never cared for the beach, much preferring the woods. The openness of the sea had always overwhelmed me. Still, this wasn't either of those things. Instead, it was desert, just flat and brown and full of spindly bushes that reminded me far too much of the dungeons for my comfort.

The air conditioner inside of the RV hummed softly, keeping us comfortable at least. I could appreciate that, since I doubted sweating like crazy would make the situation any better.

When tossing and turning didn't resolve anything — and in fact I ended up with Ingram muttering so many times I was pretty sure he'd come down one bunk and smack me if I kept it up—I gave up and rolled out of the bed.

I'd gotten the bottom given my size, plus my lack of physical skills meant it was better for one of the others to climb. No one wanted me toppling down.

I didn't bother to put my shoes on, instead creeping as quietly as I could move my rather large and unwieldy body. No reason to risk waking Yun—she'd struck me as exhausted lately.

The door creaked softly as I closed it behind me. Grains of sand stuck to the soles of my feet, despite the large section of fake grass set down, like that tricked anyone into thinking this was more homey with the greenery. Due to the sand, however, brown rested between the blades of faded grass.

The lights that hung from the awning spread a glow across the make-shift patio, the same picnic table we'd sat at for most dinners right there.

I stepped beyond, onto the patio, the moon large in the open sky. I had to admit, the lack of light pollution gave for one hell of a view of the darkness above.

The air was dry and dirty, and a part of me felt as though it might have coated my lungs when I breathed it in. All we had to do was get through this damn dungeon, and I could go back to somewhere else, somewhere better.

My senses weren't as great as Carter or Ingram's, but they weren't useless, either, a point proven when movement to the side of the RV caught my attention.

A figure moved there, in the darkness, outside the circle of light spread from the patio. Despite not being combat, instinct proved stronger than skills as I moved.

The idea of someone against the RV—not just anywhere, but hands gripping the window edge that led into the room where Yun slept—infuriated me.

I grabbed the person and twisted them, slamming them against the dirt. They had a small, thin frame—a woman? I'd learned not to worry too much about that when it came to potential espers, because size didn't mean a damn thing. A female esper could kill me just as fast as a male could.

And I had no intention of fucking around when it came to Yun's safety.

The new position—flat on their back and with my hand around their throat—put them in enough light for me to make sense of their face.

Yun.

My brain stalled. As much as people made fun of me for it not working at all, the truth was that it usually worked well enough. That wasn't the case right now. It seemed to fully shut down, like the view of Yun's wide, frightened eyes and my hand around her thin throat was enough to derail me. I couldn't work out that, couldn't believe it was true.

Until my all but useless mind stuttered to a rough start yet again and I wondered what the fuck I was doing.

I yanked backward, pulling away from her, hasty and frantic words falling from my lips. An apology? An explanation? I had no idea what they meant, but I still offered them like pointless gifts.

She rolled over and scooted backward in the dirt, putting space between us—space I didn't reclaim. Instead, I lifted my hands, palms out, trying to slow my own breathing just as much as reassure her.

Funny that I seemed just as thrown as her, like we both needed to sit down and take one big breath.

Until I focused my attention on her fully, ignoring my own hesitations, and realized we were actually *nothing* alike. While it threw me a bit, the way her heart raced, the rise in blood pressure, all the signs of stress on her body went to show she was in a significantly worse position.

So I pulled myself together, focusing instead on Yun. I crouched, then dropped to my knees. It had seemed to help before when I'd tried to look smaller, so maybe it would this time?

"I'm sorry," I said, keeping my voice quiet. "I didn't know it was you. I just saw someone at your window and thought someone was breaking in."

She lifted her gaze to mine, the dim light making her eyes look almost fully black. Worse, the small bit of light showed off darkness around her throat.

A bruise?

I gulped down a curse, not wanting to frighten her anymore by showing just how that bruise affected me. The last thing I'd ever want was to leave such an ugly mark on a guide—especially *this* guide.

"Why don't you try to slow down your breathing, huh?"

She narrowed her eyes, and that spark of anger did me some good, at least. It said she wasn't in a full blown panic attack. Sure, I'd fucked up, but seeing her crying and shaking would have been really fucking hard to stomach.

"Don't tell me how to breathe."

"Sorry," I said, rubbing a hand against the back of my neck. "I can just tell you're pretty close to passing out, and I figured you probably didn't want that to happen."

She didn't dare close her eyes, as though she needed to keep an eye on me, but she did try to draw air in and out slowly. The breathing was stilted, not nearly so smooth as I'd prefer, but better than nothing. After a long moment, her heart didn't race quite so fast and her blood pressure had dropped. Still elevated, but it didn't seem that she would lose consciousness now.

"I didn't hurt you," she said, voice soft.

"What?"

"You had your hand on my throat, but I didn't use my power against you."

"Oh." The stupid response had me recognizing for the first time that she was right. I'd heard exactly what this guide could do to an esper when she wanted, but I had no desire to see it firsthand. So why, when I had handled her so roughly, hadn't she done it to me? I'd been so focused on her that I'd entirely forgotten her ability to put me flat on my ass. "Maybe you like me?"

The way she tilted her head screamed that wasn't it, and I was dumber than she thought for suggesting it.

Which…was fair.

"I mean, not that you like me especially, more that maybe you knew I wouldn't actually hurt you. It's the difference between if *my* dog runs up to me barking or a strange dog does. I'm not gonna worry when it's my dog, but if it's a random dog, well, I might not trust that it won't bite me."

She said nothing at first, staring back at me as though working that idea through her head. It was a time when I wished I had Shear's ability, that I could peek inside her head and see what she thought about it. I wanted to understand her, and I knew damn well she wasn't intending to go exposing those secret parts of her mind.

I gave her the time to consider it, though I doubted she'd quite accept it.

Sure enough, she frowned. "I don't think that's it. I have no reason to think you wouldn't hurt me."

"Have I done it yet?"

"Everyone is innocent — until they aren't." She paused, her shoulders slumping. "Don't misunderstand me, please. I know that you — all of you — have taken good care of me. I am appreciative of that. I know that I could have had things much worse, and that's because of you all that I don't. I just don't want you thinking that means I'm going to forget everything I've experienced, everything I've learned."

"Can't you learn different things, though?"

She laughed, the sound quiet and full of pain. "No, I can't. Those lessons came at too high a price for me to ever risk having to learn them again. I suffered far too much for me to toss it all away and just hope things are different, hope *you're* all different."

Her words stilled me, made me think about what Shear had said before. Clearly, she had a past that wasn't good, one we didn't know about, one we could only guess about, and the whole not knowing thing was getting to me.

"What happened?" I found myself asking even if I knew damn well she wouldn't actually answer me. She held that secret so tight that nothing could pry it from her fingers, and even if we had our guesses, we didn't really know.

She didn't respond with an insult or a quick shut down — progress? — but instead stared down at her own hands as though she couldn't see them, like she stared at something else instead. Was it her past? Whatever horrors she'd gone through, was that where her mind took her?

"I'm not gonna judge you," I pressed when I wasn't sure she even really heard me anymore. "No matter what else is true, we're working together, right? That makes us a team, so I want to be able to help you, to understand you. I want to know what it is that's made you feel this way."

She shook her head, the motion soft and slow. "Why? What does that change? You knowing why I don't trust espers doesn't change that I don't trust you. If I let you poke around in my past, how does that make anything better? Last I checked, the great Reject Squad had plenty of their own past you all don't go around talking about, but you want me to do it?"

Did she think *that* was a good game to play? Too bad for her that I wasn't nearly so sensitive. "You want to know? You think that I care about telling you? I figured you already knew—everyone else does."

"They know the story, but the story isn't ever the truth."

"The truth is pretty simple. We were in The Pitt when it last opened, and we made a choice. We were told to do one thing, and we didn't follow those orders. Was it the right choice?" I shrugged. "I don't know, but I know it's the choice we could live with. It was the only choice I could make and still look at myself in the mirror. So we did that, and we lost everything because of it."

She listened to my words, not pulling away, not stopping me or calling me out on the vagueness of it. I *could* have given her more details, but that felt like making an excuse, like trying to pretty up the truth of what happened. At the end of the day, whether or not our choice was the moral one or the right one or anything else, we'd betrayed the Guild and done as we pleased. *That* was the reality, and I saw no good reason to dress it up, to paint ourselves as anything but the fuckups we were.

In the quiet that followed, I thought she wouldn't respond. Or maybe she'd tell me that I was an idiot for thinking that this was a tit-for-tat sort of deal. That was fair, as she hadn't agreed to some deal there. I couldn't really offer and expect her to just do as I wanted because I'd shared some.

"I don't want to go back to there," she said, her voice so quiet I had to strain to make out the words. "Do you know why I was sneaking out? Because I had another nightmare, another time when I had to go back there and relive it all again. The absolute last thing I want to do right now is talk about it. I want a break, to get to be free from it for at least a little while. I don't want to *feel* like that same person, to be trapped all over again." Her voice rose as she spoke, the words stronger at the end, the frustration clear enough that I didn't need to be a mentalist to hear it.

And I understood that better than I wanted to admit. There were times after everything that had happened in The Pitt when I wanted nothing more than a day off, then to not hear about it on the news, not get spat on by others, to just forget about it.

"You have nightmares that often?"

She nodded, then tucked her hair back behind her ear so it didn't fall into her face. "Every damn night I have them. It's like there's no way to escape it. And then I'm here, surrounded by espers, and the Guild needs so much, and they keep wanting to know how I can guide the way I do, and it's just all too much. It feels like everyone is taking a piece of me, yanking them away until I have nothing left. So, I'm sorry, maybe it isn't fair, but I just don't want to go back to that hell for a moment longer than I have to."

"I get it. I'm sorry, I didn't mean to push." And, worse, I really *did* feel bad about it. My curiosity was hardly sated, of course, but the last thing I'd wanted was to cause her *more* pain.

Which, to be fair, was *exactly* what I'd done. On purpose or not, I'd managed to throw her on the ground by her throat, terrify her, then ask her to talk about one of the most painful things she likely had ever experienced. My intent wasn't that important when I looked at what had come from it.

She shook her head, appearing suddenly smaller and far more tired than she had before. "It's not your fault. I know I got my nickname for a fair reason, and as much as I hate it, it fits. I shouldn't have been sneaking out, anyway."

"Want to take a walk? I can make sure you're safe if you want to clear your head."

She got to her feet, brushing the sand that had clung to her. "No, that's okay. I think I'll just go lie down." She headed toward the door, not giving me nearly as large a margin as I would have expected, before pausing. "And thank you."

I didn't get a chance to ask what the thank you was for — and it probably didn't really matter — before she disappeared back into the RV, leaving me out front on my own.

Which had me leaning back, wondering just how I'd screwed *this* up that badly.

And also had me thinking about how I could make it up to her...

Chapter Thirty-Nine

Yun

The marks on my neck ached, but not as badly as the span of color that rested on my back, across my shoulder blades. It went to show that no matter how much I wanted to think Kenyon was just a healer — and an idiot — he was more than strong enough to cause me problems. That fact always humbled me, the moment when I realized that even normal men could be such a danger to me.

After dealing with espers with superhuman strength and fantastical abilities, I hated the reminder that just regular male strength could so easily overpower me.

That wasn't what really got to me, though.

Why hadn't I reacted?

That question plagued me, keeping me up even after I'd returned to my own bed. I'd put espers on their asses for far less, yet I hadn't done that to him. Why not? What made him different?

Did I trust him?

That didn't seem likely. I refused to even entertain that, because of any option, any possibility, that one seemed the most dangerous. Me being so frightened as to not fight back, me being afraid of getting kicked out of another squad, those I could handle. The idea that I *trusted* these men, however?

That would lead to a lot more pain than I could handle, which meant I outright rejected the entire theory.

However, even without an answer, I couldn't avoid the situation, a point made clear as I walked with Ingram to one side, Shear to the other, Carter in front of us. Kenyon trailed behind, his expression sullen since he'd spotted me walking out of the RV about ten minutes previously. His gaze had landed on my throat, and he'd actually flinched, like a full-body rejection of the fact he'd done that.

"Where are we going?" I asked again, though didn't expect much more of an answer. Carter had that expression he wore when he was up to no good, and I had a feeling me asking too much would only please him, as though it all fall into the game he played.

Sure enough, Carter turned and glanced over his shoulder, a suspicious hop in his step. "We're going on an outing."

"An outing? I thought we had to stay here for training." Just the thought of another meeting with medical, another time where they asked me — again — how I'd guided as quickly as I had made me shudder.

"Do you really *want* to spend the day here?" he asked.

"Well, no, not especially."

"Then stop complaining," Ingram chimed in from beside me. "If you don't want to be here anyway, why would you bitch about leaving?"

"I don't want to get in trouble."

"We're always in trouble," Ingram pointed out. "If they're mad anyway, why the fuck does it matter? I mean, what are they going to do? Yell at us?" He snickered at the idea, as though he found it hilarious.

I didn't find getting yelled at nearly as fun as he did, clearly, but he had a point.

And to be honest, I really didn't want to be here. Going somewhere — *anywhere* — sounded amazing, so I stopped fighting it and followed them the rest of the short walk toward the outer edge of the compound.

It was huge, spread out over the vast desert, but lacked fences. No one in their right mind would dare attack a compound full of espers, after all, so security just wasn't an issue. It meant there was no large fence, no guards, nothing of the sort. When we reached the parking lot, I frowned.

We'd been driven here from the airport in a transport van with other espers. We didn't have a car.

I almost asked what we were going to do when Carter paused beside an SUV. After a quick glance around, he struck the window with his palm, the glass shattering as though he'd hit it with a battering ram rather than his hand. He reached in, unlocked the door, opened it, and brushed glass from the seat like it was nothing.

Ingram moved from my side and leaned into the car, crouching down beside it to look under the steering wheel.

"Wait, we can't steal this," I argued.

"Oh, sure we can," Carter said. "Ingram's done this lots of times." He leaned against the side of the car, his arms crossed, a crooked smile like some sort of delinquent trying to impress a girl.

And me? Well, I just never could stay quiet while people were being stupid. I reached in and flipped the visor down, a set of keys falling out and striking Ingram in the back of the head.

He cursed, then sat up, rubbing the spot. "Well, fuck."

"People are careful with keys when they're worried about theft. In a place like this, where all the cars are owned by the Guild, expediency is more important than safety. No one wants to be searching around for whoever has the keys later."

Ingram got up and snatched the keys from the floorboard where they'd fallen. "So you're smarter than you look," he said.

"That's not a nice thing to say," Kenyon snapped.

"You just think that because no one says it to you." Ingram's lips curled up on one side, the way the four interacted causing a sting in my chest.

The more I relaxed around them, the more comfortable I got, the more I recognized how close the four really were. It made me wonder what it would feel like to have that, to feel so connected to others. Even before everything had happened, back when I'd had a family, I doubted I'd ever felt like that. I'd had parents, of course, as much as I tried to forget about them. Remembering, going back to the years I'd been normal, those memories hurt. It only reminded me of everything I'd lost, so I pretended at times that it had never happened.

Staring at them, though, listening to the way they bickered with affection layered into the words, it made it more difficult to forget my life before it had all changed.

I recalled sitting down for dinner, the way the spice of the soup floated in the air, the easy, pointless conversation. I'd talk about my day—when I felt like it—and they'd smile and listen and ask questions. I remembered the comforting feeling of walking past the threshold of our apartment, the way it *felt* like home. The place had been small, decorated as cheaply as possible, but it had always been warm and welcoming. We hadn't had much, but it had still always made me feel safe.

Until it wasn't...

The juxtaposition between the life I'd had before and the one that had come after dizzied me. It made *everything* feel so uncertain, unsettled, like the ground could open up and swallow me down into the depths of it.

A hand touched my arm, a similar sense of calm washing over me. I glanced to my side to find Shear there, those eerie, bright blue eyes boring into my own. Strange that his powers, which normally I hated, managed to soothe me so well here. It gave me that same feeling I'd forced myself to forget.

I even managed to sag back, my knees weakening, Shear bracing me with the hand on my arm so I didn't end up on my ass. He didn't bring attention to the little mishap, instead opening the back door beside us so it appeared he simply helped me into the car.

My body went along with it, not so much my brain, and before I knew it, I had Shear to one side, Carter to the other, with Ingram driving and Kenyon upfront.

Right, just stealing a car, escaping a training base full of superhumans, with a group of espers.

When had my life gotten so damn weird?

Chapter Forty

Ingram

Every last time I looked at the woman across the table from me, my brain about shorted out and fucked right off. It was like she held some weird control over me, and I didn't even have it in me to try to fight. Fuck, I think I rather liked it. The world quieted down, that gnawing, all-consuming pain inside of me, went dormant in a way it *never* did normally.

Even the things I did to fill it, to quiet it, only hushed it for such a short time I wondered if it were useful at all. The moment it was over, the moment the tattoo gun stopped running or I pulled out of a willing body, it all started right back up, demanding more, never satiated, never enough.

Except with her.

I hadn't even gotten my dick *into her*, but my body had stayed quiet and happy all damn night. It even went back to that same place when I looked at her, like she'd tamed it into a fucking little puppy to wag its tail at her feet. Just how the fuck had she managed to do what nothing else ever had?

It was only when she narrowed her eyes like a challenge that I realized I stared at her. Then again, that sure as fuck was my preferred reaction. I *liked* that she didn't wilt, that she stood toe-to-toe with me even when terrified. I liked that she snapped, that despite the way she'd tremble, she didn't back down.

And just like that, I was hard again, the memory of her scent in that room, the guiding that had happened just from being close to her. I groaned and shifted in my seat, trying to get a little more comfortable.

"Could you try *not* popping a boner in a nice restaurant like this?" Carter asked with a bright smile on.

"Like you're any better," I snapped back.

"Want to come check?" Carter actually batted his lashes at that, like he was flirting with me. I knew better than to trust anything that came out of the consummate liar's mouth — and never to put anything in there, either. Anyone who would trust that man with their dick was an idiot and had far too much faith in others.

"I want table-side guac," Kenyon said, telling me he hadn't been paying any attention to the conversation. Not exactly a surprise — he rarely followed along with any conversation unless he found a reason to. "And a strawberry margarita."

"What are you, a teen girl?" I asked when he suggested the dumb choice, as though I weren't used to this nonsense from him.

Kenyon shrugged, not the least bit bothered. "What? They're good."

"Little girls drink flavored drinks like that. Men drink liquor."

"You took a sip of my margarita last time and you loved it!"

"I was already drunk! I would have loved random stickiness licked off the floor by that point."

Kenyon snorted softly. "Don't worry, I'll share my drink if you want."

I didn't bother to argue with him over it—no point. Arguing with Kenyon was like kicking a dog—no one learned anything from it and it was just mean.

The server—a pretty girl in her twenties with hair so red it was clearly dyed—came to the table. "Sorry for the wait—we've been really busy."

In reality, it had only been a few minutes. Of course, we often got pretty good service when we went out. Espers, even those who didn't flaunt what they were, got noticed. It wasn't even just our appearance that caused it, but something else, something deeper. It was like humans could still *feel* the corruption that had become a part of us. It should have signaled danger, but often drew interest along with it. I had to imagine it was like watching a tiger or a cobra—humans were fascinated by that which could kill them.

"What can I get you all?" Her voice was upbeat and friendly, balancing on the line between professional and flirting. Whether she did that for tips or because she was actually interested, I had no idea.

Of course, before, I would have jumped all over that option. How many servers had given me at least a short reprieve? In a dark corner, a bathroom, a maintenance closet. Location didn't matter, because I could get exactly as creative as I needed to.

So why was it when she leaned in closer to me, when a glance down her shirt revealed a lacy bra, I felt exactly nothing? No heat, no desire, no clawing need that made me desperate to get her somewhere private.

Or not private at all. I'd never minded an audience, after all. I didn't give a fuck if people watched, and in fact enjoyed that particular kink from time to time.

This time, however, I didn't feel that need. She struck me about as appetizing as an overcooked, cold steak. Nothing about her called to me, even though on the surface, I couldn't deny she was pretty enough, that on paper, she had everything I needed.

So why the fuck wasn't I interested?

The answer sat across the table, ordering a water rather than anything with alcohol, seemingly oblivious to my confusion.

Girl had no idea the chaos she caused, did she?

The server took the orders and left, returning fast enough that it was clear she was going to be giving us the lion's share of her attention during our meal. Of course, the way she responded to Yun was a far cry from the rest of us.

We got smiles and lingering glances — Yun got water in a cup with a big ol' smudge on it.

Kenyon took the glass and wiped it clean with his napkin, then pushed it back over to her. "You know, you could have had an actual drink."

"I don't drink," she said.

"Why the fuck not?" I asked, voice sharp even if I knew I should have eased it a bit.

At least she didn't flinch, instead giving me one of those heated glares that blurred the line between hatred and sexual attraction. "I don't like to feel out of control."

"Yeah, well, in my opinion you'd do well to be far *looo* controlled."

She pressed her lips together, frustration etched across her lovely features. "What does it matter to you?"

"Just figured if you got that stick out of your ass, you'd be a bit more fun to be around." I shrugged, lifting my glass of tequila to my lips.

"I'm not *not* fun. I'm sorry that not all of us can be out there drinking and whoring."

"Well, you *could be*, but instead you choose this bullshit."

"What bullshit?"

"Prudish, hates everyone, untrusting bullshit, that's what."

"Knock it off," Carter said, his voice somehow friendly despite the clear threat there. It was always impressive the way he could both sound terrifying and cordial at the same time. "This isn't why we took her out today."

Yun sat up straighter at that. "Why did you take me out, then?"

And just like that, we all froze like we'd gotten caught. Leave it to one scrap of a female to put a group of dangerous espers in our places, our gazes all down to not make eye contact.

"You told them, huh?" Her question could have been to anyone, but the way Kenyon responded said he knew *exactly* who she meant.

"I just said you were a little stressed." His words came out sullen and apologetic. "Figured a day away from the compound would do you well. Stress isn't good on the body, you know."

I could almost *hear* her grinding her molars at that, a pretty good indication she didn't agree. Or, at least, that she didn't want to have everyone in her business.

Which I got. Carter and Kenyon had some idea of why I acted the way I did, but only Shear had gotten a first row seat to it. Only he knew exactly how fucked up I really was, only he'd gotten to experience it at it's worse. I wasn't all that interested in broadcasting it, so I understood why she might not love it, either.

"Yeah, well, you suck," Yun muttered, words soft and angry, before she reached out, across the table to snag my glass of tequila right from my hand. She tipped it back, downing one hell of a large gulp, followed by a cough that Kenyon tried to help by hitting his palm against her back. Once she'd ended the coughing fit, she didn't slow at all, swallowing two more gulps that finished the entire glass.

She slammed it against the table, her gaze locked on me like one hell of a challenge.

And it seemed like my erection was going exactly nowhere anytime soon.

Chapter Forty-One

Carter

The way Yun went from sitting up straight to leaning against the table happened so quickly that it was like I blinked and she was down for the count.

Then again, she'd downed that tequila in just a few big gulps, and she was hardly above a hundred pounds, so it wasn't a shock that she might not handle her liquor that well. Ingram normally sipped the stuff, taking his time to finish it off, sticking to one for the whole night. No one needed a blackout-drunk esper, after all. We could cause problems all on our own — reducing our mental faculties wasn't a great idea.

I recalled the time when we were still at Diamond, and another squad had managed to smuggle in a bottle of vodka. They'd drunk to their little stupid hearts' content and had managed to level an entire dormitory. It had taught me that drinking that much was a horrible idea.

Occasionally alcohol could help me with others, but more often than not, it simply made people unpredictable, which was the last thing I wanted. I'd much prefer to be able to predict them, to know what they might do and guard against it. Drunkenness caused people to act in ways they never would otherwise.

Much like Yun, who hadn't seemed this comfortable in her entire time around us.

Her cheek rested against the wood of the table, as though the coolness helped her flushed skin. She smiled, listening to the conversation between Ingram and Kenyon about whether a bear or a gorilla would win in a fight as though that were the most interesting conversation she'd ever heard.

Her plate of food had been pushed forward, out of her way, after she'd eaten a few bites of the cheese enchiladas. I would have preferred she eat more, but she hadn't seemed to have any more interest. Pushing someone to eat after drinking that much often didn't go well, and she seemed content enough just to listen.

Did she enjoy hearing such an idiotic conversation that much? It made no sense to me, but her gaze bounced back and forth, following the two men and their inane comments about everything like it fascinated her.

It made me stare and try to work out what went on in her mind. Was she that happy just to be here? What I'd found with her thus far was that she wanted connection. It terrified her, but that didn't stop her from craving it. I'd watch the way her expression changed when she'd witness any of us bickering back and forth, as though there was some enviable closeness between us that she desperately wished she could experience.

And yet, even if it were right before her, her own fears kept her from reaching out and placing herself inside that, keeping her on the sidelines to watch with that same longing.

Kenyon paused as he looked to the side, noticing that Yun no longer sat upright. His gaze moved over her, his powers taking in her state, evaluating it in a fraction of the time it would take anyone else. The way he nodded said he'd found nothing seriously wrong — just drunkenness, no doubt.

"You look tired," he said, his voice soft and kind.

At least he'd actually talked to her. Since their little run in the night before, he'd kept her at a bit of a distance. Then again, if I'd left bruises like that on someone, I think even I would feel guilty no matter how unintended they were. I knew what had happened, didn't blame him, but it would still hang on him more than most. He was just such a bleeding heart that the thought of causing harm to a guide would stick harder with him.

Yun turned her head slightly to see him, with that same smile on her sweet lips that made her appear softer overall. Damn did that do things to me, the way it was so unlike her usual edges, the way she typically seemed ready to take on the entire world by sheer will. It wasn't that I preferred her this way so much as I enjoyed witnessing something about her that I doubted she showed to many people.

"A little." Even her answering that without a cutting jab went to show the tequila running through her system had altered her behavior. She sat up, then put her palms on the table and pushed herself to her feet.

She teetered, swaying side to side, but kept her balance due to the table. "I have to go to the bathroom."

She didn't wait for anyone to give her permission or tell her where it was, instead stumbling off in a direction that I was pretty damn sure the bathroom wasn't. I already considered having to rescue her and help her find the way. Before I had to do that, however, her feet caught up on nothing but each other, and she toppled.

If she'd pulled this anywhere else, she'd have ended up flat on her face. She didn't even attempt to catch herself, to break the fall using her arms, too drunk to maneuver her body in a useful way. Fortunately for her, she stood beside a table full of espers, and I was faster than her drunken ass. I caught her, my chair falling back and striking the floor.

Fuck the chair, though. Let the whole damn place look at us — I didn't care.

I expected her to yank away, to curse at me for touching her — even if it was for her own good. Instead, when I stared down at her face, she looked back at me with the sweetest expression I'd ever seen, her pretty lips tipped up in a charming, confused smile.

Which went straight to places on me I doubted she wanted anything to do with. The fact that she would give me that look, it shoved me over the line of sanity and had me picturing a future so different from anything I'd had before. I saw her living in our home, not as a temporary measure but permanently. I pictured her smiling like that when we got home, being actually happy to see me, to see us, instead of that trepidation she normally wore.

It made me think maybe she was getting better, maybe we were making progress. Maybe that picture I had in my head could actually happen.

At least until she twisted her head to the side and promptly threw up on me.

Well… that's something.

Chapter Forty-Two

Carter

I stepped out of the shower after washing off, having sent my clothes down to get cleaned in the hotel that sat across the street from the Mexican restaurant we'd eaten at. With Yun in her condition, I saw no reason to drag her ass back to the compound tonight, figuring letting her sleep the tequila off was a far better plan. Besides, I didn't want to make that trip covered in her puke, either. We'd taken the penthouse suite of the fancy hotel, giving us enough room for us to all sleep comfortably.

Well, as comfortably as we could in tight quarters with Yun.

She napped in the master bedroom where I'd left her, while I showered in the attached bathroom. I trusted the others, but not enough to leave a drunken Yun with them. Or maybe it was just selfishness that had me wanting her close.

The towel hung low on my hips, tied there to keep me somewhat covered. I'd have walked around without a stitch if I didn't think she'd react rather poorly to that. Room service would bring my clothes, once cleaned, back to the room, which left me stuck until then. The steam rolled from the bathroom when I opened the door, my hair damp, having been only towel dried well enough so that it wouldn't drip.

The idea of leaving Yun for longer than I had to felt entirely bad. It made my skin itch, made me uneasy, drawing me back toward her.

Was that because she was our guide? Was it more?

Fuck, did I *want* it to be more?

That answer was pretty damn obvious, wasn't it?

My chest tightened when my gaze landed on the bed to find Yun no longer lying down, snoring and sleeping soundly. Instead, she sat up, wrestling around like something attacked her.

The villain in question?

Her shirt. She yanked at it, twisting her frame in ways that made my body ache. "Hot," she muttered.

Stripping her down wasn't a great idea, but neither was letting this go on. If she kept on with her epic battle against her shirt, she'd end up falling off the bed and hurting herself.

I went over and set my hands on her arms, hoping she wouldn't decide to scramble my brain for the help. "You're going to fall," I warned, hoping my voice helped her relax, as though knowing it was me might calm her down.

"It's hot," she complained again, jerking hard, locked inside the fabric like a little self-made prison. The fabric muffled her words.

The entire situation drew a chuckle before I grasped the hem of her shirt and helped strip it off her. I never expected that getting a girl out of her clothes could be *this* unsexy, but Yun's absurd behavior made it so. The strangest thing about it, though, was how endearing I found that. Seeing this side of her, a part she'd never willingly show to us, it had me far more interested than simply spreading her legs would have.

"What are you doing?" Kenyon snapped from the doorway, his voice far angrier than was typical for the usually easygoing man. "She's *drunk*."

"I'm not doing anything," I pressed. "She's hot." At that, I sighed. "I don't mean it like that. I mean literally, she says she's hot and was rolling around to get her shirt off."

I had no reason to explain anything else since Yun took that chance to lean back and work at the button of her pants. She lifted her hips in a way that wasn't quite so childlike as her other actions, and the exposure of her bare stomach, the way the points of her hips shown through the gapping space of the zipper was far more adult.

She'd kept herself covered most of the time, which meant this was my first chance to get a good look at her. She didn't pose, didn't try to look sexy, and somehow that all hit me so much harder. She had a slim build, which I'd known already, but it had never felt as obvious as right now. A basic black bra still covered her, the fabric pulled across her entire chest rather than two individual cups. It was far from seductive, but fuck if it didn't give me the same general feeling. Matching black panties peeked out through the exposed area where she'd unzipped her pants, her shoes already off since I'd removed them when I'd put her into the bed.

The underwear was practical, like Yun, and I never thought I had a kink for the practical, but look at that…

Kenyon sighed and came over, Ingram and Shear peeking in through the doorway. "Yun, you don't want to get naked here, do you?"

"It's hot," she complained again. "I feel hot all over."

I let my head drop back, closed my eyes and rubbed my hands over my face, trying to get my brain to work.

She was drunk. I wasn't about to fucking jump on her when she wasn't anywhere near in her right mind. I might have been a shit person, but that was *way* too far.

Something touched my bare stomach, drawing my attention back, making me wonder why Kenyon was manhandling me like that. To my shock, I found Yun's small hands tracing the valleys and rises of my stomach, the muscles there, like they fascinated her.

"Whoa, now," I said, all those things I'd just told myself a lot more challenging. "I'm pretty sure this isn't what you want to do."

"Why not? Isn't it what you want?" Her words were soft and slightly slurred, her gaze on her work rather than up on my face, like I was just a toy for her. "It's what espers *always* want."

"Yeah, but not when you're drunk."

"It's easier when I'm drunk."

"Easy isn't that important to me. I just know exactly what you can do and don't really want to deal with you pissed off tomorrow when you wake up sober and angry."

She blinked slowly, curling her fingers over my skin. "Do you know how much I've thought about this? It's just quiet inside my head right now, so I can."

And, yeah, fuck, *that* proved so much harder to reject. There was this sweetness in her voice, this longing that I understood pretty well. If it were up to me, I would have probably given in right then and there. How could someone reject a girl in that state? Who would possibly just give that up and tell her no when she pleaded so prettily?

It seemed Kenyon could, since he stepped closer and caught her chin, turning her face so she focused on him rather than me. It didn't stop the way she traced my abs, of course, but she locked her gaze on Kenyon. "Hey there," he said in that gentle way he spoke.

"Please?" Her fingers moved down to run along the edge of my towel, the touch downright scandalous.

Kenyon's gaze darted over to catch what she was up to, his fingers flexing to hold her chin a bit tighter. "I can't sober you up entirely, but I *can* clear your head for a minute."

The electric feeling in the air said he was using his powers, helping her to think clearer, to lessen some of the fog from the alcohol. He couldn't fully remove it, since the alcohol was still in her system, but he could at least reduce the effects for a short while.

Yun blinked quickly, some of that wariness returning to her gaze, and damn I missed the sweet innocence, the desire without fear. I much preferred that, even if it was caused by the liquor.

"Better?" Kenyon asked before removing his hand from her chin. "It won't last more than a few minutes, but it should help you get some of your senses back."

"What if I don't want them back?" Her words were still soft, less certain, but they held sanity that she'd lacked before. When no one responded, she went on. "I don't want to feel like this, okay? I don't want to keep questioning everything, to have to doubt myself. Why can't it just be easy? Why can't my head be clouded so I can just be normal for a little while?"

Kenyon turned his gaze toward me, unsure.

Ingram came in, but he didn't touch her, didn't crowd her. "You know what you're asking for, don't you? Last thing I want is for you to come to tomorrow and start playing the victim, hating us for any of this."

She nodded, her hair falling forward to obscure her eyes. "I know. I know what I'm asking for, okay? Like we didn't realize it was going to go this way eventually, I mean, *you* said that yourself, Ingram. So if it's going to happen, why can't I use a little extra liquid courage, huh?" She shot the words like bullets, voice quiet but strong, gaze down.

I exchanged a loaded glance with Kenyon, Ingram and Shear, the question we all faced.

Sure, we fucking wanted this. Who wouldn't? And she was clearheaded at the moment, so maybe that was the okay we needed? But, fuck, a part of it felt bad…

The idea that to do this she needed to be drunk, that didn't settle well. Would agreeing just make this shit all the more difficult later? Would it give her reason to distrust us later? To run? To shove us further away?

I liked my plans, even if I never seemed that on top of them to others, so going into this having no real idea if it would get us closer to or farther from our goal wasn't my favorite idea ever.

She dipped two fingers beneath the edge of my towel, the action loosening the terrycloth until the tuck job I'd done gave up the good fight. It left the towel covering me only because her hand held it, like some white flag between us.

"Please?" she asked again before dropping the towel, letting it fall to the ground as though it didn't matter anymore, like it had done its job and was useless now.

And just like that, I knew we'd lost. No matter what other plans we had, what reservations about it, Yun's sweet little please took all the control. She'd been so afraid that we'd control her, that she'd wilt beneath us, but when push came to shove, when it came right down to it, look what happened.

She wrested all the control right away from us.

"You'd better not regret this," I said, forgoing that jovial attitude I usually put on, letting her see the truth beneath the mask I usually wore. "Because *you* started this."

Chapter Forty-Three

Yun

The wave of confusion hit me again, numbing the fear and pain inside me. It still existed, that edge I'd lived with since The Pitt, but the alcohol helped it to drift to the background. Instead of a bear tearing through my world, it was like one locked away inside a cage.

Close enough it could endanger me, close enough I could hear it, but still held apart so I could try to ignore it.

That moment of sobriety, where Kenyon had removed the fog, had terrified me. It had forced me to acknowledge what I'd known from the moment I'd drunk that alcohol.

I wasn't an idiot—I'd known exactly what I was doing when I'd done that. Sitting there with them, hearing them, spending more time with them, it made me acknowledge just how much I wanted more. I recalled the look other guides got, this wistful expression when they thought about how much they enjoyed guiding, how much pleasure it brought them.

Was that really what guiding was supposed to be? And I'd simply been denied it because of all I'd gone through? That thought plagued me more and more as I spent time with these men, as I wondered what exactly I'd missed out on.

So I'd said yes, using every bit of my courage in those moments before the wonderful haze took me again, when the tequila kept everything else at bay.

Once it did, the world felt quieter, smoother, as though all the hard, sharp edges had been filed down.

Carter still hadn't moved, now entirely naked, and for the first time I gave myself over to curiosity.

Men were strange to me, so different from myself and something I'd never really gotten the chance to explore. I hooked my fingers around his waist and pulled him closer, until his knees touched the edge of the mattress and nothing kept me from him. He didn't object, didn't try to hide himself, to keep anything from me.

His body fascinated me, each hard line of it, the scars that covered him. Espers scarred still, just less often, and they were less noticeable than on humans. It meant that while a human might have ended up a gnarled mess, Carter only carried light raised lines no matter how dramatic the injury. Being combat, he took more damage than the others, and it showed on his body.

I traced the history of those wounds, wondering how he'd gotten each. It was so easy to see espers as powerful and dangerous, but he had earned each of these fighting monsters, protecting civilians. Before I knew what I was doing, I leaned forward and followed one line with my tongue. It started at his hip, then moved across his lower stomach and down to the junction of his leg. His skin was still damp from his shower, and the scent of something floral clung to him — probably the body wash from the hotel.

He released a groan that vibrated so I could feel it through my tongue, my lips.

A hand ran down my back, and without turning my head, I knew it was Kenyon. While It might have set me off before, the alcohol did its job and dulled those old fears, so I arched into it instead, begging for more with my body.

While I touched Carter and Kenyon teased me, another sensation took over — guiding. The movement of corruption from the men to me, a steady flow of it that I didn't have to try to pull, didn't need to think about. The connection that physical touch had given us made it even easier, even more effective than before.

It made me dizzier than the alcohol, forging this string between us more powerful than anything I'd felt before.

Well...once...

The memory sat at the periphery of my mind, as though it — and he — watched me through that darkness, mocking me, laughing at me, taunting me.

"Stay here." Shear's voice in my head helped to anchor me, seeming to rush away those memories before they could take hold. I couldn't even find any anger with him over it, so I allowed it.

Kenyon leaned in further, moving behind me, his large hands grasping the bottom of my bra and waiting. For permission? He got it when I lifted my arms and pulled back from Carter long enough for Kenyon to remove the clothing.

I didn't lean back toward Carter, though, because he came forward this time as though drawn by the loss of my heat. Kenyon scooted backward on the bed, his large hands grasping my waist and pulling me with him until I rested between his spread thighs, my back to his broad, hard chest, and Carter perched between my legs.

I was hopelessly surrounded by these men, and yet I couldn't find any fear inside me. Not even when Carter curled his fingers into the waist of my pants along with my underwear and tugged them down my legs, stripping me of everything else.

No one had *ever* seen me like this, so defenseless, entirely naked.

Of course, these men had seen countless women in such a state, a fact that nearly had me trying to cover myself, until I let myself look into Carter's gaze.

Pure, unadulterated desire rested there, and he dragged his tongue across his lips as though he could already taste me there, like he was so hungry for me that he couldn't bring himself to wait even a moment longer. Any nerves I'd had, any fears about my appearance died with that move.

"Fucking hell," Ingram said as the bed dipped beneath his weight to my left, his words as filthy as his mind, no doubt. "She's about the prettiest little disaster I've ever seen." The words weren't sweet, but they were honest, and they got me all the same.

Shear said nothing, but those blue eyes of his bore into me, as though he hardly saw my skin, like my tits and my cunt meant nothing compared to everything else he could glimpse. He sat next to Ingram, the two close as they always were, nearly touching.

Carter stretched out his body until he lay flat on his stomach, his face a breath from my exposed pussy. "Remember, Yun, you were the one who asked for this." The words made me think he'd dive in, that he'd overwhelm me from the start, which left me startled when instead, he dragged his fingers up, just to the left of my cunt, with a touch so soft it tickled. It felt like offering me a taste of something to get me desperate.

Which seemed a stupid idea as I was already beyond desperate. It was like all those years of self-denial, all the years when I'd thought myself broken and damaged beyond repair, collapsed in the face of that one touch.

He repeated it on the other side until I arched my hips to *try* to get him where I wanted.

"How long has it been?" Kenyon asked, his lips brushing my ear as he spoke in a whisper.

How long? At first I couldn't understand the question, between the needs of my body and the tequila. Then it hit me, and I flushed, the heat spreading down my face, my throat, my chest. I didn't want to admit the truth, worried they'd somehow turn me down.

"That long?" Carter asked with a chuckle, blowing warm air against my folds as he laughed.

"Years?" Kenyon pressed. "Just want to make sure we're careful with you, so we need to know."

I wanted to keep the answer to myself, but something about the teasing way Carter kept stroking me just outside of where I wanted, the warmth of Kenyon's body behind mine, the heated gaze of Ingram's and Shear's unnerving eyes had my lips parting and the truth spilling out. "Never."

Just like that, it all stopped, like the collective air had gotten removed, like all four men existed in a vacuum, unable to move or speak. That one word had stopped it all, and I cursed myself for the stupidity of it.

Had I just ruined my one shot?

Chapter Forty-Four

Kenyon

"Never." The word that slipped from Yun was so unexpected that I went entirely still.

Never? It was like I couldn't come to terms with that, didn't understand it, refused to believe it. She was nearly thirty, and a guide. *Never?* How could that even happen?

Suddenly the idea of touching her felt almost wrong, sacrilegious. Had I ever even been with a virgin? That wasn't really my thing, since I'd always known it was temporary. I'd never seen how a person could fit into our lives, so I wouldn't want to sleep with a virgin, to take that, yet here I was, with Yun, in such a position?

And while she was drunk?

It felt like we'd tripped right into a minefield we'd never seen coming.

I looked past her, at Carter, who had gone just as still.

"Never?" Carter asked. "You're telling me you're a virgin?"

Yun tried to sit up, those defenses of hers alive and well, it seemed. However, sandwiched between us, she didn't have room to do much. "Never mind."

"Don't pull that shit," Ingram said, his voice harsh as ever. "How the fuck can you still be a virgin? As a guide?"

She nailed him with a look that said the alcohol could not only make her sweet but also just as feisty as ever. "If you don't want to do this, fine."

"We never said that," Carter said. "Just trying to make sure we've got it clear. I get it, you've never had sex. Just how far have you gone?"

Yun turned her face away from Carter, to the other side away from Ingram and Shear as well. I might not have been that smart, but even I could understand exactly what that look meant.

My cock ached with the realization that everything we did to this woman, we would be the first—and fucking last if I had my way—to touch her. Each kiss, each touch, each taste would be what no one else had ever had, how no one else had ever seen her. That astounded me, seemed impossible, and yet it made me ravenous in a way I hardly recognized.

Sure, sex felt good, but I'd never been desperate for it. I'd never felt some huge drive like Ingram did, where I needed it.

At least, not until now.

"Well then, I guess this'll be extra special for you," Carter said, a playful tone to his voice that hardly covered the hunger resting in those words. I knew him well enough to read it, to hear what he tried so hard to hide from Yun, to keep from scaring her.

He followed that up by pressing his palms to her thighs and leaning in, swiping his tongue up her pussy, no longer playing the teasing game. He lessened the touch at her clit, but used his hands to keep her still. The sight enraptured me, and I found myself unwilling to look away, instead pressing my lips to her throat, teasing her pulse with my kisses.

Carter moved his hands in, using his thumbs to spread her pussy before he explored her folds with his tongue, eating her out with a single-minded focus he usually reserved for fighting. Yun's moans said it worked perfectly well for her.

Ingram reached out, cupping her breast with one of his tattoo-covered hands, the difference between her flawless, pale skin and his colorful, ink-coated skin beautiful. He used the tips of his fingers to tease her nipples until they hardened beneath his touch, until she bent forward, seeking more but not knowing what exactly that might mean.

Unable to help it, I pulled her tighter to me to add friction to my cock, letting me roll my hips up to feel as though I fucked her—even if it was just the space between her body and my own.

Added to the physical sensations, to the view, was the guiding. The corruption flowed from me, toward Yun, through where we touched, leaving voids in their wake. Lust filled all the now empty spaces inside me, creating a cycle that grew that need. Each touch drew more corruption from me and into her, and each new void filled with desire until I couldn't separate them at all anymore.

It made me twist just enough, using my hand on her cheek to turn her face toward mine, to steal her first kiss. I should have taken it easy, gone slowly, but I lacked the ability. Instead, I devoured her with that kiss, slipping my tongue past her lips, claiming her in a way I'd never wanted to do before.

And Yun, for all her inexperience and hang-ups, met me all the way. She didn't wilt, taking just as much as she gave, whimpered moans leaving her for me to swallow down. She gasped, drawing a laugh from me.

Poor girl had no idea how to breathe while kissing, did she? It reminded me of all the things I wanted to teach her, that I wanted to do with her, that I wanted to show her.

Ingram leaned forward, slipping into the space between us, but he didn't claim her lips as I had. Instead, he dragged his tongue across her pebbled nipple, the one he'd already teased into a point.

Yun reached out and slid her fingers through his hair, pinning him to her as though afraid he'd escape.

It was only then I realized that he'd stripped down, just like Carter. It left Shear the only entirely dressed one, since I'd undone my pants at least, and rarely wore a shirt at home. Seeing the others like that was hardly new, and especially with Ingram, given his tattoos, he hardly ever seemed naked.

He reached for his cock, wrapping his hand around it with a low, frustrated sound that said he wasn't getting all he wanted.

Me either, buddy.

Still, he focused his attention on her, just like Carter.

Yun threw her head back, nearly smacking me in the face. I avoided it, so she rested the back of her head against my shoulder, her stomach muscles tensing as she tried to roll her hips. Carter's strong grasp kept her still, however, and he never let up as he licked and sucked at every inch of her cunt. He teased her folds, dipped his tongue inside, then licked across her hard clit.

Even still, he kept her on the edge, seeming content to tease her, to edge her rather than let her come.

"Just do it," Yun panted, shoving the words through her teeth. "Stop playing around."

Carter paused his focus, looking up her body and into her eyes. "Do what?"

"You know what."

"Do I?" He nipped at the inside of her thigh, leaving a tiny red mark in his wake. "I mean, you could mean so many things. You'll need to be more specific, I think."

"Aren't you going to fuck me?" she finally said, the words clearly spawned from the tequila, as most bad decisions were.

He laughed, the sound making it seem as though he did really care — though his eyes told a very different story. "No, Yun, we aren't going to be doing that today."

"Why not?"

He smirked, the lopsided grin full of mischief. "When we finally fuck you, sweetheart, you're going to be completely sober. I want to hear you begging us for it, want you to dream of it beforehand, want you so ready for it that you're dripping wet and squirming and crying for it."

A full shudder ran through Yun, as though she could picture it already, and I knew that resisting her tonight was going to take everything I had.

Chapter Forty-Five

Ingram

This fucking girl was going to be the death of me. Normally, she silenced that void inside of me. She forced it under, let me control myself, but right now? I felt no control at all.

I stroked my cock, but it wasn't enough, not nearly. That voice inside me that always wanted more screamed between my temples, made me desperate to sink into her. I wanted all of her, more, everything. I sucked on her nipple, teasing it with my lips, scraping it with my teeth, but it just wasn't enough.

I got Carter's point, even agreed with it in a totally hypothetical way, but in reality?

It fucking sucked.

I wanted nothing more than to sink into her tight heat, to feel the way her cunt would wrap around my cock, to fuck her until I could fill her with my seed. Fuck, a part of me even wanted to knock her up even if

I knew damn well it wasn't possible, if I knew I couldn't do that.

Something touched my cock, and at first, I thought it was her. Was she reaching for me? The idea had me pulling back, away from her. Except, it wasn't. Yun remained where she had been, and instead Shear had reached from the side and wrapped his cool palm against my cock, teasing the places where the barbells sat along the bottom edge.

It was far from the first time he'd touched me like this, but it *was* the first time we had an audience for it.

Still, I wasn't about to tell him to stop, not when I so badly wanted to fuck Yun and knew I couldn't. Shear's hand was a hell of a lot better than my own.

So I leaned back in and raked my teeth across Yun's nipple as Shear stroked me.

The mixing of stimuli, the sensation of not only Shear's hand but the guiding from Yun, the lust as that corruption shifted through me, out of me, had me on edge already. Sure, I was hungry, wanted more, but it wasn't quite that gnawing need of before. This felt almost normal.

The sweet moans that left Yun's lips drove me deeper, higher. They were quiet, as though she tried to hold them back but couldn't. It was the nice thing about alcohol, that ability to let go — or rather the inability to hold on. She sounded like the classical music that Carter liked to put on from time to time, something I almost felt more than heard, something that reached deeper than anything else.

I released her nipple to take her lips, wanting to feel something different, wanting to taste those sounds she made. She didn't keep from me, parting her lips and slipping her tongue into the heat of my mouth, teasing my own tongue, having me groan as it all overwhelmed me. The idea that she'd never done this revved me up all the more.

She moved with clumsy motions, a clear indicator that she hadn't lied about that. Some women liked to pretend to be a virgin, playing up their innocence, thinking it tempted men. The way Yun's teeth hit mine, the way she broke the kiss to gasp in air, it all said this was new to her, that she had no idea what she was doing, that instinct alone drove her forward.

Yun arched her back, her fingers grasping and digging into my arm so hard that her blunt little nails broke skin as she came and she whimpered out a broken, desperate little sound past my lips.

I'd seen her come before, back in the RV, but I hadn't gotten to touch her back then. I'd felt more removed, just a witness to something instead of a participant. I broke the kiss to see the flush on her cheeks, the way she panted hard with every breath, the rapid rise and fall of her bare chest.

She was beautiful. No, more than that, more than any of the stupid fucking words I'd ever had before, that I could hold on to or utter. She was something greater than anything else, the thing I'd strived for but never could find before, the thing I searched for, that I craved but couldn't identify.

Then she was gone, had moved so quickly that I bared my teeth in frustration.

Kenyon had flipped her, moving her light form until she was on all fours in front of him. For a moment, I feared he'd take it too far, that he'd do something we'd already said he wouldn't.

The worry was ill-founded, however, as he slipped his cock between her thighs, then tapped her leg. "Keep them tight."

Yun did as he said, squeezing her legs together to allow Kenyon to fuck the tight space between them, his large hands grasping her hips making her look somehow even smaller.

Carter leaned back, watching, as though the sight alone got him off.

Then again, maybe it did. Who knew what that twisted, secretive fucker thought?

Right then, something hot and soft moved up the underside of my cock, the familiar sensation enough to get me to release a gasping, shuddering breath. Shear's black hair obscured my view, but I'd recognize his tongue anywhere, the way his lips played across the Jacob's ladder piercings that adorned the length of my cock.

While this was usually done when I needed it, when my body and his mind were so out of sorts we couldn't regulate any other way, *this time* felt oddly different. Even if the touch was similar, neither of us felt as broken as usual.

Or, fuck, maybe I was being stupid and romantic with all the guiding.

I rested on my knees, spreading my thighs to give him access and room, letting my head fall back and surrendering to the feeling, the scents in the room, to it all. Sure, I'd fucked guides with the others before. It shouldn't have felt new, but fuck…it did.

This felt so different, as though Yun had a compatibility with us that I had never experienced before. She moved with us, made me feel as though she connected us in a way we'd never been before. She served as a bridge to bind us together, to cross the inevitable distance between us.

Fuck, it was like she was the water around us, like we were islands and she gave us a way to reach the others.

I shook my head, hating the way I'd just gone fucking romantic and philosophical.

How fucking embarrassing.

At least until the bed shifted, and I forced my eyes open again to find not just Shear leaning down before me, but Yun as well.

So, this is what kills me in the end?

Chapter Forty-Six

Yun

Each time Kenyon thrust forward, his body slammed against mine, and his cock stroked along my clit. I arched my back to ensure he rubbed harder against that one perfect spot. That startled me more than anything else, how quickly I gave in to this, to them, to the feelings. I wanted to blame it on the alcohol, and sure, that probably played a part, but it was so much more than that.

And so much less.

It was the overwhelming instinct inside me. It was the sparks of pleasure in my body, the things I didn't think I was capable of feeling. It confused me, changing what I'd always believed. I'd thought myself broken, thought that I'd been shattered so fully that I would never be able to feel this way, to want this, to enjoy this. I'd given up before ever trying, but here I was, entirely enthralled by the touch of each of them. Even the guiding added to it, made me lose myself deeper in this sensation.

In this moment there was no room for my past, for the horrors I'd lived through, none of that.

My gaze found a sight before me that stopped all that noise in my head, all the confusion. Shear crouched down on the bed, his lips moving up Ingram's shaft, his pink tongue wrapping around each piercing to tease it. There was a comfort in the motions, suggesting it was far from the first time they'd done this.

It drew me in, creating a desire inside me that I didn't recognize. Before I knew it, I arched forward, into the space beside Shear, and ran my tongue along the bottom of Ingram's cock, following the same route Shear had taken. It put us side by side, my cheek brushing his, and when we both turned our heads slightly, I touched his tongue with my own. All the while, I lavished attention to Ingram's cock, the scent of him drugging me as much as the alcohol, the strange feeling of being powerless and in control all at once.

I toyed with one of the barbells with my lips, the dichotomy between the cool metal and the heat of his skin fascinating. It again made me wonder just why the hell he would ever consider getting such a thing, but I saw no reason to waste time or energy actually asking. Did it really matter? Why he'd done it, how he felt about it, whether it had hurt when he'd had it done, none of that mattered.

Instead, I committed myself fully to the action, to the kisses I indulged in from Shear as we both lavished attention on Ingram's thick cock.

"Fuck," Ingram said, his voice low, the darkness inside him slipping out through that one word. I *felt* it inside him, the shadows, the void, the need for more that pulled him under. His actions made so much more sense when I truly saw what rested beneath his skin. It might have terrified me at any other time, the idea that something that dark, that twisted could exist within the confines of another, the thought that something like *that* attempted to control him.

With the taste of his cock, however, I couldn't bring myself to care. Instead, I gave myself over to the feelings, to the guiding, to it all. The corruption that swam through me already twisted, my body filtering it, changing it, turning it inane and harmless by my powers. Guiding exhausted me, but it felt like a big meal, both tiring me out and making me feel better, nourished.

It reminded me of why I had to get this to work, because I had no idea what I would do if I was kicked from the Guild, if I lacked access to espers for this feeling. If they tossed me away, if they decided I wasn't worth the effort it took to deal with me, what then?

Sure, I had no idea where I would go, how I would care for myself, and it would cause a problem if I lacked for espers, but beyond that? In this moment, my mind clouded by need and liquor and corruption, I had no idea how I would separate from *them*.

That thought scared me the most, the idea that I actually wanted them—for what, in what way, how it would all work, those answers evaded me. I only knew that I didn't want to wake up tomorrow to find them gone. I knew I didn't want to end things even if I had little idea where this all could go.

Kenyon's fingers tightened at my hips, gripping me in a way that I would have found suffocating any other time. He held me fast, his body slamming against mine, a reminder of just how strong he was by virtue of his size alone. My cunt tightened helplessly, wishing that instead of his cock rubbing between my thighs, he'd slipped it inside me. Even if I knew that, were I in my right mind, I'd not be ready for that, this drunken side of me craved it so badly.

I wanted to know what it felt like, to experience that overwhelming sensation that no toy could quite replicate. He was thick, my thighs burning despite how wet I was as he fucked between them, and I wondered how that would feel if he plunged himself into me. I'd used toys, but my own nervousness meant I'd never tried anything that thick. Instead, I'd stuck with newbie items, barely thicker or longer than my finger. Kenyon was nothing like that, and I had no doubt that he'd stretch me in a way that would be entirely unlike anything I'd experienced.

Beyond that, the idea of losing that bit of control, of allowing someone else to take me, it filled my mind. I struggled to keep my thighs tight, wanting to spread them, to beg him for more. Before I could give into such a thing, before I could ignore all the warnings and lessons I'd learned, Kenyon slammed against me, his cock twitching and warmth coating my stomach. I moaned, the sound rumbling out through my lips.

Ingram groaned, the sound making mine sound soft and sweet. Shear took Ingram's cock into his mouth, deeply, as though he'd done it a million times before. Ingram's hips jerked forward, his teeth bared, his muscles tight. After a moment, he pulled back, withdrawing his cock from Shear's lips.

And me? For a reason I didn't understand, with a bravery — or stupidity — that I'd never expected, I leaned in and kissed Shear. It wasn't some quick peck, my tongue dived past his lips and into the heat of his mouth. I caught Ingram's cum, the salty taste of it familiar in a primal way.

Kenyon pulled away from me, the action causing his softening cock to stroke against my clit enough to get me off once more, as though the mixture of that taste of Ingram's cum, the warmth of Shear's kiss, and the overwhelming sparks from Kenyon's cock brushing my already over-stimulated nub pushed me beyond my limits.

I gasped or whimpered or something into Shear's mouth, my brain so foggy that I couldn't even understand the sound I had made. It all seemed so unlike me so different, so distant from what I understood about myself.

I'd always been one thing. I knew myself, who I was, the good and the bad. I was frigid and difficult and talented and prickly. I was a woman who avoided entanglements like this no matter what, a woman who knew exactly what they could lead to.

Yet here I was, indulging in them like a fool, like someone who had forgotten all the suffering I had gone through, who failed to realize that it could all happen again.

The questions, the shame, the anger at myself didn't come, however, my body and mind too muddled to make sense of it. Instead, I found myself so exhausted that I closed my eyes, Shear's lips the last thing I recalled before I drifted into a deep sleep.

When I woke, I'd have to deal with this all, would have to suffer the consequences of my own recklessness, but for tonight? Tonight, I would pretend the world was a different place than it was.

Chapter Forty-Seven

Carter

The coffee burned. I didn't mind drinking it before it cooled, however. Anything to jumpstart my mind and erase the fog in my head.

It was strange how I could feel so much better and like absolute shit at the same time. Had my corruption levels *ever* been this low? I doubted it, not since I'd changed, not since I'd started to use my powers, at least. Nothing hurt inside me, no gnawing pain from the corruption, no tightness at the back of my neck that never fully left me, none of that.

Was this how people normally felt?

It reminded me again exactly how important guides were, why they were valued. At times I forgot, given how fraught that entire situation tended to be for us. Guides didn't want to join our squad, only did so when they lacked other options or were forced as some sort of punishment for something else they'd done. It meant that while they did their jobs, they did it with only minimal effort.

Yun had gone above and beyond, pulling every speck of corruption from the four of us in a way I had no idea was even possible. It reminded me of the test she'd taken, the reality of her skills. The woman was astonishing, and the fact she'd all but fallen into our laps felt like a miracle I knew we hadn't deserved.

It had been even better than when she'd guided us before, when she'd still held back a part of herself. She'd held nothing back this time, and it showed in lightness of my body. Strange that each time I thought it couldn't get any better, she went and proved me wrong.

Still, while I felt great physically, the lack of sleep and questions inside me had sent me off to get this coffee, to try to spark awake my brain until it could work out the next step.

Yun would wake soon, and I doubted she'd be happy. Sure, she'd chosen that, but I was smart enough to know backslides were a part of life. Before last night, I'd thought using her as long as possible was good, but the idea of bonding us, of being together, of planning for any sort of a future, those things weren't likely. They hadn't been anywhere in my mind, really.

After experiencing the way I felt, though, the way she guided, I knew better.

We could *never* let her go. Her skills plus our compatibility meant we'd never find another guide like her — and given our reputation, even if one existed, I doubted they'd ever get assigned to us. It meant that no matter what happened, we had to find a way to get her to want to stay, to draw her in, to keep her close.

"You're thinking too fucking hard for this early in the morning." Ingram stretched as he walked past me in the large dining area of the hotel lobby, set up with a continental breakfast. He didn't bother with the food, however, instead going for the coffee just like I had. "Especially after a night like that."

"After a night like that is *exactly* the time we have to think about it. It's the right time to make a plan, to figure out where to go from here."

He added nothing to the coffee, grimacing when he took a gulp of the hot and far-too-strong drink. After a moment, he pinned me with a knowing look. "Sometimes your brain is a thing of fucking beauty and other times, you fuck shit up by overthinking."

"When have I ever done that?"

"Remember when we were young and wanted to buy alcohol with our fake IDs? All you had to do was show it, pay, walk out. Instead you went into some big explanation about why the guy in the photo looked different but you were for sure the same fucking person."

"Yeah, well, it all worked out."

"Because I snuck in and stole it."

I cast him a lopsided grin. "Exactly. It worked out."

He blew out a low breath, then stood beside me. "She's up."

"She say anything?"

"Nope. Got in the shower, probably to avoid any of us. Kenyon was gonna tell her about breakfast, then head down. Shear's...well, who the fuck knows?"

"When she gets down here, act normal."

"What's normal?"

"I'd say that if it's something you'd normally say, don't say that."

Ingram bobbed his head from side to side, his lips moving as he muttered the words back.

I would have kept bothering him, but a strange feeling ran up my spine, a sort of warning. As a combat esper, I had great senses, and they often caught things my logical brain couldn't make heads or tails of, at least not at first. Instead, I got this shiver, this tightening of the muscles in my back as though my body prepared for danger even if my conscious mind hadn't identified it yet.

And in all the years I had been an esper, it had *never* been wrong.

I jerked my hand out to the side, something large and hard striking it instead of Ingram.

A table?

Had someone just thrown a whole ass table at me? I peered across the large room to find the culprit, his stance making it damn clear who had done it.

It was a man—at least, he had been at one time. He had long black hair, tied back at the nape of his neck, and wore a black shirt and black jeans. It wasn't the gothic emo outfit that stood out the most, though. Instead, it was the way his eyes shone pure purple, and black spidered out across his face.

Corrupted were easy to identify. Sure, any esper could balance on that edge, and I'd had a face like that more than a few times. The difference was perhaps not so easy to tell by sight, especially at first, but by feeling. Once an esper crossed that line, once they lost themselves, that corruption no longer existed within them, but poured out all around them. Often electricity would flicker, people would feel this sudden unease, and I could spot the signs with him.

The whole throwing a table had been a pretty good indicator as well.

Ingram shifted his gaze between me and the corrupted, appearing less ruffled and more mildly annoyed. He took another drink of his coffee, then set it down with a drawn-out sigh, as though not getting to drink it were the most troublesome part of this whole thing.

The other patrons in the dining area rushed out, but their screams hardly reached me. I filtered it out as unimportant, focusing instead on the corrupted who stood there, clearly looking for a fight. That was the threat, the only thing that mattered at the moment.

Corrupted were out of their fucking minds, but in addition to that, they were arguably more powerful than espers. With a larger capacity with which to hold corruption, they could wipe the floor with a similarly ranked esper. It meant that it was good I wouldn't have had to deal with this asshole all on my own.

"You want a cup?" I held up my drink. "I feel like that when I haven't had my coffee yet, too."

He smirked, and if I was into his type, I might have fallen for that sort of bad boy look. He walked forward, tossing anything in his way to the side as he went. Thankfully, the civilians had taken off, which meant the flying chairs, tables and random breakfast items only struck other furniture or made it to the wall. "What rank are you?"

"Isn't that a little personal? Come on, wine-and-dine a boy before you get to those sort of questions." I caught a chair that came sailing my way, then set it down.

"Combat?" the man asked.

"Obviously. Now, what's crawled up your ass? I'm pretty sure I'd know if I'd done something to personally offend you."

"I saw you all walk in here like you matter. Like you're special. What, because the Guild is willing to suck your cocks, you think that means anything?"

"The Guild sucks cocks now? I must have missed that because I'm pretty sure no one's done that for me yet." I walked forward, closing the distance, Ingram remaining slightly behind me. I could take far more damage, after all, so it made sense to keep the asshole's focus on me. "So who are you?"

"Daniel," the man said, though he twitched at the name, as though it hurt. Then again, the exact connection between the person someone was before they corrupted and after was hardly studied or understood. Even if they were the same person, the cracks that occurred in their psyche ran so deep that their old self was all but gone. Whoever they had been disappeared beneath the anger and hunger and madness of the corruption.

Which was exactly why guides mattered so much, to keep us from turning into *that*.

I didn't recognize his name, but why would I? Unless I'd dealt with him personally, I tended to avoid espers—or anything that might complicate my life. Still, they didn't usually have espers walking around who might go corrupt like this, were careful to keep an eye on levels of those using their powers.

It meant this sort of thing—an esper corrupting out of the blue, in public—tended to only happen with espers who had hidden what they really were. I had to guess that meant him, that he'd wanted to use those skills for whatever the fuck he wanted without the complication of the Guild, or their oversight.

That didn't tend to go so well for people, a point he proved pretty damn well.

"How old are you?" I asked, trying to keep him distracted and off guard. If he had to think about those answers, if he had to focus on his disjointed memories, we stood a much better chance.

I was pretty sure we could take him on, but I would prefer no one get hurt — including us.

"Twenty-five," the man said, again jerking as though the answers didn't come easily.

"So what are you doing here, huh? What are you hoping out of this?"

He went still, a sign that didn't bode well. When anything stopped moving, it was a threat, a preparation. "I want you to pay for *everything* the Guild takes from us."

The last word left his lips as he came forward, faster than the items he'd thrown, and slammed into me *far* harder. Judging an opponent was one of the most important things I could do, to determine how powerful, to figure out the best way to counter, and it took only one strike from this corrupted to know one thing for sure.

We were in a lot of fucking trouble...

Chapter Forty-Eight

Shear

The overwhelming anger struck me before I stepped into the dining room, before I knew what had happened. It was how I lived my life, how I moved through the world. I saw things, sure, but I felt them more. That was how I experienced everything, through the minds and feelings of others.

So when I moved past those running away, through the lobby, when the chaos appeared in the dining space, I was already prepared for something bad. Few things got Carter's mind moving this fast, and Ingram didn't seem much calmer.

Worse, there was something else in that room, something dark and swimming with corruption, like a void threatening to pull me below if I ventured too close. I knew the cause without seeing the corrupted, since few things could create an energy pattern like this.

And one look at the room gave me a pretty good idea of the danger.

Carter had blood leaking down his face, and he hardly had the time to spit before reengaging with the corrupted. Ingram drifted in and out of shadows, but neither man could gain an upper hand on the corrupted.

He had to be an S-Rank, and a powerful one at that. Carter and Ingram together could easily take on about anything. It meant that their struggle went to show just how much of a problem this corrupted was.

Worse, there wasn't much I could do. My powers were useless against corrupted espers. Their minds were too twisted, and trying to interact would only draw me in, burying me beneath their madness. It meant I stayed close, but without physical prowess, I couldn't exactly jump in.

When the corrupted struck Carter hard enough to send him across the room, throwing his body against a table, I cursed my lack of other skills. One hit like that to me and it was possible I wouldn't get up.

"This is not good." Kenyon's voice from beside me went to show how focused on the fight I'd been—I hadn't even noticed him arriving. Usually his idiotic thoughts always annoyed me.

Right then, Ingram caught his fingers around the man's throat from behind. I'd watched Ingram end enough people through that little move, watching him strip the life from them, but that didn't happen this time. Just when I thought it was over, a blast of power sent Ingram sailing backward, flung as though he weighed nothing, as though his attempt had meant nothing.

Which went to show *exactly* how bad this was.

The man turned his attention toward Kenyon and me, stalking forward.

Well, it had been a pretty good life.

I paused, nearly releasing a rough laugh.

That wasn't true. It had been a fairly terrible life, one fraught with pain and trauma no person should have had to deal with. I thought about getting shipped off to Obsidian as a kid, about trying to survive while so many thoughts and feelings that weren't my own poured into me. Really, things had been rather unfair, and maybe this was the first time I'd truly considered it.

In fact, I wasn't sure there was one bright spot in the whole mess of my life.

A flash of my tongue entwined with Yun's, her sweet breath, the way she'd swallowed Ingram's cum from my mouth filtered through my mind. Was this just a moment of nostalgia?

Whatever it was, a discomfort settled in my stomach over the idea that there might have been one thing worth all that hell, and that I was losing it *far* too soon. Thankfully, with Yun up in the room, she was out of danger. The Guild had already been alerted, so they'd send more espers, and given the number of espers at the compound, they could deal with this asshole pretty easily.

Still, it was fairly irksome that after everything we'd done, after surviving The Pitt, *this* would take us down. It should have been better, should have been at least memorable. Reject Squad would go down as failures who never gained ground again, who never managed to come out on top again.

At least, that was my thought as I pulled my shoulders back, as I readied myself for whatever this corrupted would dish out—and I had no doubts it would be highly unpleasant—when someone else stepped forward, past me.

Familiar dark hair, a figure that was already trapped in my psyche, sure steps.

It startled me so much that I failed to react, as though so unexpected that I *couldn't* react. It felt like if the sky had suddenly fallen, the event so impossible, so unprecedented that no one would know how to respond. Likewise, I just watched as Yun stepped forward, past Kenyon and me, her steps quick.

Ingram tried to pick himself up off the ground, arms giving out, and Carter had not moved since the last strike. It was then I recognized that neither of them would stop this.

If that corrupted could take me out in one hit, the damage he could do to Yun was unfathomable.

My throat strangled the words, but I shoved her name out, surprised by the panic in my voice. I didn't panic. I didn't feel much of anything.

Or perhaps I'd just never recognized it before now. Maybe it had never been strong enough for me to identify it clearly, but I certainly did now.

Yun didn't react, her gaze shifting around to the men on the floor, but she didn't stop until just before the corrupted.

Despite the way she stood, her shoulders back, her chin held high, the fear that poured off her was impossible to miss. It bathed the room, thick and acidic and choking to me. I couldn't ignore it, the fact that she wasn't foolish enough to think this was safe.

"A guide?" The man let his lips quirk up on one side, a sickening smile that made my stomach clench in anger. "Don't you know that guides should stay back and not get in the way?"

"What exactly are you wanting here?" Her voice was strong despite the waves of panic that rolled off her.

"What else? Just to prove something, to show that no matter how much the Guild wants to control us, it can't."

"And you think that causing a scene here does that? All it does is prove *why* we need the Guild. It just scares civilians and makes them give more money and more power to the Guilds. It tells them we're uncontrollable and that there's no good reason to give us freedom."

He narrowed his eyes until nothing but purple shone out through them. He bent down slightly, to meet her gaze head on. "You're worse, you know that? Espers, the Guild, they're powerful, but *you?* Guides benefit from everything else but they don't bring much to the table. They don't matter, not really. You just lie to yourself and the world helps out and tells you how vital you are, but really? You're fucking useless, just a tool to get used, nothing else."

On the surface, Yun made no visible reaction. Nothing went to show that the words hit, but her mental waves moved out of control, shifting around, showing that the insult landed.

I wanted to do something, but nothing came to mind, nothing useful. She stood so close to the corrupted that he could erase her life before I could *do* anything. Even a wrong word could make this go bad so much faster.

"If you had more respect for guides, maybe you wouldn't have ended up here," Yun shot back.

I winced at her honesty and lack of tact. Couldn't she have been a little gentler in this moment? Her cutting wit normally pleased me, but right now was not the best time for it.

Lines etched in his face, making the black spidering evidence of corruption more evident. "We're stronger when we're like this. You're nothing but a way to control espers, to weaken them. You have *no* idea what it feels like now, to let the corruption take over. It's only called corruption because civilians want to demonize it, want to make it seem terrible, but the truth is that it is amazing. It makes us more, not less. I wouldn't let something like you weaken me."

With that, he snapped his hand out and wrapped his fingers around her throat.

Fuck.

Chapter Forty-Nine

Yun

The moment he touched me, it was over.

Despite the panic that rushed through me, the fear that came from knowing exactly what he could do, I focused only on what *I* could do.

The sight of Ingram and Carter down echoed around in my head, pushing me onward, forcing me past my own fears. My blood raced, sweat beading at the back of my neck and creeping down my spine.

I'd been *so* angry with them, but seeing them like this, witnessing them unmoving, unsure if they were alive or not, the thought of not hearing them again, clawed deep inside me. I didn't care how much I disliked them at times, how frustrated they made me. None of it mattered as I thought about them not getting back up.

Not seeing Carter making his stupid jokes, not having Ingram making filthy comments, not to have

Kenyon just being dumb in general, or Shear freaking me out… That suddenly struck me as unacceptable.

I had survived what a corrupted could do. I was stronger than most people knew, than he knew.

So when his fingers wrapped around my throat, when my air closed off, I tapped into my own past. I recalled that horrible, clawing sensation from before and opened that gate.

Where the corruption had been forced into me before, where I'd dealt with how *he* had poured it into me, this time I created that link on my side.

Corruption flowed into me, the same strange way it always did, though the corruption was far more wild. It was feral, scratching and burning and tearing as it filled me.

Corrupted were *not* espers at the end of the day. They were different, something between esper and monster, consumed by that twisted, dark energy. They gave themselves over it, couldn't survive without it, their bodies so entwined with it that my forcing it from them *hurt*.

He tried to move away, but I wasn't done. I wrapped my fingers around his wrist, a mirror of how he'd grabbed me, and held on even as he panicked, desperate to withdraw. Even still, I pulled the corruption from him, every speck of it rushing from him to me, my head dizzy, my thoughts sluggish.

It overwhelmed me, but I didn't stop. If anything, I pulled more, opened myself more. The black on his face, the purple of his eyes, they both receded, dimming.

He yanked harder, stumbling until he tripped backward, taking me down with him. I fell on top of him, but still kept my grasp on his wrist, refusing to let him escape. If he did, he'd recover, he'd come back worse. I couldn't let that happen, not after what he'd already done to Carter and Ingram.

He stared up at me, his eyes wide, his lips parted in something between horror and amazement. I didn't stop, though, even when the corruption thinned to a trickle, when it was nearly gone from his body, when it filled me until I feared I might split apart from the pressure.

"How?" he asked, his voice weaker. Of course, animals fought the hardest when they knew they'd nearly lost, when things were the most impossible. Sure enough, he swung, hitting me hard enough to send me flying and skidding across the floor, the air forced from my lungs at the impact.

Even as my body screamed, I twisted, trying to keep him in sight. The past mixed with the present, so much worse than it ever had been before, probably because of the corruption my body struggled to filter through. I saw this man, but overlaid on that I saw the other, my own nightmare.

The man came toward me, steps uneven, feet catching on the floor when he couldn't even fully lift them. It went to show just how much I'd taken from him.

I couldn't lift myself, the horrors playing in my head from my past, my body here but my mind trapped in the dungeon from so many years ago, at the mercy of another corrupted.

Before the man came more than a few steps, darkness surrounded him. At first I thought I was losing consciousness, that the visual disturbance was nothing more than my brain giving out, but something familiar about it comforted me. As quickly as the dark mist consumed him, it coalesced into a figure.

Ingram. He appeared just behind the man, blood on his face, fury in those depthless eyes, not a speck of mercy or kindness in them. He lifted his hand, grasped the man by the chin and yanked. A sickening crack came first, but it wasn't all. Ingram gripped the front of the now limp man's throat, his fingers curling in before he ripped his throat out as though unwilling to take the slightest chance of a repeat.

Blood spread from the man, pooling on the floor, his body dropped like trash, and it only added to the heaviness inside me. With the threat gone, my mind lost its ability to hold onto the present at all, and I lost myself to the memories, the horrors.

Chapter Fifty

Kenyon

Yun hadn't woken. The Guild had shown up, taken care of the mess. The corrupted was dead.

Not just sort of dead, not just barely having passed, but fully and completely gone. Even my skills couldn't have saved him, not with what Ingram did to him.

"How is she?" Carter walked in, though he didn't walk well. I'd healed him as well, but that wouldn't stop all the aches from the injuries he'd sustained.

"Healed, but she hasn't woken."

Shear sat in the corner of the hotel room, silent as he'd been since the Guild had come, since we had somehow survived this entire mess. He was always quiet, but this felt suffocating.

"How much do they know?" I asked.

"The cameras told them everything, even if we hadn't. They know she took down a corrupted who handed two S-Rank espers our asses, that she somehow stripped nearly every atom of corruption from him."

"They aren't going to fucking let this go." Ingram strolled in not so much as limping. Then again, he'd gotten thrown around a lot less, and he was so prideful that he wouldn't limp if he could avoid it. "Should have fucking hidden it."

"Not enough time. I don't like it either, but we're going to have to deal with this." Carter sighed and dropped himself into one of the chairs in the room. Just doing that went to show how bad he still felt. "The Guild is going to want to get their claws into her."

"They assigned her to us. They can't remove her for no good reason," I argued, more because I didn't like the implication rather than because I honestly believed it. I knew as well as anyone else exactly what the Guild could do when they wanted.

"They can't take her, sure, but they can make things *really* uncomfortable for us until they get what they want, and what they're going to want is to figure out what makes Yun different, what exactly she did and how she did it." Carter leaned forward, then let out a long, frustrated breath. "I don't even know what she did, so how the hell can we do anything to protect her? How the hell can a guide do that to a corrupted?"

"She's done it before." Shear's voice came out soft, the way he interjected into conversations as though he'd been part of them all along. It drew the attention of all three of us.

"What?" I asked.

"Afterward, just before she passed out, I slipped into her mind. She doesn't know, probably too distracted with what she went through, but I saw it."

"What did you see?"

"The dungeon, again, the same one from her nightmare before. She relived it there, for a few seconds before she lost consciousness, and I saw it. A corrupted forced her into guiding inside a dungeon. *That* is why she's different, why her guiding is different, and why she could do what she did today—because she's been forced to do it before."

Silence met the information, all of it too horrible for me—for any of us—to accept.

Even the idea that a guide might have gotten sucked into a dungeon was bad enough, but to think a corrupted would do that? My stomach rolled at the wrongness of it, the sickening truth of it.

It explained so much, though.

Her fear, her abilities, her distrust.

And yet, despite her having every reason to have turned around and left us to our fate, she hadn't.

I turned and stared at her, her eyes closed tight, her lids shifting as though she dreamed.

"So what now?" I asked.

No one answered at first, the reality of the situation so heavy, the lack of easy solutions, all of it crushing.

"We accepted a long time ago that we weren't the Guild's golden children anymore, that we didn't want to be. Nothing's different now," Carter said.

"The Guild won't just let it go," Ingram pressed.

"They're going to want to get their hands on her, and trust me, that isn't a fate we want to let her suffer," Shear said.

"She can't trust them," I agreed, knowing better than most exactly how much the bottom line mattered to the Guild. They would trample anyone if they thought it was worth it.

Carter, wearing a strangely serious expression, moved over and brushed Yun's hair from her face. For a man who rarely stopped smiling, who never appeared to take anything to heart, he showed no signs of that happy-go-lucky man then. "They won't touch her, and we'll make damn sure of it."

"What if they don't accept that?" Ingram asked.

He smiled that time, but it wasn't playful, not funny. Instead, it felt like a threat. "Then we'll show them exactly why our squad used to be on top. If they think we've been a problem before, they have *no* idea what we'll burn down for her."

Sign up for our newsletter and find out about all our romance book releases, eBook sales and promotions, sneak peeks and FREE romance books!

Want to see more from this author? Here's a taster for you to enjoy!

Reject Squad: Collateral Attraction
Jayce Carter

Excerpt

Yun

"You are mine." The voice repeated in my head, reaching deep inside me, a whisper that never fully went away.

It was only in very rare nightmares at first, then later in most dreams, and now? I heard it—no, felt it—on the outskirts of waking, like a piece of string that kept tightening around me, dragging me back to a place I never wanted to return to.

There, in the depths of my mind, the horrors surrounded me. A hand reached for me, clawing through the darkness, always getting closer. I remembered when it could grab me, when I had no chance to escape it, and everything it had taken from me.

I jerked backward, my eyes snapping open to find myself in a dim room, orange sunlight from the rising sun pouring in through a window. I had no idea where I was, didn't recognize anything around me, couldn't make out enough details to know if I'd been here before.

I twisted, then froze when a pair of purple, glowing eyes met mine. They were so bright in the room that they cast deeper shadows on the outskirts.

Did he find me?

I scrambled over the soft surface of what had to be a mattress. At the end, I toppled, trying to catch myself, reaching blindly for anything. He'd said I was his, that he was coming back. Was this another dream, or had I finally lost my mind, or maybe it was all real and he'd done what was impossible?

Light filled the space, so bright I had to shield my eyes from it. It took a moment to adjust, but when I did, the terror from before washed away.

It wasn't *him* in the room, not my nightmare, not my past, but Carter. He'd turned the light on, and there was a familiar smile painted across his lips.

With his face came back the events from…whenever it had been.

What happened in the lobby with that corrupted—along with my time with the entire squad before that.

Heat flamed across my cheeks at the reminder of how I'd lost myself to them, to the feelings, to things I'd never experienced before.

Worse, I felt so much better than I had recently. I wasn't even sore, which didn't seem possible given just how many rounds we'd gone. Even if none of them had actually fucked me, I should have hurt.

"Kenyon healed you."

How did he always know what I was thinking?

Instead of addressing that—doing so would mean me having to think about and acknowledge what we'd done—I ignored his statement. "What happened to the corrupted?"

"Dead."

Right. I recalled the sickening crack when Ingram had snapped his neck. While it was needed, that didn't mean I had to like it.

I tried to slow my still-racing heart, standing up straight so I could figure out where I was.

It appeared similar to the hotel room from before, with the same general decor to suggest the same building, but it wasn't *quite* the same. "Where are we?"

"Same hotel, but different room. The other needed…cleaning." The way he said that last word said it all, right?

Then again, after all we'd done, it wasn't a shock that it might need some work. I tried to ignore what the staff would think of the state of the room, however, and prayed I didn't run into a single person.

"How long was I out?"

"Almost a full day."

"A day and the Guild hasn't been here yet?"

"Oh, they were, but I refused them access to you."

That surprised me. In my experience, squads gave in to whatever the Guild wanted, always too afraid of screwing up their ranking to refuse.

Then again, hadn't Reject Squad proven they didn't a fuck about their place in the Guild or how others viewed them? The exact same trait that bothered me so much before now seemed like an unexpected benefit.

"Aren't you going to ask?"

"Do you want me to?"

Did I? I wasn't sure. Perhaps I just expected it so much that the idea of him not questioning what I'd done to that corrupted, of not addressing it, felt strange and oddly unfinished. He cared about little, but did that really go that far? That he didn't give a damn how I'd done something previously thought impossible?

"You told me not to ask questions I don't really want the answer to. Is that all this is?"

He smirked, his smile seeming slightly more genuine than before. "You want to hear the other part of that advice? Don't ask questions you already know the answer to."

"So you know what I did? And how?"

He plopped himself down in a chair, far enough away to keep me relaxed. "What you did was pretty damn obvious, don't you think? You pulled the corruption out of a corrupted until they were so weak they were almost dead. You also nearly got yourself killed doing that." He leveled a not-at-all friendly look my way, an expression that sat strangely on his face. "Don't do that again."

"Trust me, I don't plan on it."

He smiled widely. "Good. Glad we're on the same page there. If that happens again, you just stay back."

"And let you die? Not a problem."

"Wonderful. Well, you haven't eaten, so let's order some food then head back to the compound." He rose slower than usual, but I took nothing for granted when it came to Carter.

He might seem stupid and slow, but I'd peeked beneath that carefully crafted exterior now and then, caught glimpses of something darker and far more dangerous beneath the surface. I got the feeling everything he did was to get others exactly where he wanted them.

And I refused to play the part of a pawn.

He opened the door to the bedroom of what had to be another suite, but instead of an empty doorway, two bodies fell into the room.

Kenyon and Ingram tangled, thankfully with Ingram on top. Kenyon's massive frame might have crushed the stealth expert, after all. Ingram hopped up and brushed himself off, looking around as though confused as to how he'd gotten here.

Smooth…

Kenyon lacked the same ability to play things off, however, and lumbered to his feet, a goofy grin on his face as he rubbed the back of his neck. "You should make more noise when you're going to open a door," Kenyon said.

"You shouldn't listen through doors."

"Listening in?" Ingram snorted, dragging his fingers along the doorframe as though that had become the answer to all questions in the universe. "We were just checking the structural surety of the building. Do *you* want to stay somewhere unsafe?"

I stared at them and wondered exactly how this could be normal already. Their absurdity helped ground me, helped to erase the nightmares, that voice. It also eased the heaviness inside me from the extra corruption that my body was still working to process and get rid of. It didn't take it away, but it gave me something else to focus on.

"And how does it rate?" Carter asked.

Ingram pressed his lips together, then shrugged. "Good enough." His answer went to show he had no damn idea what he was talking about, something that I found charming for a reason I couldn't understand.

"Since the hotel isn't going to fall apart, why don't you all help me order and set up food before we leave?"

Ingram and Kenyon's expressions reminded me of children given a task when they were bored — begrudging acceptance. Still, they followed him out, the door open.

Just when I thought it was over, when their voices trailed off to parts of the suite I couldn't see, when I released a breath, I spotted one more.

Shear stood just outside the door, behind where the others had been. He stared at me with an intensity that said he hadn't been part of their conversation, perhaps hadn't even heard it at all. Something about that expression had me wrapping my arms around myself, as though that shielded me, as though it somehow protected me from those piercing, shockingly blue eyes of his.

He knows.

The words whispered through my mind — mine, not his — drawing a shiver through me. It was in his expression, in the serious set of his features, in the way he studied me. I didn't know exactly what he'd seen, what he'd figured out, but I knew he'd picked up something he didn't care for.

I had secrets, but I didn't think they'd stay secret for long.

And when they come out?

Everything would change...

About the Author

Jayce Carter lives in Southern California with her husband and two spawns. She originally wanted to take over the world but realized that would require wearing pants. This led her to choosing writing, a completely pants-free occupation. She has a fear of heights yet rock climbs for fun and enjoys making up excuses for not going out and socializing.

Jayce loves to hear from readers. You can find her contact information, website details and author profile page at https://www.firstforromance.com

ENTWINED PUBLISHING